يا الله
لا اله الا الله محمد رسول الله
صلى الله عليه وسلم

By Jane Downing

FICTION
The Lost Tribe
The Trickster
Searching for the Volcano and other Stories

POETRY
When Figs Fly

NON-FICTION
Lavington: What's in a Name?

FOR CHILDREN
The Whale and the Sandpiper
The Hermit Crab and the Needlefish

THE SULTAN'S DAUGHTER

- A NOVEL -

JANE DOWNING

Obiter Publishing

Published by Obiter Publishing
PO Box 5133
Braddon ACT 2612
info@obiterpublishing.com.au
www.obiterpublishing.com.au

ISBN-13: 978-0-6481742-9-5

A catalogue record for this book is available from the National Library of Australia

Cover design by Giraffe
Design by Karen Downing
Printed by Ingram Spark

For my mother
who visited Zanzibar when I was a child
and brought me back some silver 'princess' bangles
sparking my imagination.

Author's Note

In the middle of the nineteenth century Zanzibar stood at the crossroads between East and West. Traders and merchants from across the British Empire, France, the Hanseatic League and the United States of America filled the harbour of this small island off the east coast of Africa. They came because here was unimaginable wealth. African gold and ivory, ebony and rhino-horn, leopard skins, and tortoiseshells all passed through Zanzibar; and most importantly slaves. The Sultan of Zanzibar was acknowledged as the greatest slave trader in the world. Queen Victoria presented him with a state coach, President John Tyler of the United States sent a luxuriously appointed ship, and he received a dinner service, especially made for him, from the Emperor of China.

The Sultan had three legal wives and unnumbered concubines spread in palaces and harems across his empire. In 1844 Jilfidân, one of his Circassian concubines, gave birth to a child. He called his newest daughter Salmé. This is her story.

PROLOGUE
1844: BET IL MTONI, ZANZIBAR

'She's not very pretty.'

Jilfidân looked at the baby in her arms. Even discounting Medine's jealousy she had to agree with her.

'She looks like her father,' Medine added.

The women's silence was deeper than a lack of words. They looked around the reception room. Only a couple of personal slaves were within eavesdropping distance; the Sultan's legal wife was holding court over by the far window. Jilfidân allowed herself a giggle. The newest baby in the harem mewed. She screwed up her monkey-round, bug-eyed, yellow-tinged baby face. It was just the face the Sultan made above Jilfidân in moments of intimacy. She glanced up to see if that was what Medine – another of the Sultan's Circassian concubines – was referring to all along. Medine moved away from the pillows where Jilfidân lounged with her baby. Jilfidân could see she was bursting with amusement, because that's exactly what she'd meant. Baby Salmé's resemblance to her father was no compliment. Medine's jewellery jangled, an amplification of her suppressed laughter.

The baby mewed again, more loudly. Fat old Bibi Azziz, the Sultan's legal wife, his childless wife, looked over. Not with understanding, nor kindness. Jilfidân knew she had to silence her baby. She rearranged her shirt and lifted tiny Salmé to her nipple and winced as she clamped on. The baby sucked with gusto. She had a keen hold on life. Jilfidân thought she would never grow tired of staring at her daughter's not very pretty but totally mesmerising face. She didn't care what Medine said about her baby.

That wasn't strictly true. She *did* care what Medine said and thought; she loved Medine. They shared a homeland, a mother tongue, a friendship, as well as a harem. But Jilfidân was more than a concubine now, she was no longer a slave. This birth made her a *suri*. She could demand as much respect as Bibi Azziz over by the window, that Omani cow. Jilfidân's daughter was a princess as good as any other: Sayyida Salmé, princess of Zanzibar and Oman.

In a few minutes the baby would have her ears pierced in the ceremony that had brought them down to the reception room with all this hoo-ha. Jilfidân hated the idea of her baby's perfect, innocent flesh broken, violated, six holes in each tiny shell-like ear, punctured with a needle and threaded with red silk until she was old enough for the heavy gold rings. But at the same time Jilfidân had been looking forward to the ceremony. Because then there'd be no mistaking her daughter for anything common, anything owned. When she grew up she'd marry a rich cousin from Oman, or at worst one of the Arab nobles fat on the slave trade of Zanzibar. She was a princess, the daughter of the Sultan. She didn't have to be pretty to be safe. Jilfidân bent and kissed her baby's fur-matted head as she suckled. Whispered a small, modest, personal prayer. The baby opened her eyes wide and dribbled thick fatty milk out around her smile.

Bibi Azziz was beside them then. Jilfidân felt coated in her heavy musk scent. The Sultana looked down on Jilfidân from a great height.

'Babies do not smile until their sixth week,' the official wife commanded. 'It is wind.'

1866

Zanzibar

Eunuchs were so opinionated. Salmé was not going to question this truth no matter how cast-down Johar looked, all quivering bulk and lowered eyes in front of her. All an act.

'No coffee,' she told him, her hands on her hips in the manner of a five-year-old having a tantrum. She remembered who she was and lowered her arms into a more graceful pose.

'No sherbet, no mint tea, no food of any kind.'

Johar opened his mouth, his right hand raised as if to physically make a way through her prohibitions for his own suggestions.

'No singers, no dancers, no storytellers,' she said over the top of him. She wasn't going to leave any possible exception for him to slip in an excuse to disturb her.

'No soothsayers, no sisters, no brothers.' She hesitated for just a moment. Of course, as chief eunuch he knew that should the Sultan arrive this didn't include him. She fixed Johar with her dark eyes. 'No apricots, no pomegranates, you understand, no interruptions.'

With a last emphatic, 'And no French lollies,' the princess turned to climb the north stairs out of the courtyard. Her right hand ran up the grain of the wooden banister as she skipped like a child and her jewellery jangled and her veil billowed. From the gallery she looked down. Johar had his *kofia* off and was rubbing his gourd-bald head. He felt her eyes and looked up. He had that if-your-father-was-alive look on; eyes raised to heaven. Then he spied a slave and started bawling about the slaughter of some poor goat to feed the household tomorrow. The albino peacocks roosting in the eaves shuffled away. The dusk turned their white translucent and their movement into a ghostly shimmer.

Salmé smiled at Johar's playacting. She felt the lassitude of the last months slip away. She was sick of going over what had happened; she wanted to know what was going to happen next.

Night fell quickly in Zanzibar. The light from the cooking fire on the far side of the courtyard didn't reach far enough to penetrate the second flight of stairs that continued up inside the palace walls. She took off her shoes at the dark entrance to the stairwell. They had hard soles that clattered on stone. She left the high *kubkâb* on the bottom step and started up barefooted: it was a sudden decision, an impulsive plan to take up her position quietly, secretly. Except she forgot the gold around her wrists, ankles, neck, dangling from her ears and hanging from the veil around her head. All tinkling away, saying, the sayyida is coming up the stairs now. With her right arm out and her crooked left arm stretched as far as it would go, she could steady some of her bells. Her knuckles gently grazed the walls on either side. Then: the roof.

Sinbad, a streak of white fur, ran down the steps as she emerged. Salmé tripped over him and tottered and the gold announced her arrival anyway. She pretended it was some orchestrated *ghazal* of the stars overhead, this chiming of gold. Maybe the foreigners across the street would not hear it – maybe *he* would not hear it – above their own chatter.

She tried to convince herself it was excuse enough to be coming up just to look out over the beauty of Stone Town. And it was beautiful. Blocks of shadow and dark, gossipy windows of yellow light, a skyline set against the blackness of the ocean;

distant drumming and the insect hum of voices; the smell of cloves blanketing it all. She'd missed the constant activity of Stone Town during her exile to her plantation.

Her women had laid out cushions when there was still enough daylight to arrange them in a comfortable heap. Salmé settled herself low to the rooftop, plumping one of the smaller *tekkies* to support her crooked arm, never the same after an accident as a child. She positioned herself low but still high enough so she could see over the parapet to the house opposite. She thought she couldn't be seen amongst the silks and satins. Voices drifted across the narrow gap between the two buildings, voices in languages she could not distinguish, one from the others. Male voices and female voices. Men and women. Together in the same room. She raised herself a little to better see down into the dining room on the second floor. The angle was steep: she could only see a truncated room, and only four and a half of the people gathered to eat there. But, yes, amongst them, definitely women. Her excitement was barely contained though none of the players opposite showed any astonishment at being in mixed company.

The voices spoke in pleasant tones, male and female. They could be English or French, though his voice, the deepest note, would be most comfortable in his mother tongue, German. She'd had her women ask at the market, sent Johar out to gather what gossip he could: the man who was in residence in the house opposite was from the Free and Hanseatic City of Hamburg. Herr Ruete, she was told – Heinrich Ruete – merchant of Zanzibar since 1855. He'd come to Stone Town as little more than a child, only sixteen, and now he had his own trading company, in cloves and other spices, nutmeg, vanilla, cardamom, and in ivory brought over from Africa. This man who drew her eyes like the North Pole drew a magnet, was said to have many languages and no wives.

Through the low points in the parapet that ringed the roof Salmé could look down on this Herr Ruete of the market gossip. He'd been alone when she first saw him three weeks before, that first night home from exile and in her new palace. He'd paced his own rooftop, smoking, not seeing her. She'd thought him a curious creature, nothing covering his floppy hair, shirt tucked into trousers. And then she had thought about him again and again; and didn't know why.

But he wasn't alone tonight. She'd heard his guests arrive, stomping up the road and knocking loud on his gate. These *kafirs* were the beautiful Europeans of the consulates and merchant houses, the foreign men and women who made the island their home. And here was Salmé, Princess of Zanzibar, watching as an uninvited guest.

The shutters were wide in the large upper room opposite. Bugs were swarming toward the lights. A thought struck her as more lamps were lit on Herr Ruete's dining table. Did he actually know she was there watching? Three weeks of watching silently and she knew his movements: the time he got home from his merchant house; the time his servants laid the table for his evening meal; the time he smoked, and the time the lights went off and she could no longer see in. This however, was the first dinner party. She briefly imagined him ordering the shutters open to allow her to watch what was going on. And better, she let her imagination run, that he'd organised the festivities simply to entertain her.

He did not look toward the window even once as she watched. Clearly he had no idea she was there. She resigned herself to her anonymity in the harem of her palace.

Every now and then recognisable words of Swahili drifted across the narrow street. Sometimes it was the only common language the residents of the island could find, both in the harem and out in the world. Salmé leant forward, wanting to be part of the conversation – if only the listening part. From what she could catch, the men were talking about dull shipping timetables. Herr Ruete was lamenting the *kasikazi* winds that blew the wrong way at the wrong time.

Salmé closed her eyes and let his voice become the only thing in her head. She had a waking dream about this infidel-neighbour. In this dream she and Herr Ruete were both on their roofs at the same time, and she leant across and reached out her hand, and he leant across the narrow street and reached out his. She judged the distance again now. Yes, their hands could meet if they both stretched out. Did meet, in this waking dream. The fingers touching, the palms. The Europeans called it a hand-shake, this meeting and touching.

To touch a man's flesh. No wonder she called it a dream. It was an unthinkable proposition from her harem, but who can control the nature of dreams?

Nonetheless, she tried to chase the trespassing, mosquito buzz of the dream away. The moon was not up and the shadows on the roof were dense. There was more laughter and a ship's bell sounded in the harbour. She regretted all the prohibitions she'd heaped on Johar. Coffee would actually be nice instead of this sudden attack of loneliness. She wanted him to appear in the stairwell and announce the arrival of a sister, who'd bustle up and plump herself amongst the pillows, singing '*jambo, jambo.*' She was ready to make a confession. Me touch a man's flesh! She'd laugh in her confession. Just Salmé being ridiculous again, Metle would say in return. She heard the word ridiculous over and over in her head, only it wasn't the imagined sister talking; the word was spoken in the snide voice of their brother, Sultan Majid.

Just Salmé being ridiculous. Again. She flushed in the dark. Yet how could she complain: this character assessment got her the punishment of exile and not death for her treason against the Sultan. Now she'd been given permission to come back, but no one seemed to have actually noticed she was home in Stone Town.

There was movement. She looked across the way, examining everything minutely. She thrust herself back into the present, the here and now, the neighbour's dinner party. Four deeply black slaves had entered the dining room opposite and were placing huge plates on the table, one in front of each guest. The slaves glided in and out of her field of sight. The guests she could see at Herr Ruete's table, all four and a half of them, reached into the food with alacrity. She assumed the same movements of the men and women further inside the room; all these funny Europeans.

She made herself feel better by putting on her own snide, cutting voice. It was bizarre: *they* were ridiculous. She compared all the certainties she'd taken for granted: eating habits, dressing habits, odd habits. She concentrated so she could dismiss her dreaming and so she could collect details to share with her sisters when she saw them next. The knives and forks the Europeans held in their hands. The squares of cloth they laid across their clothing in case of spills. Metle would say, 'No, I don't believe you,' and roll her eyes and ask for more details. She would say, 'Why would you have a set plate, only for you, when you can share everything and eat what you want when you want?' It was a good question. Salmé watched the foreigners doing it anyway.

This was of course distracting trivia compared to that one completely astonishing thing. Those three women she'd seen arrive at Herr Ruete's house, the one and a half she could now see clearly, were seated at his table, were dining in the presence of men not their husbands and not their fathers and not their brothers. It was barbaric – acting like the slaves in their enclaves. Her sisters would shake their heads until the combined bells at their ankles and bangles would drown out any further descriptions. She didn't know if she believed it herself and it was there in front of her.

She let herself feel superior. She liked the feeling, this mocking height. Remembered a time when she didn't question her right to this feeling. Look at their immodesty, she told herself snidely, all that flesh, pale, paler still in the candlelight. Their arms, the colour of alabaster, their breasts bursting from silk organza and stiff taffeta. Their hair pulled back to sit in mounds on their lower necks, exposing so much of their faces, big like mules. All their facial features indiscreetly unmasked. That this could exist in the heart of Stone Town was like a tall story from when she was a child at Bet il Mtoni, one of the tales from Arabia or the fables her nurse whispered to her in Swahili. Women in the presence of men indeed. Women unveiled in public.

Salmé felt her superiority slip a little as she watched the one and half women bow their heads together, the half becoming a whole as she leaned in. Then they both threw back their heads again in laughter. It made her wonder why she had to wear her veil even in the company of her brothers. Her eyes, her mouth, the tip of her nose were always left free of course: even with her veil on she could see, she could speak and she could smell as well as any of the women opposite. She reminded herself, and said a small prayer, that she also had behind her veil the advantage of being obedient to Allah. And that had to be a comforting thought.

Herr Ruete rose from his chair then and left the part of the room she could see from her position. His chair was left pushed back from the table. Salmé felt herself falling from Allah's grace. If only she could be more like her saintly mother, but she couldn't stop herself thinking: the chair is probably warm from the fleshy cheeks of his bottom. She giggled softly. Clapped her hands over her mouth and echoed her giggle in golden bells.

The furniture. That was safe to mock. She'd tell Metle and their cousins about it when she went over to Metle's palace again. They'd be the ones laughing. She'd shriek, 'Can you imagine the furniture? It's high and hard and unbending. The only cushions are round, upholstered seats. Not even silk.' But the little scene of imagined collusion and sisterly secrets faded. There could be no mention of residual warmth and rounded buttocks.

Herr Ruete was seated again and a new round of plates were set before the guests. She could see something soft on the plates, something pink that wobbled when attacked by a spoon. Yet the chairs sat the poor people rigid and let only their feet touch the ground. Their elbows had nowhere to lean.

Salmé was not completely ignorant of the ways of the Europeans. She wasn't a child. Her father the Great Sultan, when he was alive, had chairs like these under the guests opposite, around the walls of his receiving room to impress the consuls and the missionaries. But the family understood it was a joke. They didn't use them. They sat on the cushions of the floor. Comfortable. She lounged, comfortably, across her pillows on the rooftop and went back to imagining Metle's black face contorting in laughter as she described this scene, eight men and women – she calculated – set around the edge of a table like chess pieces. Then she would tell her sister about the dresses on the European women that kept them even more rigid than the furniture. Their bodices were so tightly fitted it was a wonder they could breathe let alone eat, and with such appetite. The woman closest scraped her plate clean of its pink flummery-dish; there'd be no work for the servants in the kitchen.

These dresses really were a sight. There was scant material about any of the women's shoulders and breasts – all that flesh – and yet beneath the table the robes jostling against each other like great voluminous bells. She remembered watching a missionary wife leave through the high gates when she lived with her mother in the Great Sultan's palace by the shoreline. The English wife looked like she had metal beneath the cloth, molding the shape. Bang, bang her shins must have gone against the frame.

Another ship's bell sounded in the darkness. The harbour was full, bringing the slaves from the mainland, taking the spices, and the ivory, and the slaves away again. Bringing the colour and all the movement Salmé missed when she'd had to leave Stone Town after the rebellion. These women opposite probably knew nothing about the brothers Majid and Barghash fighting over the Sultancy. Would not know her name, or how she helped the wrong brother, the one who failed to take the throne.

They did not even know the thing closest to them, right in front of their mulish noses. They had no idea she was watching. 'I'm here, look at me,' she wanted to shout, because Herr Ruete was looking into the room at them not up at her, and they were so dowdy in their dull hues, blues and greys, the colours of the bruises they must have on their shins. Great blocks of monotony they were, not a broken line amongst them, no beautiful, gorgeous, clashing war of colours and designs that gave life to any gathering of her family.

She heard furniture moving and she looked and she saw him stand up and his presence filled the room and the women no longer existed. Ridiculous, she chanted to herself. Go to bed, she told herself, this show is not for you.

She rolled onto her back, stretching her legs freely within her long shirt and trousers, felt the softness of the thick carpet between her toes. The carpet's crimsons and rubies had darkened to the colour of dried blood in the night. She turned her attention away from the distractions in the building opposite and upwards to the stars. The enormity of them made her suddenly serious. She set about counting Allah's blessings as she counted the stars and shaped the constellations.

On dark, moonless nights like tonight, the stars were so close she felt she could reach out and touch them. They had the illusion of being as close as they'd been when she looked through the telescope at Bet il Mtoni, the palace of her childhood. Back when her father was Sultan, alive and in control, and when her mother was alive and carrying a pious quote for every occasion. When Salmé was part of a big boisterous world called her family.

Count your blessings, she warned herself again. She ran her silk scarf between her fingers as if its length was the rosary-beads carried by one of the Christian missionaries. Beautiful tender silk. Don't tempt fate with bitterness, she prayed. *Nothing shall ever happen to us except what Allah has ordained for us. He is our Lord, Helper and Protector.*

She wondered what exactly the Lord had mapped out for her from this point on. Her mother would disown her for such temerity. Jilfidân had taken life as it was handed to her, from being captured and sold into slavery as a child, to entering the Sultan's harem, to the birth of only one child, to her widowhood, and even the cholera that came and took her, probably – Salmé imagined with a slight blasphemous sigh – straight into the presence of the Prophets. 'You are not a slave,' she'd told her daughter throughout her life. 'Count your blessings every day.'

But did Allah really intend her to grow old alone, unmarried, the forgotten little sister? Her other sisters had been found husbands. Even fat Metle had one, though Salmé wasn't going to covet that particular example. Still, she addressed the stars, surely my happiness isn't too trivial a matter for the universe?

Her mother Jilfidân had a quote for that too, a favourite. *And everything, small and big is written.* Small and big. All written down.

Perhaps it was about the writing after all. She should have left it to Allah and the men. She decided that night as she lay on her back under the dome of the universe – and not for the first time – that she should never have turned her nose up at the rules and taught herself to write.

Such regrets bred the listlessness that had anchored her too often to her bed since the rebellion. It was natural that one brother fight against the other to be Sultan; it was almost obligatory in their family's history. However, for their sister to act as scribe to the rebellion was most definitely not.

His voice stirred Salmé from the past. The sound tugged on a little string on her chest. She forgave herself a little for this feeling, because his voice was now raised in song and it was enough to divert the dead.

She propped herself more openly above the crenellations of the parapet to watch the performance. Heinrich Ruete was standing and unaccountably singing an after-dinner aria. He stood back from the table so she had a clear line of sight. She could let her eyes linger over every detail: the black suit that sculptured his body and his legs, that clung to every bit of him. His buttons shone like stars, burnished gold, holding tight the cloth across his chest and his heart. The white collar was so very stiff it was as if it was designed to hold his head high through every adversity. They should, she realised, fear any nation that could maintain such a hideous, heavy costume in the African heat.

When the singing ended Salmé wanted to clap along with the others. He seemed shy in the praise they threw at him in their applause. His face was pink. He grabbed up a bottle and walked around the table – he was doing the work of a slave, pouring piss-coloured waterfalls into glasses. It had to be alcohol, another astounding forbidden on show in front of her. She wetted her lips with her tongue as she watched the loudest and closest woman shut up for a moment to sip the wine.

Then he tripped. On the edge of the carpet perhaps, or the edge of inebriation. Herr Ruete's hand brushed the arm of the loud-woman as he righted himself. Her head came back, with a bright smile around her white teeth. What on earth could they be saying at such a moment?

'Oh, can I paw your flesh dear?'

'Of course, my good man.'

'And would you like some more alcohol with that, the quicker to get us both to hell?'

'Don't mind if I do.'

Salmé watched as he laughed. And the woman laughed. Murmured, entwined laughs. He moved on to the next guest. The touch was brushed away as nothing. The man beside the fleshy woman, the husband surely, watched with perfect equanimity. If this was play-acting, it was of the highest quality. Could the touch between an unmarried man and woman be such a nothing? She couldn't believe it. But the little scream she let out had nothing to do with the antics opposite. Light flooded around her. She'd missed Johar's panting as he made it to the top of the stairs carrying too much bulk, too much age, and a bright lamp. Salmé swung around. 'Away,' she hissed.

'But Bibi Salmé.'

She could not have light. She'd told her women to set down

pillows, cushions, but no lamps, because lamplight would make her as obvious as a *dhow* in the harbour, pendulums of light swinging from the middlemast. But, of course, Johar would not be purposefully disobedient: she'd forgotten to stipulate lamps in her list of prohibitions to him.

'I could whip you,' she whispered anyway. 'I'll sell you. Away, away,' she said, her hands shooing him off in a jangle of gold clipping gold. The light failed back down the staircase. He made his displeasure obvious in the set of his shoulders as he retreated. I have been faithful your whole life, his shoulders said, now look how I'm rewarded.

The night felt suddenly darker after the intrusion. Her land of make-believe had been revealed briefly for what it was in the eunuch's lamp. A transitory silliness only. She lay back and closed her eyes and refused to look anymore. Eventually she heard the European voices in various words of departure, *auf wiedersehen, au revoir*, goodbye. They faded down the narrow street and around a corner into the labyrinth of Stone Town. Bedtime. Lights were going out up and down the building opposite.

The first time she'd seen him – when she was full of joy at being back in Stone Town – she'd watched him walking across his roof, to the edge and then to the far edge and back. He'd been smoking, but, for an Arab, a walk must have a better purpose than simply a chance to smoke. This man could be heading nowhere on a rooftop – there could be no earthly destination – so the pacing had inspired thoughts in her of strange Christian practices. Maybe it was part of their prayers, she'd wondered.

Now, after the dinner party she hoped he would come again to his roof, to smoke, to pray. But the last visible light was snuffed across the way and then all the noises were lulled into a hum as peaceful as insects. There was no reason to stay on the roof. She'd see nothing more of the German tonight. Yet, the return of her listlessness kept her there. The tiredness that had haunted her since the failed rebellion took hold again.

She woke before she knew she'd slept. She listened. All quiet. She was completely alone in the universe. So she got up. She gathered herself together, straightened her shirt as it fell back to her ankles, stretched her legs within their silk trousers, righted herself to the tune of her jewellery. Gusts of amber and musk, jessamine and orange blossom wafted out from her clothes into the night. The moon was finally up. It must be well past midnight she calculated. No wonder Johar had intruded.

Only as she straightened fully did she see him on his roof. The man Ruete. He was not pacing tonight. He'd set a flame to a cigar and was blowing smoke, setting it in great eddies toward the constellations. The end of the cigar burned red. Red as a devil's eye. He turned towards her on the pull of her movements. His eye caught hers, knocking her pulse into a clip-clop panic.

'*Jambo*,' he called softly.

'*Jambo*,' she called back.

Swahili would be their shared language too. But of course she could never talk to him again. She remembered who she was. She clapped her hands across her face to cover where her mask should be and ran down the steps two at a time.

Her slaves were asleep in a heap like puppies when she got to her bedchamber. The women disentangled themselves and stretched and lit the brass lamp hanging in the window and the candles around her bed. The wind generated by her body as she threw herself melodramatically up onto the plump mattress of her rosewood bed snuffed several of the candles out again. The Nubian patiently lit her brand in the flame of one of the survivors and relit the rest.

Salmé rubbed her face into her pillow, as if friction could scrape off her blush. She could feel the slaves hovering. They knew what she'd been doing. The youngest one, Zada, beat the fan a little too wildly, hoping perhaps that the princess's mood could be pushed away along with the heat. The oldest of the slaves stood at the foot of the bed and stroked her feet.

'Where are your *kubkâb*,' she asked gently.

'At the bottom of the steps,' Salmé mumbled. She'd forgotten her shoes in her rush and run to bed barefoot. She felt the slave wipe the bird shit off her soles. Peacock probably. The geese were less keen on adventuring in the upstairs galleries.

'Have you said your prayers?' Nashwa interjected from over by the window. She'd been Salmé's wet-nurse and was allowed almost as much impertinence as her sulky eunuch.

It seemed like a lifetime ago, but Salmé was able to say truthfully, 'Yes, before I went up on the roof.'

Then they began the nightly massage, her two chamber slaves, one for each side, massaging each ankle under its band of gold and bells, and then more firmly, her calves. The fanning of the third slave slowed to beat with the rhythm of their hands. But she was not going to find comfort in rituals. She lay rigid on her belly wondering what on earth and in the heavens possessed her to say hello to an infidel.

The slaves moved up every inch of her body. Rubbing her calves, one for each side, and then her thighs where the flesh was softer and more compliant. Their hands pushed deeply through the cloth of her trousers and shirt that was stiff with the day's perfumes. The movement released the smells yet again, those competing scents of amber and musk, jessamine and orange blossom, each simultaneously containing memory and masking memories. One slave stood back and the other gently kneaded the small of her back and Salmé finally relaxed. Then an image flooded her mind and she was tense again. His hand falling onto the woman's arm. His hand stroking down her bare milky flesh.

'Sayyida,' whispered the slave whose breath brushed the back of her neck. 'Little *bibi* princess, it is time to sleep.' The slave stroked the slight dip in her shoulders.

You can't make me, Salmé thought rebelliously. Then remembered where rebellion had got her.

The slave had each thumb moving lightly across to the humps of Salmé's shoulder blades. In slow circles, they kneaded deep, and Salmé's mind moved in the same circles and she tried to imagine how her exposed and bleached bones would look beside those of a camel. She'd used the shoulder bone of a camel as a slate when she was teaching herself to write. Would she and the camel be the same underneath? The camel bone was for once a safer image to dwell on, safer than the one she'd shooed away. His hand falling onto the woman's arm. His hand stroking down her bare milky flesh.

As the slave's two hands merged to touch a place at the back of her neck she finally gave up, and closed her eyes. She gave up on Ruete's hands too. 'So go away Herr Ruete,' she told the image in her head. '*Hello* is impossible.' She even had a story to illustrate this now she'd given into the massage and let the memories surface.

It was actually a story told by her mother because she had been too sick to remember the events herself: the time Salmé was actually subjected to a white man's touch. She let herself travel through the story as her mother had told it. It was comforting, the cadence of Jilfidân's voice, her certainties. She missed her mother, not in the sharp way of the first grief when she was sixteen, but quietly, inescapably with every single breath.

Her breathing shallowed. She felt the slaves withdraw and heard the hissing sizzle of candles going out.

This was actually a story from the good times, the big boisterous family good times. The irony of it: good times and a time of life-threatening fever linked in her mind. That's what stories could do.

The typhoid fever never distinguished between rank. The slave quarters were a den of sickness and now young Sayyida Salmé – *you my darling*, said Jilfidân – was raving. None of the Arab or Swahili remedies had done any good and her mother – *that's me, though I'm sure your other mothers were very concerned too*, said Jilfidân – was more than worried. This was her only daughter.

'Do we need to send for the doctor?' Jilfidân asked. It was a bold suggestion that she was careful to couch as a question because the Sultan's sister was the one to decide. Asche looked at her sick niece.

'And I'm sure she thought you were as good as dead.' That was the exact way Jilfidân described the look, every time she told the story. 'It could be the only reason she consented to letting the English doctor come to the palace.'

The other women of Bet il Watoro were told to hide themselves in their apartments at the approach of the foreigner. So, Jilfidân mused in her telling, he would have thought it a quiet place and a quiet life in the harem. With the women hidden away he missed the laughter and busyness of a usual day, the shouting for coffee and lemonade, the gossip over the new jewellery, the children underfoot.

The doctor climbed the stairs from the deathly quiet courtyard and was led to the princess's room. 'We wrapped you in every part in your *schele*,' Jilfidân assured Salmé when she first told her the story after her recovery. 'Your shawl was round and round and around you, as if you were in public.'

Her mother didn't say, 'Round and round you like a funeral shroud.' Salmé didn't think she imagined the shadow of these words.

The gold borders of the *schele* snaked over a shoulder, under her thigh, partly haloed her covered head. The eunuchs surrounded her also. They stood by the door and hovering at the end of the bed, leaving room only for her aunt Asche and the doctor. Salmé had been in other sickrooms since and knew how muggy it could get. The women insisted on closing up the room of anyone ill, sealing it from the outside world. And once every breath of fresh air was banished, the remaining air was thickened with ritual fumigations of combined and competing perfumes. Though the result never defeated the smell of sickness.

The doctor spoke to aunt Asche in Swahili. Asked questions. Perhaps because he had little knowledge of Arab customs – Jilfidân's version of the story always gave him the benefit of the doubt – the doctor insisted on feeling Salmé's pulse.

Asche stood in long consideration as Salmé tossed in her shroud-*schele*. Agonisingly long, Jilfidân thought under the circumstances: the prohibition on touch surely didn't count now. Finally Asche allowed it.

Salmé had no memory of the touch. Of the doctor taking her wrist and placing two fingers against the vulnerable inner side.

She rolled over in her bed now as an adult who had survived the typhoid. She held up her arm. Moonlight was the only illumination with the slaves gone and the candles gutted. She trailed the fingers of her left hand down her right wrist, tracing by touch the delta of blue veins. Her pale skin glowed. She was white – her skin inherited from her Circassian mother. In fact she was almost as fair as the women drinking wine in Herr Ruete's dining room. As fair as the one his hand brushed against.

She felt the blood pulsing in the veins under her fingertips. She had a fever now as well. One that had to be cured swiftly. She was ridiculous but not that ridiculous.

The European doctor ended up doing nothing to help at Bet il Watoro anyway. He stormed out without a diagnosis or a prescription, banging down the stairs, swinging a black leather case full of poisons and cures, watched from behind screens and doorways. His cranky exit was talked about for days.

There was compromise, and there was one step too far. After touching the princess's wrist, the doctor had the temerity to ask to see Salmé's tongue. Johar, not yet chief of her eunuchs but vociferous nonetheless, put a stop to the examination before Asche had time to decide. The English doctor was ejected and Salmé's recovery was left to Allah.

This was always the way Jilfidân's stories ended. With Allah. With a moral to live by and a standard Salmé felt she had never quite lived up to, though her pious mother forgave her that too. The word of Allah is powerful, was the moral of this one as it turned out. Funny how often it was.

After any hope of powerful western medicine was ushered unceremoniously out of the harem, calming passages of the Qur'an were written on a white plate, not with ink, but with a solution of saffron. The words were then dissolved in rosewater, and the mixture forced between Salmé's lips. Asche and Johar and Jilfidân in turn stuck the spoon on her tongue and watched her gag and swallow.

Salmé got better, of course, otherwise she wouldn't have been lying in her own small palace, alone. In that, her worst illness, the written word had come to her aid.

Maybe I shouldn't have taught myself to write, she thought yet again as she drifted into a deeper dreaming. But she saw another truth here too: writing *is* powerful.

Metle visited the next evening. Salmé had resolved never to go onto her roof again – or not for at least a week – so her sister was a welcome distraction.

'I brought a fortune teller,' Metle announced before the whole retinue was through the palace gates. The heap of street shoes was growing near the doorway, Metle's *kosch* in the centre, just as she was in the centre of all the hubbub. Two tall Nubians extinguished the lanterns, which were left to roll against the wall like severed heads and the fortune teller stood beside them, hooded, in black, and looming.

'Now you're back here, it'll be nice to see our future,' Metle explained, sure that fortune would be agreeable, and completely oblivious to the fortune teller's foreboding aura. She herself, once unwound from her *schele*, was a joy in crimson and green, a quail egg-sized ruby lolling across her bosom and an emerald in the dip of her nose.

Salmé stood back from the confusion of bodies and voices. 'And you've brought a fish,' she said loudly. The smell had announced itself. Two slaves were needed to carry the kingfish through into the courtyard.

'Supper,' Metle cried. 'Johar,' she called. 'With ginger. Yes?'

All the visitors were still shouting their greetings over the top of each other when they finally got to the reception room. Welcome, hello, the rain has held off, I like your new shirt, slave take the *schele*, hello, one more shawl, come this way, hello to you too. The noise was enormous. Metle's guards and cooks and chamber women had retreated into the kitchen and the slave quarters but there were a sizable number of bodies settling around the room, taking coffee and rosewater jellies as they plumped down on the cushions. Metle lived with seven of their female cousins and nieces and they weren't going to miss out on an outing. Nor the children. Metle's two-year-old toddled over and collapsed on her mother's lap as if she was just another of the comfortable cushions. She was not the most beautiful of the sisters – the Great Sultan was generous in handing down his protruding fish-eyes and Metle hadn't any advantage from her Abyssinian mother either. And then bearing children had made her round. Salmé watched Metle bend her head slightly and smell the top of her son's head. An intoxicated smile skipped across Metle's lips and Salmé was very glad she had come. She no longer wanted to tell her anything about the entertainment from her rooftop the night before: she wanted to hear all the gossip from the real world.

'Tell me about,' Salmé shouted, only the hubbub was abating and she sounded overloud like a market fishmonger and the room erupted again in laughter.

'No, no,' Metle interrupted, her mouth full of jellies. 'I said I brought a fortune teller. She will tell our fortune. Come, come.'

The swathed black presence materialised out of the shadow of the arched doorway and hovered. The tiny diamonds of light that fell through the fretwork doorframe seemed to avoid the figure. Salmé felt a shiver prickle over her scalp. She remembered the time they went as children to their father's *shamba* at Ngambo, the time there was the dead donkey on the road with its ribs showing. When they got to the clove plantation the prophetess was there with a monstrosity she called her unborn child in her arms, and this stomach-churning apparition of a foetus spoke to the Great Sultan of calamities. Of course, calamities had indeed come.

A high turbulent crown of black hair appeared when the fortune teller pushed back her hood. It bobbed and swayed as the old woman squatted in front of Metle and stroked her hand as if she was painting it with henna. Salmé sat upright, close by, suddenly anxious. They'd only just arrived; it was all too much. Fortune needed more preamble, more time to prepare.

'I see many children in your future,' rasped the fortune teller. 'All of them boys.'

Salmé collapsed against the wall and laughed at the relief of it. There was no great power here. Metle's child, limpet close, was clearly a boy, and her belly was big enough to contain no secrets about more to come. But Metle was hugely pleased. 'See, see,' she nodded. 'Now the Sayyida Salmé's turn. What is going to become of our dear little sister just back from Bububu. It is a pretty spot on the water's edge but so far away from us all. Tell us what she will find now she is home?'

'Metle, let the fortune teller discover my past without your chitter-chatter,' Salmé chastised. Metle would know she was mocking her: Salmé had called her the naïve one of the family often enough. Metle grimaced and waved the old woman on to her sister.

Obediently, the fortune teller turned and knelt down in front of Salmé. She had thick, pink lips and shrewd eyes. Salmé was sure she would have gathered all the personal history of every woman in the Sultan's family before she came tonight and didn't need a blabbermouth to make her job easier. Salmé let the woman assess her. Let her see that she too had shrewd eyes.

Then Salmé lent forward and offered her hand and let herself be part of the game. The crone's fingers traced the bones under her flesh, turned her hand over and rubbed her palm until the skin tingled. Salmé heard the rustle of cloth as the women in the room leaned closer to hear what would come next.

'You will surely marry one of your cousins from Oman,' the fortune teller announced.

There were several snorts and a chorus of giggles.

'I doubt it,' sighed Salmé melodramatically. She retrieved her hand and played to the audience. 'What would the Princes of Oman want with one of their barbaric African relatives?' Even Metle could see the sport in this. There'd been no love lost since the Great Sultan divided his kingdom between two sons, and there'd been even less truck with Arabia since their eldest brother Thuwayni sent a fleet of *dhows* from Oman to try and take Zanzibar back by force. Memories erupted in circles of umbraged memory sharing. The younger brother Barghash's later rebellion was nothing to this attack.

'No,' said the fortune teller, interrupting her betters. Salmé stopped her acting and looked back at the conviction on the old woman's face. If nothing else, she believed in her own pronouncements. Salmé raised her hand to quiet her gabbling relatives. 'No,' the fortune teller said. 'I see you crossing the ocean. You will leave Zanzibar.'

Salmé told Johar to give the fortune teller double the Maria Therese *thalers* of the agreed price. She'd been good entertainment. They were to have sons and husbands and riches and new donkeys and long lives. It was worth a few extra coins. She watched the gaunt old woman hobble into the slave quarters beside the lumbering weight of Johar. The slaves would be happy tomorrow with the chance of dreams fulfilled in her prophecies too.

The kitchen slaves set up the *sefra* and placed the steaming fish on the low table. There was every type of vegetable and a pyramid of glowing pomegranates and too much talking for Salmé to keep up with any one conversation. Not that she wanted to keep up, she was happy bathed in the noise. She was parched and wanted to absorb every single voice to make up for the lonely nights at Bububu. The musicians were reduced to a tidal wash of sound under all the voices. She dipped in and out, the benign hostess.

'The ruby?' needled cousin Sharifa.

'Yes, from the funny old Banyan on the east side of the marketplace. I don't know where these Indians find such good gems,' confessed Metle.

'There's a ship from France due,' said one niece.

'Did you order any china?' asked another.

'Said-boy, show Auntie Salmé your doll,' said Metle over the top of them. 'From France, when he was born.'

The little boy shyly approached her with his eyes downcast. Salmé tried to coax him in with a square of baklava off the *sefra*, but he stopped a few feet away and stretched his arms fully in front, the doll an extension that just reached her waiting hands. She had missed his birth, and had only met him in the last couple of weeks. She was a stranger. She reached out her right arm and the boy rushed over to a cousin and dived into her lap and buried his head into the familiar smells of orange blossom and jessamine.

Salmé was left with the French doll. She tipped it towards herself to see its face better, and the eyes blinked at her. She tipped it back, the eyes opened, she tipped it forward, the eyelids dropped again with a tiny clicking snap. Metle was watching everything, 'Who does it remind you of?' she laughed.

'Khole!' Salmé said immediately, without consciously considering the question. The doll didn't really look like their sister Khole – the doll was hard and porcelain and had rounded cheeks – but she knew exactly what Metle meant. The resemblance was in the saucy eyes and the thick lashes that fell to brush the pink cheeks.

Metle may not be beautiful, nor Salmé, she was willing to admit, but Khole was acknowledged as the loveliest of the Great Sultan's daughters. Khole was thus his favourite. Their father had called her *Nidjim il subh*, his Morning Star, and he'd given her custody of the keys to his Treasury in the last years of his life. No one was immune: she seduced them all. Salmé had thought herself blessed when Khole took her in after her mother's death.

Metle leaned over the *sefra* and lowered her voice. 'Did you hear what they are saying about her now?' Salmé leaned into their imagined dome of privacy. 'They say Khole is planting peach trees along the drive to her palace. It's right in the interior, remember the largest of her *shambas*? It's a long road in there. They say she is planting one for every…'

A loud growling sound shot Metle's head away and the trace of her thoughts with it. She was laughing and her belly was jolting and they were all pointing at poor old Zemzem, a spinster niece, twenty years older than Salmé and fast asleep. She'd moved away from the *sefra* with its remnants of supper and let her curly, Nubian head fall back against the mosaic tiles of the wall. Her mouth was wide. She snored again as they watched.

'It is late,' Salmé said to quell the laughter. 'Zemzem,' she said louder, 'it is time to go.' Zemzem's eyes opened and her mouth immediately formed a smile. Salmé wondered at her dreams. 'Home?' she suggested to all her guests.

Zemzem was not the only one overtaken with fatigue. The three youngest children were found in curled heaps, smelling of sherbet and slightly of urine, and impossible to wake. Slaves were summoned to carry them. The wet-nurses lifted them effortlessly. The youngest girl rested against the shoulder of her *yaya*, deep, round imprints revealed on her cheek where the coins at the bottom of each plait had dug in. Salmé remembered the same marks from her childhood as she kissed the soft cheek goodbye.

Metle held back while the rest changed shoes and wrapped themselves in their *schele*, taking back their correct shawls from the pile by smell.

'I'm so glad you're back,' Metle whispered to Salmé alone. 'He'll send for you eventually you know. The Sultan didn't have to give your Bububu to the British Consul. It is such a sweet place but there are many spots along the coast as pretty. This must be our brother's way of bringing you back to Stone Town. It is six years since, since the upset. Even Barghash is back from exile in Bombay, why should you stay away?' Metle let each of her sentences trip over the one in front, eager to get them all out. 'You were so young. Remember how much Majid loved you when you were living with him at Bet il Watoro. Majid has to forgive you.'

Salmé blinked like Said-boy's doll to clear her eyes of threatened tears. 'Yes, yes,' she reassured Metle in return, though she didn't believe it.

And then the guards led the retinue out of the gates with their round lanterns hanging in front like a pair of harvest moons. It wasn't quite two by two behind them – the women were not soldiers, they were not a phalanx – they were only forced into lines by the narrow streets as they snaked back to Metle's palace that squatted closer to the shoreline. On the way they'd have to squeeze single file if they met another retinue going to the Sultan's palace. The princesses would nod companionably. They might not be able to go abroad in daylight, but they made use of the moons, real and manmade.

Salmé watched Johar lock the gate behind the rearguards. She felt the weight of absence. The knowledge that she'd been left behind, alone. When she'd lived with Khole every night had been as lively as this one. Regrets were hard to blink away. She distracted herself with Metle's half-told then forgotten revelation.

'Johar, when you are out tomorrow, see if you can find out about Sayyida Khole's peach trees,' she said as they walked back through the courtyard, Johar calibrating his gait to her shorter steps. The palace keys clanged in a bunch from his waist, a lower note to her tinkling gold bells.

'Everyone has gone?' she asked. 'The fortune teller too?'

He nodded. 'Anything else Bibi?' He walked tall with a firm set across his plump shoulders. Salmé noticed: he looked happy. Maybe he had enjoyed the night. Maybe he too regretted the loss of company in exile. He'd never said, always seeming to look to the future, not back. He would have enjoyed the entertainment Metle brought along.

'Ah,' she smiled, 'you saw the fortune teller. And what did she say? What is your fortune?'

A screech of bats broke the square of night sky above them. She stopped. They were in the centre of the courtyard, a still, calm centre after the unexpected bustle of the evening. She turned to face Johar as he paused too. His shoulders slumped slightly and he looked resolutely down at his broad feet and talon long toenails. Salmé guessed immediately. 'That old crone told you you'd be free!'

He didn't look up. His bald head nodded almost imperceptibly. She reached out and touched his arm to reassure him that it was all a joke. 'Yes Johar, you will be free when I go across the ocean.'

They both laughed. They were safe together. It was reassuring to know that he would be her chief eunuch until the day he died.

'Sleep well, Bibi Salmé.'

Salmé counted the steps as she climbed, as she had as a child to teach herself her numbers. Twenty-five up the first flight to the gallery, a few more steps with her hand running along the grain of the balustrade to her bedchamber. Nashwa was laying out a change of clothing for the next day. The old wet-nurse carefully draped them across the sandalwood chest in a manner to suggest they contained an extraordinarily thin princess. Salmé knew each garment intimately, the long trousers, the shirt to the knee, the swooping scarf, from the many times she'd worn them before, in this combination and with other pieces. She wanted something new.

'There's a ship coming from France. Make sure I get some new cloth,' she directed two of the younger bedchamber slaves who were as pretty as peacocks and knew about quality. She considered how she wanted to look. 'Blues. Lots of blues.'

Then she let them fan her and massage her and slip away from her, all the time thinking, see Herr Heinrich Ruete of The Free and Hanseatic City of Hamburg, I didn't think of you once all evening.

It was a battle every day not to think about this man. That's how she thought of it anyway. It was language she understood – theirs was a family of battles and fighting. The Great Sultan had gone back to Oman when Salmé was just getting to marriageable age because he said he had battles to fight. She always pictured her father on top of the blackest of his stallions, swinging his scimitar and shouting – she couldn't imagine the curses of men but they'd have to be strong enough to make a polite woman blush. Sultan Sa'id won this war against the perfidious Persians. For two days she won her own battle too. She was her father's daughter.

She snorted, an encouraging sound, like a whistle in the dark, each time she passed the stairwell up to the roof. Go up! The very idea of it! But this was harder than she imagined any Arabian skirmish. She had no voice to scream obscenities, she only had the uncontrollable urge to climb the steps, that she had to control nonetheless. 'Ten types of pigeon poop,' she said as an experiment. It only made her sound like a child.

As a child she'd always got her way. She thought, Maybe the problem is I don't know what I want. Because she wanted more than anything to go up to the roof, and equally, she never wanted to see that man again. Why in the name of Allah would I want to see him – what sort of an idiot am I? she asked herself. The albino peacock shuffled along the gallery railing, its silvery crown bobbing about knowingly. 'Don't answer that,' she squawked at the bird. It looked affronted then pretended to be a statue.

Salmé spent that afternoon in imitation of the peacock. Aloof from it all. Sewing, reading the Qur'an, walking along the balconies looking down. Staying in her palace. And not on the roof.

It'll be okay to go up during the day, she told herself the next morning. The German will be in his merchant house. Making money.

She tied on her mask and let the golden chains hang down behind her ears. Just in case one of his servants was up on the roof opposite. A whole phalanx of her slaves raced up the last flight of steps in front of her, big with pillows and tall with tasseled sunshades and wide with coarse-woven fans. Stickybeaks every one of them.

There were seven slave-women on the roof when she emerged from the stairwell and yet all she could see was the background figure. He was eating something. He used it to wave in a gesture that just made it across the rooftops. A chicken leg waved.

'Hello there,' Herr Ruete called in Arabic. 'We meet again,' he added in Swahili.

'How can we meet again when we have never met a first time?' Salmé asked in the most Sayyida-dripping voice she could muster, a direct imitation of the dreadful legal wife Bibi Azziz.

Before the man could think this was anything more than a rhetorical question, she turned away. Slow down, she told herself. Don't run like last time, after we last met. She did not miss the irony in her thought. But she managed to obey her inner monologue and left the roof at a haughty pace. She fled, but only one step at a time, not two.

'Dignity,' she whispered to herself. Her back, which she hoped would speak volumes on this theme, was unfortunately and instantly hidden by her cavalcade of slaves clumping and smashing down the steps behind her. She kept going down the next flight of stairs to the courtyard to pick a fight with Johar. 'I hate goose,' she told him, as he stood with the limp necks of two of the creatures in his plump hands. 'I never want goose again.'

She couldn't work out if he was good looking or not. This man she was determined not to think about. His eyes were small, set between a high forehead and a pair of red and round cheeks. His swollen pink lips were enclosed in a forest of short, thick beard. And his hair was uncovered. Brown, with a sheen to it like a horse after a long run.

Salmé only had her brothers to compare him with, and he wasn't like any of them. The uncovered hair for one thing. She hadn't seen a brother without a turban since they were children on the beach at Bet il Mtoni. The eunuchs said all the princes were good looking then but Salmé had her doubts. Majid was admittedly more and more handsome now he was elevated to Sultan – that went without saying: she knew there were no ugly Sultans in history. He was tall and pale-skinned with intelligent eyes. Or had been last time she saw him, before her exile from Stone Town. He had a Circassian mother like herself, making them both the envied 'cats' of the harem. The aristocrats amongst all the royal blood. 'You cats,' she heard Barghash hissing at them. 'Lazy, treacherous cats.'

Then of course who could deny the looks of Barghash? She hadn't, sister Khole hadn't, the other conspirators who followed him into revolution hadn't. A magical black brother in amongst the Omani children. She remembered clearly the charismatic quirk at each end of his lips. She wondered about the lines around her neighbour's lips. They were yet too finely etched to make out across a Zanzibar street no matter how narrow. Up close, would there be wrinkles that spoke of a life of smiles and happiness? He was round and upholstered like the seat of his dining chairs, that at least was clear from where she spied on him. But he was not quite the roly-poly bundle of mischief that was big-bottomed Hamdan, a beloved brother, before he died too young. Herr Ruete was swift in his movements, from his dining room to the roof, across to the edge, but didn't have the elegance of Mohammed, her nephew who kept greyhounds and fed them champagne. This man, she concluded, was nothing like any of her male relatives. Herr Ruete was only himself.

It wasn't any wonder, with all this going on in her mind, that she made slow progress on her sewing that day. The cloth from the French ship was quickly turned into clothes, with the fine detail left to the princess and her chamber slaves. They'd given her the embroidery around the hem of one sleeve to finish. It wasn't much. Some thread, some seed pearls from the pot at her knee. Zada laid the other sleeve beside her so she could follow the pattern. For two hours they matched, green and orange thread written in loops with the buds of seed pearls nestled along the hem. Salmé felt a sense of accomplishment though it took a moment to recognise the feeling. She thought she'd go and visit Metle that night and wear her new outfit and hear the latest gossip.

It was only when she stood up that she realised her mistake. A few loose pearls pinged to the tiled floor, then she walked two steps and the new shirt came with her. It flapped like a kite caught on a prevailing wind. She brushed at it to dislodge it, but it stuck, it dangled, it came with her still. Three sets of hands appeared and tugged and pulled and Salmé burst into tears. Over all the hours of work she had sewn the new shirt through to the old. She pulled the whole thing off over her head to get rid of the blunder. It was an awkward manoeuvre with her crooked arm. She shrugged and her naked belly quivered like that of some slave belly dancer.

'Another shirt,' she shouted. She stood with her arms in the air so it could be pulled on. As she waited she knew she wasn't going to visit Metle or anyone that night. 'A thousand types of pigeon poop,' she cursed Herr Ruete, under her breath so the slaves would not hear.

That night she hated herself, but she was back on the roof. The afternoon rains had left pools that reflected back the stars. She stared at them so long they were no longer beautiful. They simply reminded her that flat roofs may be perfect for her Father's desert kingdom but bringing the architecture from Oman to Zanzibar had to be a mistake. All the palaces of her childhood were crumbling from wet rot.

She decided she did not want to go to Oman to see her

father's old palace that would last beyond anything in Africa. She did not want her brother Sultan Majid to find her an Omani cousin for a husband and send her away. The fortune teller was a fake. Her brother did not even remember she was here.

The Christian bells tolled slowly in the distance. The rhythm suggested sadness and mourning, a sound that could enter the soul. A few cries carried off the harbour, more alive but disturbing in their growling tone. She stopped propping herself up to see across the street. Her new clothes, now complete, were scratchy where they touched her neck and shoulder blades. There was nothing to see across in her neighbour's house to take her mind off the irritations.

She woke up to find Johar carrying her into her bedchamber.

The rain made her restless. The sun made her restless. Two evenings running she surrounded herself with her women and guards and went visiting. She visited Metle and pushed away from her sister's cheerfulness without telling her anything about the odd life of her *kafir* neighbour. She visited their mad sister Shewane, the closest to her age, who said she was going to leave all her money and *shambas* to her slaves. As if that was ever going to work. She stayed in her palace then and prayed five times a day and ate goose when it was set on the *sefra* in front of her. She watched the rain and she had Zada draw the shutters against the noontime sun and she had them opened again and she waited for the sun to go down. Waiting, when there is nothing to wait for, is a physical ache. She knew Sinbad would give her comfort.

'Sinbad, Sinbad,' she called but her cat didn't come. So, or so she told herself, she had to go up onto her roof again. Just to find Sinbad, the naughty cat. He'd been sent from Persia as a present after her mother died. As comfort. He'd been with her through all her adventures.

'Sinbad, Sinbad,' she called as she climbed. See, I am only coming up here for Sinbad, the call actually said.

He was talking, almost shouting, before she was fully onto the roof. 'I apologise for my rudeness,' the man from Hamburg shouted across the roofs. 'I do not know the etiquette with an Oriental princess. It is not taught to us. We do not expect to meet one.'

His Arabic accent was awful. Salmé strained to understand, and did not turn and run. The sun was on the horizon turning all the buildings pink. Sinbad was the only pure white thing around, sitting on the top of the parapet like a Sultan on a throne. The cat did not run at the man's voice. And at least the man was showing deference.

From halfway onto the roof, her legs still in the stairwell, she almost failed to find words to reply. She hadn't been taught how to talk to a strange man either, and not by omission. This should not happen.

'There is no etiquette. I do not know you exist,' she called across to him.

Herr Ruete laughed then. Was he laughing at her? She didn't think she liked being laughed at. Did he think an Oriental princess was something as cute and exotic as a pedigree cat? She climbed the last steps and walked over to the parapet, securing her veil as she went.

Herr Heinrich Ruete was coming to the edge of his roof as she approached hers. He got there first and suddenly knelt and leaned against the lowest part of one of the crenellations. His wide chest only just fitted through; he squeezed until his body reached halfway across the divide, his arm outstretched from it. Sinbad stretched from the warmth of the stone on the other side and leaned just a little toward him. Herr Ruete stretched another inch. The cat nudged his face into the offered hand. Sinbad's purr was loud above the dusk whispers of bats and boatmen. They'd done this before.

'Sinbad is Persian isn't he? I thought the Persians were your enemy?'

Salmé stopped at the edge. 'Not the cats,' she said.

Her sudden anger at being laughed at, was as suddenly gone. It was a very funny situation she had to admit, this situation that could never exist. She nevertheless wanted him to know she was a woman the same as his dinner guests, that she wasn't a barbarian, a strange exotic. She wasn't a mist of perfumes without any centre. She wanted him to know everything about her. A tumble of words was trying to get out.

'I can read and write you know.' She cursed herself. Of all the things she wanted to say, what a nonsensical thing to come out. What a *ridiculous* thing to say. True to character again. Sinbad jumped over to Herr Ruete's roof, turned and blinked at her, casting low beams of light at the end of the day.

'Will you write me a letter then?' the man asked.

'Isn't it enough that we speak?' she said and she heard him laugh again.

'If we do speak,' he said quietly. He wasn't moving. She

suspected he was using the same tactics he'd used to gain the confidence of her cat. Calm, patience, persistence.

The sky turned from pink to black in those moments of silence.

'Bibi Salmé! Bibi?' came a call from below.

Salmé swung her head around. It took Johar an age to get up all the flights but he would be there soon.

'What do I call you?'

'Sayyida. Princess. You cannot call me anything else.' Stupid me, she remembered, he cannot call me anything at all.

'I am Ruete, call me Ruete,' he said as she left to waylay Johar.

The sky did not fall. Allah and the angels did not send a plague on her house. This was a revelation.

Salmé slept late after a dreamless night and busied herself sorting her jewellery to take up the hours of the afternoon. The contents of her ebony box could become a tangle and she didn't trust any of the slaves to look after everything right. She sorted her childhood jewellery, which had become too small for her earlobes and ankles and wrists, and wondered if she should give it away. She could not let herself imagine a daughter wearing the bangles and bells. She sifted out her mother's favourites, the pieces Jilfidân was given when she was raised from slave to the status of *suri*. They were too special to give away despite their old-fashioned design. Status didn't simply equate to a few rubies and emeralds, but they could symbolise it. She held the newest necklace against her skin and wondered why she'd bought it.

And suspected boredom. The gold really was too heavy to be comfortable.

Her anticipation weighed as heavily between the points of her collarbone. 'Don't get excited,' she told herself. 'Don't get excited. He might not be there tonight.'

As she put the gold and silver away in the box, it chimed, metal against metal, in time with the bells that hung from so many of the pieces. She picked out her biggest diamond stud for her nose and called for Johar to arrange the cushions and lights on the roof. The slaves rushed up and down the steps. They all knew anyway.

Salmé went upstairs as soon as her last prayers were finished. The rote verses meant nothing tonight as she recited them, and yet they connected her by association to a deep well of comfort. She climbed almost joyfully. And he was there.

'Ruete?' The moon was a scythe offering little light. It helped that she was talking to a shadow.

'So will you write to me?' he asked in Arabic as if their last conversation had never been interrupted.

She settled herself on the cushions closest to the parapet, wedged a *tekkie* against her belly and rested her elbows on the stone. I'm just being polite answering his questions, she reasoned. She dropped into Swahili to encourage him to do likewise.

'I'm not supposed to write. Girls don't. Only my brothers were taught.'

'Is that in the Qur'an? I didn't know.' Herr Ruete too was now seated, on his roof edge, astride, one leg hanging over. The leg swung as he spoke, knocking slightly against the wall at intervals like someone gently urging their horse forward. He took her lead with the language. Swahili would be their language after all.

'*Hapana*. No it is not written,' she answered his question. 'But it is what we are told. Girls do not write. I didn't like being told. Hamdan was so stupid and he still got to learn. But Bibi Toad – that's what we called our teacher. You know a toad?' She puffed up her cheeks and vibrated her lips though she doubted he could see her in the dark. 'We got to read, but then, *no, no, no*, the teacher said, *go sit over there*. The boys got slates and pencils. It looked so exciting.'

'So weren't you punished?'

She tried to remember. She'd always been in trouble as a child for doing the wrong thing, but the anger never lasted. Her mother was a saint and her father had so many children, what was one naughty girl in the youngest set? He had battles to fight. Persians to conquer.

'They were all very angry at the time but we can't unlearn things can we?'

She didn't tell him about all the lonely, boring times she sat in her mother's apartments practicing, those interminable hours with only a pencil and a smooth camel bone for company, listening to the shouts of the other children whooping and swooping up from the courtyard with the pigeons and ricebirds. She would have given up except for the fact she wasn't one to give up. As stubborn as one of the sayyida's donkeys, her mother always said. Maybe if she'd been prettier than a donkey she wouldn't have had to play with the boys, or wanted to be like the boys.

He was looking across at her patiently waiting for more words out loud. Perhaps he imagined she *was* pretty under her veil.

'Who taught you? Didn't they get punished?'

'You have some funny ideas about us Arabs and our desire to punish,' she chastised. 'As it happens I taught myself on a camel bone.'

He was definitely laughing. 'A camel bone. Do they leave camel bones lying around in the harem?'

She took umbrage. 'You don't believe me do you?' She put her hand up to her shoulder, massaged the bones under her shirt and flesh. 'It was a long one. Worn down. Like this I think.' She leant her shoulder forward.

'The shoulder bone of a camel?'

'I can't be absolutely sure. I've never fondled a camel's neck,' she protested in her own defense. 'Is it the Germanic way to always be so precise and definitive?'

'Perhaps you should come over so I can…' In the dark of the night she could barely make out that the man was touching his hand to his own shoulder, in mirror image to her movement. Salmé didn't know what to think then. Was he implying he wanted to touch her shoulder bone – to touch her?

'No, you tell me about how you learned to write!'

As she listened to a description of school desks and ink pens and insufficient fires in darkened grates, she thought again of her father's failure to find her a husband. Was it a punishment because she was the difficult daughter who'd taught herself to write, or simply an omission? She listened to Ruete's voice, and was glad of her father's neglect.

The sound of singing rose to the rooftops where they sat. A band of men rounded the corner and snaked their way along the street below, singing a deep and soulful lament, then they turned the next corner and went on their way.

'Zanzibar is beautiful,' Ruete interrupted himself to say. 'I was very glad to come here.'

Salmé stopped going to visit Metle, she stopped waiting for the Sultan to contact her – which he didn't anyway. She bathed and perfumed and dressed and waited for the sun to dip below the skyline. Johar alone kept her in her world. Her eunuch insisted she sit down in the secure room off the courtyard where her wealth was stored and listen to reports from her *shambas* when she really didn't care about the harvest and the tree yields and the price of cinnamon in Europe. Her property was her inheritance from her father, her rightful portion. She thought about it little or not at all when Johar wasn't wittering on about it.

He sat cross-legged in front of the locked chests, one of the ledgers planked across his lap. He did his duty and told her she was doing well from the plantation Sultan Majid had given her in return for pretty Bububu. He told her the cloves this year were magnificent, Allah be praised. That there were two slave girls at her other estate on the eastern side of Zanzibar who were nearing ten.

'Is it time to bring them here to teach them sewing and embroidery?'

Salmé agreed it was. There was no point keeping her slaves ignorant. When the noble, a distant cousin, originally built this palace, he'd tiled the room with even more exhortations from the Qur'an than the others. She was reminded, if she cared to read, to be wise in the use of her riches. The blue letters jumping from the clean white of the tiles. *Allah will deprive usury of all blessing, but will give increase for deeds of charity.*

'And I have a report on the peach trees you asked about.'

'Peach trees?' It took Johar a little more prompting for her to remember. She'd forgotten Metle's stray remark and her own request for market gossip.

'It is said,' he said, and she was left to imagine who was doing the saying and where, 'that your sister has planted a line of large peach trees along the road to her estate.'

'Yes, that's what Sayyida Metle told me. She wouldn't plant seeds or saplings would she, not Khole. How large are the trees?'

'The size of each tree is perhaps not the nub of this story Bibi.'

He paused. He was doing this for effect and she humoured him. 'The size of the peaches?' she asked like a child being teased.

'No. There is no report on the size of the peaches, nor their juiciness nor taste. However, it is said, she has planted one peach tree for every man in her life.'

Salmé moved to get up, resting the hand of her good arm on the floor as leverage. So it was all about her brothers. She didn't want to hear about Majid and Barghash and the others and the ones she'd never met in Oman. She commented, to end the audience, 'Well that will be a lot of trees with all our brothers, and one for the Great Sultan our father, I suppose, may Allah the most Merciful, the most Beneficent preserve his soul.'

'Not for your brothers.' He did not move to get up. 'One for each of her man friends.' He had his mistress's full attention for the first time that morning.

'Friends?' she whispered though no one in the courtyard could possibly overhear them unless they were being very naughty pressed up against the wall by the door.

'More than friends.' Johar's eyebrows were doing a dance on his huge expanse of bald head. She still felt she was missing something. Princesses of Zanzibar and Oman did not have friends who were also men. 'Lovers.' His eyes were cast down at the ledger. At what was not beneath the ledger. She let herself acknowledge what he was saying. *More* than friends. She slumped back on the cushions. She remembered then the very first story gossipy Metle told her about Khole when she came to town from Bet il Mtoni. Salmé, the silly country sister who knew nothing, listened wide mouthed to anything her city sister said. This story was about an Arab chieftain who accidentally caught sight of lovely Khole on a feast day many years ago, probably before both Metle and Salmé were even born. In shock at her overwhelming beauty, and inadvertently, so Metle's story went, he drove his iron-pointed lance into his own foot. The story sounded like it had become embellished over the years, Metle was sure to have added to it when she happily told Salmé. In this version, the poor man was left to stand, wounded, but so enchanted by Khole's beauty he failed to notice the blood pooling the dust into rusty mud at his feet. Of course Salmé hadn't actually believed Metle back then. Khole was perfect, their father's favourite. She did not have admirers.

'Lovers?' Salmé asked to be completely sure about this latest story.

'They say the road to Sayyida Khole's *shamba* is very long and shady.'

'How could I have been so naïve?' she asked, though she did not expect an answer. Johar knew her well enough to stay silent now. He pretended to write something in the ledger to give her time for her blushes to subside. 'Lovers?' she chanted softly, as if to etch the meaning of the word in her brain.

Khole, always so elegant, always eloquent in her movements as well as her words. Lovers? The story of the chieftain and the lance – well if it wasn't true, it now seemed at least a myth to capture a truth. Lovers. Possibilities awoke as Salmé sat fidgeting each of the six earrings in her left ear in turn.

'Did you say you *will* come across here?' He sounded startled.

'Why did you ask if you didn't think I'd say yes?'

'In case, I don't know, because I wanted...' Ruete didn't finish his sentence because he was moving away. 'I have to find something to, well for you to walk across. The jump, maybe – well, too dangerous.'

Salmé laughed at the agitated hiccups in his voice. She heard his shoes on the stone steps leading down into his house. He was back so quickly she didn't have time to change her mind. Not that she intended to – she was no waverer – but he didn't know that.

He was a rectangular block with arms rather than a man as he approached the edge again. The shape of his face peered out from behind the plank. 'You're still here.'

'I could go down and cross the road,' she suggested after he'd lowered the piece of wood in the manner of a gangplank to a ship. It didn't look terribly wide once it was over the gap.

'More likely, you know, to be seen though,' he said.

She liked him for this. He knew the risk she was taking. That this had to be their secret. So she hoisted herself up onto the parapet and took the first step onto the plank. It was a risk, but for the moment, one foot on stone, one on wood, the risk felt as if it was all in the vertiginous glance down to the street. It was a coincidence that this was a moonless night: she had not planned to move under the cover of total dark. Without light, the fall beneath her looked less like two flights and more like a chasm straight to the centre of the earth. She paused, then took the second step without flinching.

The wood of the plank was smooth and cool against her bare feet. She knew she should be scared of heights after the time she climbed the palm tree as a child and couldn't get down again. A slave helped her then, so she'd learned to trust help would be there when she needed it. She stepped twice more quickly and found that her heart was beating like an unanchored rowing boat caught in the driving *mwaka* rains. She half-fell onto the opposite roof.

'Welcome aboard,' he said. So they were both thinking of boats: a synchronicity. He stood back a little from where she landed. His hands stretched toward her and fell back again; unsure hands. She was suddenly shy of him too, now she was close enough to actually see his features clearly. And to smell him. Sweat and some sort of sweet cologne. She was awkward, back to the moment of the surprised *jambo* across the night. The tinkling of her jewellery subsided into a new silence. He said nothing. She searched his face, still rounded from youth but with an indication his hair would soon start to recede. His hair, floppy, brown, invited a hand for confirmation of its silkiness.

'Well I'd better put the plank down until it's needed again,' he said at last. He bent to remove her means of escape.

'No, it's not a plank, it's a gangplank,' she said as he propped the wood lengthwise across the edge of his roof. 'My palace and your house are like ships in the harbour.'

'Palace?' he snorted.

The palace, now a dangerous jump across the gap, was a house only slightly larger than his. 'Are you teasing me?' she asked.

'Why is it called a palace? Do you have plumbing?'

'It is called a palace because a princess lives there,' Salmé said in her best Bibi Azziz voice.

He must have recognised the haughty tone. 'So have we met now?' he asked. He held out his hand toward her with conviction this time. She ignored it. His moustache twitched as his upper lip seemed to be making up its mind what to do next.

'Come. Come down. I have tea,' he finally invited, remembering his position as host perhaps, even though his guest was unlikely and suddenly imperious. 'We will drink tea from India,' he said, pointing to his stairwell.

Ruete took her down to the dining room that was now clear of silver tableware and bosomy guests. Salmé felt she was entering the stage for one of the annual puppet plays. It was not a real room: it was where stories came to life.

All her senses were alert. She'd experienced this feeling before, in times of danger, British shells slamming into Khole's palace, the rebellion lost. She knew she'd be able to describe every inch and every moment of this night. She gathered in the detail while she was ready at the sound of a footfall to flee. The teak of the table, now without the linen tablecloth of the dinner party, was polished until it reflected the room. The prismic chandelier was a miniature night sky on the table's surface. There was a lot of other furniture, side-tables and side-cabinets of equally heavy wood, and too many chairs.

'So much furniture.' He didn't seem to understand what she meant.

'It was sent from Hamburg,' he explained. He indicated one of the chairs and hovered behind her as she sat. 'I will go and get the tea. I think it best the servants don't come up. Just us.' He was gone and she was alone. 'I could go now and not come back. There is no harm done.' But she didn't move.

She was opposite a painting in a gilt frame. She looked at it because she did not want to leave. The painting was florid with roses and globular fruit and a hanging hare, ears forlornly guiding her gaze to a knife amongst the flowers. It was not art as she knew it. She wondered whether she liked it or not. She shifted in her seat.

The chair was not uncomfortable of itself she discovered. She leant back, was supported by hard wood. She wriggled a little but could not sit still. She got up, but only to go and look over at her palace. There were few lights on this side of the building. Most of the life would be in the courtyard, the cooks cleaning up, the butchers hanging new meat, the children being hurried away to bed. A lamp flitted from one window to the next. Then another. Then the light trickled out from behind the shutters of her bedchamber. Her women would be setting out her clothes for tomorrow and preparing her bed. The light winked every time one of them passed between the lamps and the window. So this was what he could see if he wanted to spy.

Her slaves were scrupulous about closing the shutters: only Allah was looking over her as she slept. She felt a little relieved, just a little disappointed. She leant forward and tilted her head to look up to her roof. A light hung there like a sentry waiting for her to come home.

There was a cough behind her. 'Thank goodness you're still here.'

She hadn't heard him come back. He was setting a tray on the edge of the table, out of the orbit of the mirrored stars.

He sat on a chair diagonally across the table from her and drew it in so his legs disappeared underneath. Salmé attempted a sitting shuffle forward to get her legs underneath the table too. She imagined this was like maneuvering one of the Sultan's elephants into line at a royal procession. Then she feared her voluminous trousers would catch under a leg, and stopped shuffling, and smiled. He was concentrating on the paraphernalia on the tray and did not smile back.

'I'll be mother,' he quoted in a strange language.

Swahili had been working well for them up to this point. 'Excuse me?' she asked. Her host paused with his bulbous teapot held high.

'It's an English saying. Mrs Seward uses the phrase – the wife of the British Consul.'

Salmé nodded, because of course she knew who Mrs Seward was: the new mistress of her estate at Bububu. Zanzibar was a small island, she knew she should not have been surprised that there was this connection between them.

'Being mother means you are going to pour the tea,' he continued. 'It is the mother's job.'

'Not the slaves?'

'There are no slaves, not even servants in many homes,' he added, tipping the pot. They were both silent to better concentrate on the stream of gold falling into one of the small cups, and for her to assimilate the idea of a home without slaves *or* servants.

The cup was of fine bone china like the pot. She watched it fill without saying anything more, though of course she could not banish all the tumbling of words in her head. She hadn't drunk from a cup before, she thought to tell him, but didn't want to appear ignorant. The glasses we use for coffee are more cylindrical, slipped into silver casings to hold the heat away, she wanted to explain but he would already know because every street coffee vendor used the same sort, though she doubted they went in for silver or gold casings. Then she remembered the cups from her childhood and wanted to tell him about the enormous quantity of china sent to her father by the Emperor of China – a perfect coincidence of words there, she would laugh if she could put it into spoken words. The Chinese china was out of bounds to the hands of the Sultan's children so she'd only seen it at a distance. How could she explain the power the Great Sultan had over his children? She doubted Majid dared use the china even now. The old Sultan's prohibitions had been unequivocal.

She found herself unable to voice any of this and about then the silence began to feel like an uninvited guest. She waited for Ruete to say something – he was the host, he was the man – but he was concentrating on filling the second cup. Then she noticed the other thing on the table, a brass-footed ceramic tile the pot had been sitting on. Designed as a surface to absorb the heat away from the table's high polish, which was a good thing surely, it depicted a little boy in breeches and peaked cap, the foreground to a one-mast sail ship. The portrayal of the human body was not allowed, yet here it was. A dishevelled boy in blue. There was no point of convergence here between his world and hers. Her palace tiles were all soothing patterns of nature and words from the Qur'an. She was shocked to see a boy pictured: But, if I am able to think this clearly, am I shocked at any deep level?

She was about to say something about the blasphemous boy when Ruete replaced the teapot on top of him. A crumpled felt shoe peeked out from under the edge of the pot. She had to chase something else to say as heat twisted off the teacups. He cleared his throat and passed one of the cups across to her. The cup chattered on the saucer making up for the lack of other conversation at the table. Then the confident precision of movement in Herr Ruete's pouring was revealed as an act.

'Sugar?' he asked, and promptly sprayed half the granules across the table like stardust. Salmé wanted to grab his shaking hand and tell him it was all right.

She didn't. She watched him spoon three teaspoons of sugar into her cup then stop. He helped himself to more. He stirred, the spoon loud against the side of his cup, looking down at the swirling tea all the while. Salmé could not see his eyes under a slipped hank of hair. It wasn't just his naked head she decided: he was completely unlike her brothers in every way. After the arrogance of self-regard amongst the male members of her family, she found his reserve singularly appealing. If he'd been more sure, less diffident, would she still be here?

Finally the silence was too much. She judged it was time to do something with her mouth – so she drew the delicate china to her lips under her mask and sipped. And immediately pulled back from the heat. The tender centre of her top lip twitched. Ruete was made of sterner stuff and slurped the tea. Two drops hung in his moustache. Her whole body ached to lean forward and wipe them away.

He made the goat-grunting throat-clearing coughing sound again. She put her cup down and sat with her hands completely still on her lap in case the tinkling of her bangles drowned out what he might say. His tongue, pink and fleshy, darted out to lick up the drops of tea in his moustache. The mugginess in the room was unrelieved by slaves rattling fans. There was too much to say and nothing to say. Salmé looked back at the hunted and slaughtered hare in the painting. This was all too silly for words, she decided. Which was obviously why words wouldn't come out.

And still they wouldn't come, and the silence went on. She whispering little cooling ripples into the tea before sipping again. I shouldn't be here, I shouldn't be here, were the inaudible whispers.

A pair of peacocks interrupted the silence then. They flew onto the windowsill and looked startled to see movement within. They bobbed their heads up and down and looked silly but she laughed merely because they were unexpected; they should have already found their roost for the night. At least now there was something to say.

'They are my peacocks, my special albino pair.' Their diadem crests quivered as they settled. The birds moved closer together:

framed by the window they were more attractive than the dead hare. 'So I am not the only one who comes across to visit you?'

'You are like them,' he said, laughing as well.

'Am I that white in the moonlight?' Salmé stretched out her arm to see.

'No, well you are pale, but I mean you are different, not like everyone around you, like an albino is different.'

She considered this. It was a compliment: she could tell by the lightness in his voice. It wasn't like Barghash sneering at her as one of the 'cats' of the harem. This was a good different.

'More tea, more sugar?' Now he'd started talking he couldn't seem to stop.

'Yes more.' He poured, he spooned. She reached across and stayed his hand. Touched his soft flesh. Finally touched him; an innocent practical gesture to hide the transgression of it. She could not as easily still her galloping pulse. When she breathed again, she spoke inanities.

'Be careful stirring the sugar, the cups are so fine they will break.'

'Bone china,' he said. 'Probably more brittle than bone but I'm sure it will withstand the assault of a few spoons.' Her hand remained resting on his. He did not move his away.

She talked to distract herself from the warmth of his flesh under her hand. She remembered some prattle from when she lived with Khole, and Barghash was always there visiting – and hatching plans – and the Europeans were the enemy of the day; behind their brother the Sultan Majid of course. 'It is very strange that you put bone in your clay,' she said, echoing Bar-ghash's mocking tone from that time. 'My brother, not the Sultan, another one, told me that it's bone ash – crushed up bone, burnt and ground bones of humans. It makes the china shine. Isn't that outlandish? You Europeans denigrate us for our benign slavery while you put your lips up against crushed men.'

Ruete laughed. His whole body shook. Her hand bumped off his and she took it back. 'It's not human bone,' he said between snorts.

Salmé wasn't used to being corrected. She wasn't used to being laughed at. She definitely didn't like it.

'Yes it is bone. Barghash told me.'

'Do you believe everything you are told?'

She thought perhaps she always had, and was startled by her gullibility. The idea made her angry, with herself, and with him. She felt she should defend herself, but instead she found herself attacking. The tension that had built since the moment she decided to cross to this stranger's house broke more easily than a bone china teacup.

'You believe everything you are told,' she accused back, her voice rising. 'All you Europeans come to Zanzibar and then you write silly treatises condemning slavery without bothering to look around and see how well our slaves are looked after. My slaves are fed until they are full and fat and they have clothes and they hardly work at all. And I teach them things.'

He'd stopped laughing but he still looked amused.

'It's true,' she continued. 'They have such an easy life. Compared to all my worries.' She scraped her chair back in his over-cluttered European dining room and stalked over to the window, shooing her peacocks away with wild arms. 'Go home,' she shouted at them. 'Get out of here.'

She did not hear his chair being pushed back above her shouting and her jangling jewellery. She did not hear his footsteps. She only knew he was there behind her because of the warmth of his body. The heat touched her before he did. He was solid. It was like standing against a wall.

Across from her was her palace full of slaves and gold, below were the narrow winding streets of her town. A turbaned Banyan wove his way through the shadows. Disembodied voices were tidal. A background.

'I'm sorry,' he whispered in her ear. 'I didn't mean to upset you. I would do anything to make you happy.'

She turned to face him. Both his hands went to her face. He did not remove her veil. He lifted the cloth briefly and lightly touched his lips to hers.

She spent the next day telling herself that if she were caught with Ruete it would not matter if she was drinking tea or kissing, or discussing Eastern philosophy, or anything else. Leaving her palace harem was the greatest sin: what was anything compared to that? There'd been no turning back from the moment she stepped onto his roof the first time.

So the next night when he embraced her as she turned to leave, she let his hands move firmly down from her shoulders. When she did not bat them away, he hesitated, and then moved his hands down further. Then he gently started to haul up her shirt, foot after foot of cloth, like pulling in a sail. She was suddenly scared: that must be the reason I can't breathe. If I do not move this is not happening, if I do not move. Her silent words crashed. Broke up. Scattered. If.

Her stomach between her trousers and her bunched up shirt was exposed now. The night air caressed it. And then the heat of his hand on her flesh was like a branding iron. Like he was a trader marking his slave. Salmé shivered: the hands stopped moving, but stayed. As if wooing a frightened animal now, his hands moved slowly, daring only a little at a time, tracing lines on her soft belly in another language. A language, she told herself, she did not understand.

Her rational mind briefly fought back. 'I have to go,' she said in her own clear language. She raised her hands to stop his, but they landed lightly and travelled with his hands over her bared flesh. The rucked cloth of her shirt fell back over their joined hands, hiding the movements: his hands moving, one higher, one changing direction and moving lower, sending a tremulous jolt through her. Her body startled her. It seemed to be responding in that same unspoken language he was using.

Her senses were alight. She could hear voices as far away as the harbour and smell the mangoes down the coast at Bet il Mtoni and feel every swirl on the fingerprint of his thumb as it searched her flesh. So *this* is what the women talked about in the *hammam* when they were naked and bathing and their fat bellies and thighs rippled with mirth. It didn't seem funny now though. She turned into his arms. He stepped back. Now she was facing him he was shy again. She couldn't catch his eyes.

'I'm sorry,' he said. 'I shouldn't.'

Salmé pushed herself forward. 'No,' she said.

He stopped. He was a statue; any minute a stray pigeon or peacock would land on his head. She had to clarify, 'Not *no* we shouldn't. *No*, don't stop.' She released the gold cord that held her mask in place and let it dangle. She was naked in front of him. Fully clothed and yet totally exposed now her face was unveiled. Her cheeks burned.

Salmé pushed herself forward again, toward him, and she angled her head up so their lips had to collide. Lips, and suddenly his tongue was forcing its way between her lips, searching. She felt like one of the big stewing pots being scrubbed by her slaves – his moustache was the big brush and his tongue the shammy cloth. She pulled away to laugh, and to breathe. The women were right – this whole business *was* funny.

'Your tongue?' she gasped. 'Is that the way you do it in Hamburg?'

'It's called French kissing,' he panted. 'I'm sorry. We can't.'

She pushed herself back into his arms. 'Try again,' she laughed. Her whole body was laughing. She pushed her tongue between his teeth and tasted the steeped tannin flavour of his mouth.

'We can't,' he said again. While his hand was back searching amongst her clothing. 'The Sultan.'

She felt a thrill of disappointment shoot up from the electric point at the bottom of her thatch of pubic hair.

'How would my brother ever find out?' she whispered into his lungs.

'We can't,' he repeated, but his body was not pulling away. 'We can't go to my bed. The plank' – another kiss – 'was from under the mattress. Not safe without it.'

'Do we need a bed?' she asked. It was an entirely innocent question. The talk of the harem was coy and exciting, but never as explicit as a lesson from Bibi Toad. Lover was a word only. Words were beginning to have meaning.

Salmé half slept the days away. They were intervals between life. She dozed in a haze of allegorical stories and images she made up to guard herself from looking directly at what she was doing. *If my palace is a dhow and his house a merchant ship, we are setting sail together into the vastness of an empty ocean.* The days passed, the daze of sated limbs and bruised lips. *The voyage of the dhow and the merchant ship rocked and swayed because the ocean was gentle to them.*

After the first week, Ruete procured a wider plank without jeopardising any of his myriad pieces of furniture. His bed was once again supported, and the way across the gap was safer. She walked from roof to roof in the dark on moonless nights, and then in the glare of the full moon that gilt her silver. They found the bed. *We are the only two people in the world to discover the body's passions,* she thought each time her foot was set on the gangplank. *This is fate: the fate her mother taught her from the Qur'an.*

There were of course doubts struggling in the haze, in the happiness: in another language, fate could translate as doom. She wasn't listening though. Most mornings she couldn't connect two thoughts together: *I am happy. What does Johar want now?* Whole minutes passed with no thoughts at all.

She wanted to spend every evening on the other side, as she came to call it. Her rare visits to her sisters were diversionary tactics, like in some British naval battle, so no one would notice her other life – on the other side. When she was exiled to Bububu she'd felt cut off from her sisters, and she felt no less so now, even when she sat in their palaces and sipped their coffee and sliced rose-jellies with her teeth. They could never imagine what was going on in her world. Look at virginal Zemzem, look at fat and thoughtless Metle, their bodies never felt like this.

Then Metle would say a kind word, something like, *You are looking almost pretty, the town air must be agreeing with you*, and Salmé would melt: I could tell her. But she didn't. She went home. For months she looked forward, not back. She looked forward, but did not see the future.

Salmé left Stone Town immediately after first prayers. She rode her favourite white donkey. The high saddle jingled with every step no matter how she positioned her bottom on it. She wanted silence, an impossible demand in the procession: the donkey's tail, dyed with henna, pointed like an arrow for all the noisy slaves to follow behind. Their horses and donkeys clattered on the stones and snuffled loudly. There were too many of them to be secret though the armed guards up ahead with Johar had been kept to a minimum, only four Nubians on foot, in a feeble attempt to avoid interest: all the market gossip that now frightened her, and the eyes of the Sultan's spies she imagined peeking from every window along the way. She muffled herself in her *schele*. It was still half-dark so she convinced herself she was cloaked a second time in shadows.

Sunrise was a mere suggestion on the horizon as the procession emerged from the narrow streets of Stone Town into the countryside. Salmé had hardly slept in the night, worrying that she'd miss the safe time to travel. A sayyida's curfew made any movement difficult – there were few hours of convenience. She noted with some ire that a female slave moved about with more independence than a princess; which made the whole daytrip to the *shamba* of Marseilles a silly undertaking, another risk in fact. But she had convinced herself that it was necessary for Ruete to see the aftermath of the rebellion so he'd understand just how serious her family was. To him Majid was a considerate host, well liked amongst the merchants of all the nations in Stone Town. They all got rich under his rule. He'd told her of several occasions when Majid had been personally affable to Ruete. She imagined visitors to Bet il Sahel could easily be tricked into believing the swords and daggers were in the same league as the women's famed jewellery: gorgeous, rich, gem-studded pieces of pure ornamentation. It's no use simply telling him. For him to understand the danger I'll have to show him what it's really like for me here.

'Do you want to come to Marseilles with me?' she'd whispered in his ear as he nuzzled her shoulder the night before.

'France?' Let him laugh at the mistake. Only make him come to the *shamba* as arranged.

She'd been out of bed that morning and demanding new clothes before her slaves had time to massage her limbs awake. 'Hurry, hurry, it's time,' she'd called to them. Because it was time, she couldn't avoid the fact. Time to go. The mistake about Marseilles was half intended.

She wondered that this hadn't come to a crisis sooner. Johar had finally told her the market was atwitter with the affair, so imperial intervention was inevitable. Why it had not come already was more the question. Amongst her other fears was the realisation that it probably had everything to do with declining status, that difference between princesses and slave girls. She may be the Great Sultan's daughter and the new Sultan's sister, but she was the naughty daughter, the rebellious sister and she'd slipped down the scale to a point of insignificance, exiled and isolated. But even a low class sister can go too far.

The narrow streets of town were succeeded by dirt-compacted pathways hemmed in on either side by trees and bushes and undergrowth. There were no roads of any width or permanence; travel by boat was far simpler. She tried to imagine what roads looked like in Europe, and failed. She'd seen a carriage at Bet il Sahel when the Great Sultan was still alive. The Queen of the British Empire, Victoria Regina, sent the royal carriage as a gift, but it turned out to be too wide for Stone Town's streets – being wider than an elephant – and had no roads to travel on over the rest of the island. Salmé never got near the thing because by the time she lived in town it was well and truly a monument rather than a notional thing of transport, but she remembered Khole boasting that as a young girl she'd sat in the back of the carriage pretending to be in London. Khole bounced up and down on the upholstered seats until the magnified heat through the windows burnt her out.

Salmé had laughed at her sister's story. Now as she passed along the uncultivated paths she didn't see anything to laugh at. The sun finally came up. The parrots were so loud in amongst the trees it was as if there was some huge, noisy winch hoisting the sun into the sky.

From up on her donkey Salmé could see the rolls of fat down the back of Johar's neck. His hand came back to swat a fly as she watched, then, as if to outstrip the fly, he moved his horse forward to the front of the line of slaves. He was really going ahead to lead the way. She wouldn't be able to flee anywhere alone, she realised. The *shamba* was somewhere to the north, but she wouldn't be able to find it. She'd always been taken places so why would she need a map in her mind? And she'd never been to Marseilles before anyway. It was a mythical place: somewhere she wrote letters to during the rebellion. Eight years ago. She hadn't wanted to see it in the intervening years. The reports were bad enough, the death toll still made her think of the deep, mournful tolling of the Christian's church bell.

They thought they'd been so clever using this *shamba* as a base for the rebellion, the closest to Stone Town owned by any of the conspirators. The estate was fortified with all the arms and munitions listed in instructions – in her handwriting. Sandbags, she remembered on the list, for the parapets and gun emplacements around the mansion. Hard-cakes ordered by the thousand, siege being such an unknowable thing.

They were moving faster now, as the undergrowth stopped pushing into the path so much. Johar bellowed a command and the animals broke into a soft canter. Salmé stretched her own neck backwards wondering if she was getting rolls around it to match the rolls she was noting elsewhere. Too much food and too little riding, she wanted to diagnose. Stretching her neck back and looking up she couldn't ignore that it was a glorious day. The uninterrupted blue of the sky made it seem more vast than usual, a sky to dwarf this speck of land called Zanzibar. Allah was not being fair making it so lovely.

Tears pricked in her eyes. Because of the rays of the sun: surely I'm not going to get emotional, she warned herself. But every nerve-end tingled. It was like her skin vibrated, prickling under the new sun. She'd seen so many women's bodies in their magical variety in the bathhouses of the harems, but she'd never imagined her own would be so intriguing. As her donkey rocked its way over the undulating dirt path, she was assaulted with messages from the backs of her thighs slipping against the leather and the weight of her feet dangling over the hind legs of the beast. Her nipples chafed against the muslin of her shirt.

Her skin was not the only thing picking up new signals. All her sensations were running amok. Her nostrils registered every new fragrance and stink. She was sure there were animals close by. The background of cloves now they were in plantation country was punctured by the smell of something deeper down the scale. Maybe a red monkey or a bushbaby, something hairy and rank. Her sense of smell was more acute; there was no denying her body was changing. What she'd suspected was now something she could not ignore. It was too late for her to have any choice about what to do next.

Johar's hand went up and the procession slowed. They came out of the trees onto a plain of blighted stumps and swaying saplings. Of course, Salmé thought, this is part of the consequences. Some of the trees had been cut for wood to stockade the villa, and the rest – and this was a clever touch hatched between Barghash and Khole – were lopped so the attacking forces had no cover during the onslaught. Five thousand men fought in all, Majid's soldiers plus the British sailors. It was a wide empty space. The ruins of the villa squatted beyond.

Johar on his horse and the armed Nubian slaves on foot, slowed to a stop. The rest of the procession had to haul at their reins. Johar turned back to face her. She knew what he was thinking. He was not stupid, he was as worried about spies as she was. There was someone already over by the ruins, a man and a horse. The figure lifted its arm. Salmé let out her breath when she recognised that it was raised in a wave of greeting.

'*Guten morgen.*' Ruete stepped forward, making himself distinct from the chestnut horse and the square of the horse's shadow. He moved quickly, puffing audibly until he got within a comfortable earshot of the princess's entourage.

She could not hide her surprise at seeing him. The plan had been for him to leave Stone Town later and to go by a different route, as if that would make them both invisible.

'I didn't want you to have to wait,' he said. He moved closer, spoke more softly. 'Don't worry. There was no one about to see me go. Only the usual men around the mosque and a few urchins.'

There were times like this when she felt she'd never be able to tear her eyes off Ruete, though, if she'd ever got up the courage to confide this to Metle or any of her other sisters she wouldn't have been able to say exactly why. He was not so good looking; he was not irresistible in that sense.

Her slaves gathered amongst the last ring of trees before the clearing opened out. The shade offered a little relief against the growing heat. Ruete followed them under the overhanging branches and as she dismounted her donkey and stamped the discomfort out of her legs she watched his face. The sum of his features gave way to two details only: the thickness of his eyelashes and fleshiness of his bottom lip. His slicked-back hair made it look like he'd emerged from a body of water and not the shadow of a horse.

'We can walk,' he said, indicating the ruins of the villa with the hand that had extended to take her arm and then sprung back as if stung by the looks of the slaves unpacking the animals around them. 'Over there,' he said. 'It's really interesting, you should see.'

Johar sent a young Nubian slave to run alongside her with a long-poled parasol. He had trouble keeping up amongst the tree stumps and exposed roots and his sayyida swam in and out of the circle of shade. His presence had another effect: the couple walked in silence.

'Oh go away,' she said at last. The young boy stood still while the couple walked on. He looked back at Johar and forward at Sayyida Salmé as if he didn't quite know whom to obey. 'Go back and help with the food,' she snapped. Ruete moved slightly away from her. Salmé felt the distance.

'It's all right,' she persuaded him. 'Slaves just don't know what to do unless you tell them exactly.'

'You are used to directing?' It was less a question and more of an observation. She realised he'd only ever seen her in his house, alone. She asked herself how much they really knew about each other before dismissing the question as useless. This wasn't why they were here. Still, the silence went on even without the boy around to eavesdrop. Salmé found she didn't need to talk. When they came to them, the ruins of Marseilles started to tell the story she'd brought him to hear. The details were in front of them and at their feet. They stepped over the low, straight foundations of the outer wall of the former villa and through dry, crackling weeds to a larger flat area.

'I did not know it was so – so destroyed,' she whispered once they were inside the circumscribed lines of the building.

'I don't think this is from the fight itself,' he said as he turned in a circle to take in all sides. 'They say this was part of the punishment afterwards. With the help of the British. Some explosives in each room and, boom, the villa was razed to the ground.'

'You know everything that happened?' She'd been so caught up in the rebellion she'd thought of it as a family saga only. She bent to run her finger over the grooves in the low remains of an exterior wall. They were like the pockmarks on a smallpox victim, though these scars had been caused by bullets and rockets and the twelve-pound howitzer.

He bent beside her and followed her fingertips over the jagged dents. 'We all followed the events keenly,' he said. 'It was a worrying time, with the mercenaries coming in from Persia and the mainland, and the El Hath tribes massing. It was bad for business. The harbour was a mess, virtually closed, and we waited though there was little doubt which of your brothers we'd be paying our customs fees to.'

Salmé knew this only as numbers: five hundred mercenaries to be paid for; three brass guns for the stockade; dates and times to tell the El Hath chiefs in the letters. It was strange to hear it told from another side.

'Then I rushed to the square in front of Bet il Sahel like most of the people in Stone Town and watched Sultan Majid return. He was showered with rice and flowers as he rode toward the palace. He looked every inch the returning hero. Your other brother didn't have a chance,' he said.

Salmé, despite the passage of time and the regrets since the rebellion, bristled. 'We thought he did.'

'Against the Sultan's guards? How many – thousands? And then the British. We knew it was all over when Lieutenant Berkeley took his sailors off the *Lynx* and marched inland.'

'So you know everything,' she conceded as she straightened. 'You know the streets of Stone Town better than I ever could. I've never been through them in daylight like you do every day of your life. And you saw all this happen, while I was in the harem waiting for news.' She paused. 'But do you know what I was doing for the rebellion?'

'Waiting in the harem?'

'Not during, I said *for* the rebellion.'

Before she could tell him, he was interrupting. 'So this is why it's called Marseilles.' They had moved beyond the outer wall into what could only have been the public reception room. The name of the *shamba* hadn't been the only thing influenced by the French. They were walking onto a glassy mosaic of smashed mirrors.

'Smashed to smithereens,' he said. 'Are your feet all right through your shoes? The bits look sharp in places. Be careful.'

Be careful, she repeated to herself. A bit late now. She almost laughed.

'It must have been beautiful,' he said as he picked his way through the shards to stand in the middle of the open-air room.

'My uncle built it after he saw palaces in France with mirrors all around the walls. My nieces were very upset to see it destroyed. They don't dare rebuild.'

'They must have been children when it happened.'

'My nieces? No they are old ladies now.'

'But.' He was facing her. He looked a bit slow when he was confused.

'The words I have to use are not explaining this.' She could feel her frustration rising. It was the heat and the tiredness from too many sleepless nights. It was from his inability to simply know her. 'My family is not like any you know. Some of my nieces were older than my mother. As some of my sisters are. My sister Sayyida Khole, who I lived with until the rebellion, was older than my mother.'

'Sayyida Khole? The one who was the accomplice to your brother Barghash?'

'Yes. The ages do make sense if you understand my mother was bought by the Great Sultan from the slave markets in Constantinople to be a companion for two of his daughters. They were all six years old. They played dolls together.'

Salmé caught a glimpse of herself in one of the larger fragments of mirror. It was like a calm pool, capturing the blue of the sky above and then her face. The reflection's steely, unwavering gaze reminded her of her father. He wasn't known as the Great Sultan for nothing. Then her face went out of focus. The tiny medallions of silver dangling from her scarf set off flashes of light as she shook her head at her reflection. The fear is getting to you, you need a cooling drink she told the face as it slipped out of the frame of broken mirror.

Ruete was a little further into the villa now, in what was once the main courtyard. His back was to her. His broad, plump back. Between them was a path of broken mirror, which looked to her like the sugar crystals he was so partial to, the ones he'd clumsily scattered across his table the night she first crossed to his house. I *do* know him and he *does* know me, she told herself. He is sweet, he is sweet, she murmured as she walked toward him. She let herself feel the imprint of his weight on top of her: her body felt the memory physically. When she caught him up she stretched up on the points of her slippers and kissed him on those fleshy lips, trusting the jagged ruins of the walls to screen them from the spying world. The bristles of his moustache itched her upper lip.

'Why are you here with me?'

'I wouldn't dare not do what you asked,' he laughed. 'You have strength, spirit.'

'Like a horse has spirit?' She didn't know whether she liked that. Why was nothing simple with him? The relationship between her father and her mother was so much less complicated. He owned her. Once she'd given him a child, he gave her every respect. Jilfidân would have done anything the Sultan asked of her in return.

'I'll tell you about the rebellion,' she said after a second kiss. She could feel his breath on her cheek. They were too close for her to see his eyes.

'I was one of Barghash's conspirators,' she confessed.

Ruete, a hand on each shoulder, pushed her back slowly. If a ghost had raised itself up out of the ground and howled she wouldn't have been surprised. Now her guilt was out she could feel the shadows moving between them. Over a hundred restless ghosts; lives as irreparably smashed as the mirrors that crunched underfoot.

'Remember how I told you I taught myself to write? Well that was the problem. Khole and Barghash used me as scribe, writing to all the conspirators.'

'I will never cease to be amazed about what goes on in your harems,' he said, jest in his voice. He didn't seem at all surprised at Salmé's past transgression, but then he'd witnessed her latest rebellion night after night for months. He pulled her back toward him and patted her on the back, as one would a child, as if that would make it better.

'I have not been forgiven,' she persisted.

Salmé pulled away first. The heat of his body was too much, and she didn't want to be made feel like a child.

'Marseilles was destroyed, Barghash was exiled to Bombay, Khole was sent away. I had to go to one of my estates. I'm only back because the Sultan wanted to give Bububu to the Consul Seward. I thought he might forgive me once I was back in Stone Town, but now,' she paused.

'But he has forgiven his brother. We found it odd, it was the talk of the merchant houses when Barghash came back from India. We couldn't see why the Sultan didn't just kill him, a traitor. But if he has allowed Barghash back, so surely you are all right?'

'Barghash is not only a traitor – he is the heir to the Sultancy. I am merely one of many little sisters and one who made a mistake.'

One mistake may eventually be forgiven, but two, she asked herself. She took a deep breath but before she could get the next part of her confession out, but before she could say even one of the words, Ruete jumped in with visions of stability and orderly progression of power from father to son in European kingdoms and principalities.

'Can't figure out, how you manage it going through the brothers instead of the sons,' he pondered. 'Even Napoleon, getting rid of the French kings, could see the point.' As he pontificated over his history lesson, he had his hands on his waist, allowing the slightest of breezes access to his already damp underarms.

Salmé was not immune to the temperature. The sun was prickling her skin under her muslin shirt and cotton trousers. She wanted to get back to the shade. She wanted to get home. She didn't know why she couldn't get to the point of any conversation with this man. Round and round we go, and he just doesn't understand. But it's my fault, she decided: I have to be more decisive. Look at him, a man who wears a coat over his shirt in this climate!

'Ruete!'

He dabbed at the slick sheen of sweat developing across his forehead.

'My princess?' His eyes snared hers. They were brown and liquid and distracting.

'I have coffee,' she offered, a sigh disguised in her voice.

The cook had set up camp in the shade and coaxed a fire into life in a brass brazier while most of Salmé's entourage disappeared into the neighbouring clove plantation to talk to the *shamba* slaves.

This was an easier story to show Ruete about Zanzibar, because it was one they shared, this story of the clove plantations that brought so much wealth to the island; especially now the British were being harsh about the slave trade. The Great Sultan had brought both the slaves and the cloves to the island. As they walked back across the bare space to the camp Salmé could see fifty or more slaves in amongst the immense trees. Some were up shaky ladders, some half hidden in the bushy foliage, while the rest stooped below collecting the snapped and dropped clove buds. The wicker baskets were huge. More than a few slaves were resting by a ring of baskets, chatting and directing anyone who would listen. It was obvious the Arab overseer was nowhere about. Johar would have seen him off so he couldn't accidentally come into the presence of a female member of the royal family: as much a point of protocol as it was of secrecy.

A soft wave of song washed across them as they got closer to the plantation. The song followed the rhythm of the slaves picking, or the other way around. The tiny flower buds were shaped like nails. Khole always joked that it was these nails that held the wealth of their family steady. Salmé felt a pinch of sadness at the sight of all the activity. The sadness of loss.

'We have set a carpet over here,' beckoned Johar.

The thick carpet of purple and red with gold thread woven through was under a cluster of parasols, propped like drooping flowers with their heads holding each other up. Salmé sat down first and then Ruete dithered and circled until he found a way to sit himself. She leaned back amongst some pillows on her good arm and watched him, reminded of a dog trying to nest on a blanket. He hadn't learned anything of the Zanzibar way in all his years on the island. She looked down to give him the privacy to get more comfortable. Her plaid shirt and trousers clashed like cymbals with the carpet. It made her think of the kind of lizard in the jungle areas whose colours changed to blend in with its surroundings. She liked the contrast of herself against the mat: it announced that she was there and would not hide like the chameleon.

One of the young boys came over with the brass coffee pot. What could have been his twin approached behind him with a tray of glasses in fine casings. She held her silence while the coffee was poured. She watched the colours on her lap and waited for the slaves to go some distance. The smell of the thick coffee competed with the cloves and the sweat, and won. Even before drinking it, the coffee made her a little heady. There was no putting it off any longer. Ruete was preoccupied, popping small squares of halva into his mouth to sweeten the coming coffee. Salmé held her glass on her lap and began. 'You know that thing you said about Mrs Seward, the words she used about pouring the tea. Being mother.'

He nodded, smiling, remembering.

'Well I'm going to be a mother now.'

She didn't quite know how she expected him to react but she watched in surprise as he calmly brought his own glass to his lips. He clearly hadn't quite found where to put his legs nor his heavy boots. The soles of his boots glittered, impregnated with granules of mirror. Like diamonds. He too had been made rich on the clove trade. He sipped his coffee cautiously through the sweet halva.

'So?' she asked, needing a reaction.

'I thought you'd want the little boys to do it, but if you want to pour the next glass...'

She couldn't tell if he was joking or not. She snorted. It was a laugh and a gasp and an animal sound. 'I am going to be a mother,' she said more loudly as if this would make him understand. 'I am going to have your child,' she said softer now, for his ears only.

Ruete spilled his coffee in his clumsy haste to lever himself up onto his knees. She watched the coffee spread and stain the pale cloth of his trousers.

'I should have known. You've been a bit strange these last few days.' He was staring at her waist not her face. 'You must marry me. Come and live with me. I'll protect you.'

Poor sweet Herr Heinrich Ruete. 'Do you really think the Sultan is going to let one of his sisters leave the harem and marry a *kafir*, a Christian?'

'You will be my wife not his sister.' He leaned forward but did not touch her. There were too many eyes around.

'You cannot think that. This picnic may look like a pure idyll but look again behind you. Marseilles. Can you not see that my family is ferocious and violent and death comes easy? Don't be beguiled into thinking the Sultan's leniency to Barghash is some honourable thing about blood being thicker than water. It is convenience only. My oldest brother, the Sultan of Oman since our father's death, was killed this year. By his own son. My nephew.'

The close harmony of the *shamba* slaves' verses filled the morning as she gathered more words to her argument. 'This is what my family does.' She waved her crooked arm in the direction of the ruins. 'This is what we do to each other.' Her hand landed again next to the other, the one still holding her hot coffee. It fluttered slightly like an injured bird. 'See?'

'If we cannot marry?' he whispered as he sat back on his heels.

'We can go to your country. I will go into exile on your word,' she prompted. Her heart was still, a tightly bound emptiness keeping doubt at bay.

The sun was dipping and would soon set. Salmé had planned this – to enter the town as she had left it, under cover of darkness. They were half an hour from Stone Town at Ngambo when the time to pray fell on them.

'I can't find it,' Johar told her as she was dismounting. He did not look well. She could see the whole day had made him fretful.

'What have you lost, Johar?' she asked kindly.

'Your prayer mat. We must have left it at Marseilles after the last prayers. Half the water bottles are missing too.'

Salmé wondered what it would be like to be a Christian, and not have this imperative to pray.

'There are other mats,' he offered though he knew her answer before she said it.

She could never use a slave's prayer mat, but she knew only too well that she could only pray on a mat made of vegetable matter as Allah decreed. If it were not carefully woven, nature would have to provide. 'A leaf,' she demanded. 'A large one.'

The tallest of the Abyssinians was sent to fetch down the

largest leaf he could reach. He stood on a Nubian guard's shoulders and tottered as he grabbed at the high branches of a moz tree. There was a murmur of appreciation in the crowd of slaves as he jumped back to the path waving an almost child-sized leaf.

Salmé knelt on the makeshift mat. She touched her nose to its dusty, earthy smell. Allah guides his faithful in the straight path, she reflected, the path of those whom He blessed. But what about those who go astray, she asked Him. She prayed with all her might. A breeze got up while she knelt. It hushed some of the heat off her back.

Her donkey prodded her shoulder and nuzzled in amongst the folds of her scarf when she went to remount. He had the longest, darkest eyelashes. She remembered the day her father gave her this new donkey, a mount high enough for a growing girl.

'I will miss you,' she told the donkey. I will not cry, she mouthed to herself.

Once again, she only saw the streets of Stone Town in the dark.

It was hardly dark the next night when Metle stormed through the gate.

'What are you doing?' Metle hissed as she struggled to get her *kosch* off her swollen feet. A slave fell to her knees in front of her and pulled at the offending shoes.

'I was just ordering the poultry we'll need for next week.' Salmé was in the courtyard. She came forward so Metle didn't have to hiss as loud as an incensed bush snake.

'That's not what I mean and you know it.' Metle righted her-self and looked directly into Salmé's face. 'And don't you lower your eyes modestly.'

Both sisters looked around to see who was hearing all this. Salmé noticed how small the crowd at her gate was. Metle had the minimum of slaves and guards that protocol would sanction, and no son, no sisters, no aunties or cousins.

'Come into the reception room.'

'No, upstairs, private, right now.' Metle threw off her *schele* and didn't look to see where it landed. She herded Salmé ahead of her. She was panting heavily. Salmé could feel her breath on the back of her neck as they climbed the steps. At the gallery she turned.

'Metle, should you be upsetting yourself and rushing around like this in your condition?'

'Don't you make this about me. This is about you girl. Move.'

Guilt made Salmé do what she was told; little else could make her do anything against her will.

'Away, away,' Metle waved at the slaves in Salmé's bed-chamber. They looked at Salmé, her old nursemaid and wide-eyed Zada, and she nodded, so they went, the slap of bare feet echoing down the gallery. Metle unhooked her veil and let it fall near the door; she was a palm tree in a typhoon shedding fronds. 'Majid has made a big mistake,' Metle moaned when they were finally alone.

Salmé felt a flood of relief. So this was something about the rebellion, not about her life now. Her secret was safe. She went over to her chest and rummaged amongst the litter of perfume bottles lying on top of it.

'What has the Sultan done now?' she asked, all innocence, dabbing a little orange blossom, reaching for the musk.

'It's what he hasn't done. He really should have made you live with one of us, or at least had one of our cousins or nephews here with you.'

Salmé's anxiety started to rise again. Metle must know. The look on her face. She was perched on Salmé's bed, her pregnancy huge now and sitting low on her lap. There was only one lamp alight in the room but Salmé could make out the dark half-moons of moisture under Metle's armpits.

'I know Majid was angry with you but you're still his little sister. Come to think of it, Barghash is as much to blame for all this. Why hasn't he taken you in and looked after you? Mind you,' Metle considered aloud every thought popping into her brain, 'I don't know how you got taken in by him over all that rebellion business. And now look at you – still the same old gullible Salmé getting caught up in things you shouldn't.'

Salmé didn't say anything. She didn't have time.

'But that's no excuse. You are old enough to know better. You've had your twentieth birthday and more. You have no excuse to be led astray. You! Don't you remember all that talk when we were little? That princess in Oman. Stoned to death.'

The musk bottle slipped from Salmé's hand. The perfume pooled at her feet and evaporated instantly and entirely off the heat of the tiles as she watched.

'But Khole got away with it,' she whispered from within the fog of scent.

'Khole gets away with everything. You can when you're the favourite. But you are the naughty little sister not *Nidjim il subh*.

Neither of us were ever destined for the firmament, as the Morning Star or any other little twinkling spot. The penalty for...' Metle hesitated, seemingly unable to say the word for what was happening with her sister, which, considering her own condition, Salmé would normally have found very funny. 'For it,' Metle said when she settled on her words. 'For consorting and relations and such and such. The penalty is death.'

The wall of words stopped and Salmé stumbled over to the bed.

'Sit, sit, my silly duck,' Metle patted the mattress. Salmé, again, did as she was told. She was suddenly very tired.

'You were bored,' Metle said, patting the same place, only it was Salmé's thigh now. 'Or you were excited to be back in Stone Town.' As if boredom and excitement could co-exist and excuse anything.

'How do you know?'

'Everyone knows. It's the talk of the marketplace. My eunuch finally gave up the information this morning but he admitted it's not new gossip. I came as soon as the curfew lifted.'

'Will the Sultan know?'

'Salmé, how can you even ask? Are you that naïve? If I know, he knows. The red monkeys on Pemba will know by now.'

They sat in silence. Voices filtered up from the courtyard. I bet they're talking about it down there too, Salmé thought.

'But we were so careful. I never went down to the street,' she said, looking out toward the window, through which, should the slaves had failed to close the shutters, she'd be able to see Ruete's lit window.

Metle's breathing had settled to a slight nasal wheeze. 'Spies, my darling,' she sighed. 'Which of your slaves do you trust?' Then she leant over and rested her head against Salmé's.

'They say he's from Europe.'

'Yes.' Salmé was suddenly bursting to tell. Her adventure would be real if she could share it. Metle kept talking though.

'One of those German places they're saying. Oh Salmé, what if it were Mr English Trader next door, or Monsieur French merchant? Would it have happened anyway?'

She didn't know how to answer that. Her passion clouded all rational thought. But was it a passion for him or passion for passion itself?

'You can't love him. He's a *kafir*. It can't go that far.' Metle was so adamant, Salmé almost believed her.

'They sent me away,' she whispered. 'They exiled me – should they be surprised?'

'Salmé, we do love you. Bring your spirit back to us.'

Tears began to sting in the corner of her eyes and deep in her nostrils. It was the kindness in Metle's words that got her.

'Maybe if you stop Majid will pretend it never happened. The Sultan has the power to do anything, even forget. And I'm sure Majid does love you.'

Salmé contemplated the word: stop.

'It is so dangerous.' Metle stroked her hand.

'I know danger,' she interrupted. 'I was there, remember, when the British opened fire on Khole's palace to stop the rebellion. The gunboat moved in as close as the German merchant's house is to us now. I know the sound of shot exploding against stone. I heard the screams. I thought I was going to die. This doesn't feel like danger, Metle. It feels…'

'It feels lovely doesn't it?' said Metle, who it seemed, understood after all. 'Which is why you are not to trust it.'

'But what if it is too late?'

The thick, sweet pink smell of spilt musk still hung in the room, blotting out all memory of the acrid stench of gunpowder.

She had one night to worry about whether she should change her plans and stop seeing Ruete. The next morning Majid's letter arrived.

A commotion in the street outside set off the dogs and then the birds and then the slaves. The gates opened and banged closed. She came out onto the first floor gallery and leaned over the balustrade. She could hear unknown voices below but the men had not moved beyond the entrance hall so she couldn't see who they were. The cook had a chicken by the neck on the other side of the courtyard near the fire. He was watching Johar greeting these new visitors. He mechanically wrung the animal's neck as he watched.

Salmé ran down the gallery until she got to the room above the gate. Nashwa was in there teaching the two young girls from the *shamba* to sew, which always started with hemming. She'd heard it so often she believed it, *Everything needs a hem, Salmé, we cannot have loose threads hanging.* The newest additions to the household were a pigeon pair of pinched faces and skinny limbs sitting awkwardly and shifting the sheets along their laps. They stopped what they were doing to watch their mistress rush through the room to the window. She positioned herself behind the fretwork frame and peered through the star-shaped holes.

The soldiers were clear enough in the street below. They wore white robes, punctuated by black – belts and hands and feet. From this angle, looking down on them, the tops of the turbans were coloured dog turds. There was no mistaking who they belonged to. She'd waited so long to hear from the Sultan she should have been thrilled. Instead dread was a rock at the bottom of her guts. As she turned back to the room she caught Nashwa's look. She could not ignore her old wet-nurse. But she could not frighten her.

'After all this peace and quiet it's like the Sultan's Custom House around here. If I only got the same two dollar head tax for every slave to pass through I'd be as rich,' she joked.

Nashwa didn't laugh.

'Well, richer anyway,' Salmé added before a renewed commotion took her back to the window. The soldiers were parading two by two, shoulders touching, down the street, with a couple of corpulent eunuchs in crimson rolling forward in the middle of the procession. Their umbrellas bobbed like lily pads on a pond.

'I had better...' She left the room without quite fixing on what she had better do.

There was a small boy at the top of the stairs. He'd survived the cholera the year before and would be forever small. His voice fitted his size. Salmé wondered if she could ignore him, tell Johar she hadn't heard.

'You are requested to come to the reception room,' the little slave said again in a brave squeak.

Johar was already seated when she got there. He had the letter open. He knew the contents. His face was giving nothing away: his fat lips sealed, his eyes blank as if helped by a pleasant drug. She waited for two of the younger slaves to rearrange the *meddes* and pillows before she sat in the imitation of comfort and ease. She noted how pleasantly the green of her shirt warred with the orange of the small pillow that supported her crooked arm. She noted how hot and stuffy it was in this room at this time of day – and how much more pleasant evening-time visits were to the daytime visits of men.

'Will I read it now?'

'Of course,' she said though she felt there was nothing ordinary about the situation.

He read without preamble and without varying his tone.

To Her Highness the noble lady Salmé, the beloved sister of Sayyid Majid ibn Sa'id ibn Sultan. May Allah preserve you and keep you as a treasure for us during the period of your life, Allah willing. Allah is the Almighty, the Noble, and for His servants He is forgiving, merciful. Peace be with you sister.

She took no comfort from these opening words. They were customary. She had written them herself. Being scribe for Barghash had taught her a lot about etiquette in written messages, whether dealing with friend or foe.

Johar coughed before going on. He managed to keep his voice steady as he read the message from Bet il Sahel. Salmé imagined Majid standing in his palace reciting the words to a sitting scribe. How much easier life would be if they talked to each other rather than going through all these intermediaries. She would then – if she'd wanted – have been able to plead and proclaim her love and willingness to do her duty. Instead she had to simply accept that the offer he was making was not up for diplomatic negotiation. More words washed around her and then the threat arrived in full:

I invite you to take a journey to Mecca. I give you permission to leave your palace harem and undertake this pilgrimage which is good in the sight of our Lord.

Johar paused. Salmé knew he was damming up a threat of tears. He finished the letter as Majid had dictated it.

I greet you as one humble before his Lord and obedient to Allah.

They sat in silence. The paper crackled as Johar placed the letter on his lap. They didn't have to discuss the offer. They both knew what it meant: it was not the first time such a proposal had been made to an unmarried woman. The daughter of one of the Sultan's overseers, ten years before, had had no choice but to go on a supposed pilgrimage. By the time she boarded the ship she was obviously with child. She never came back. Salmé's mother was appalled at the time: the Holy City should never be used in a ruse to remove a woman from the world.

Two of the slave women began to sing outside in the court-yard. They were cutting up vegetables and fruits for the midday meal. Coconuts needed force to give up their milk and flesh and singing helped. The song was from somewhere far in the north of Africa. Salmé did not understand the words but they sounded joyful. An honest, rhythmic, working chant.

'It is a death sentence,' she said at last. 'He knows.'

'They say he has an executioner ready,' Johar said now they were being honest.

'Who does?'

'The gossip in the market.'

'It is much talked about?'

'They say the executioner is six-foot-four inches tall.'

The silence fell again, much like an executioner's axe really.

It gave her time to consider the truth of the gossip. Stories with such detail had to be true.

That night as she crossed to Ruete's roof she had a sudden image of herself walking along a rope – she was a tightrope walker over a chasm of nothingness.

'You looked like you were going to fall,' he said as he caught her on the other side. 'I missed you last night. I was worried. After our picnic. I thought.'

'My sister came. We have to talk,' she said once his lips let go of hers.

'After.'

That was the way of it, the pattern of their nights. Their bodies talked first and then, only after they were finished, their voices were heard in the drowsy glow. So she fell into the embrace of routine – blessed as it was – and, without wanting to, fell immediately into sleep after. It was deep and impenetrable sleep. She hadn't been able to sleep after Metle's visit and needed this respite.

'My Sleeping Beauty,' he said as she stirred much later. 'I've been watching you. Doesn't all that jewellery poke into you? Do you ever take it off?'

He was propped on a pile of pillows with a candle and a book beside him. She smiled at his innocence. 'A sayyida is never without her gold.' She lifted her right arm and shook it as if it was a musical instrument.

'I thought I was going to have to kiss you to wake you up like the real Sleeping Beauty.'

She knew she should talk to him about the Sultan's ultimatum but that would be the end of this story and she wanted to put off the new urgency and linger within the moment for a while longer. So she asked, 'And who was she, this beauty you keep talking about?'

'Sleeping Beauty? But of course you don't know. She was a princess, like you. She was cursed and fell asleep and only the kiss of a prince could wake her.' He bent over and kissed her, a light gentle brush on one corner of her mouth and then on the other. 'My mother told me the stories when I was a child. The stories of Mother Goose.'

'You have geese that tell stories in Hamburg?'

He laughed. 'Yes. These are the stories we can tell our child.' He reached out and stroked the slight swell of her stomach. 'Are you hungry? Some food? I'll go and get some.'

She held his arm to keep him in the bed. 'Our children's stories were told by Scheherazade who was, I'm sure, far more beautiful than a goose.'

'Yes I know. I've read them,' he said and she believed him because he had many books in his house and often had one beside the bed. '*A Thousand and One Nights* isn't it? She kept her Sultan awake night after night with her stories.'

'I had a mother called Scheherazade.'

'I thought her name was Jilfidân?'

'I had many mothers,' she said patiently. 'My father had many wives. Bibi Jilfidân gave birth to me. She was one of the slaves, over seventy-five of them in his harems. And then there were the legal wives.'

She sat up then and pulled a pillow in front of her breasts

and belly as a modesty shield because she felt less like Salmé and more like the courtly fictional Scheherazade as she told him about her mothers. He put his head back on his pillow to listen. His eyes closed but she knew he was listening from the quirk of his moustache, riding the movement of his upper lip.

'We lived with one of the legal wives when I was a child at Bet il Mtoni. She was fat and proud and ruled us severely. She was my mother's bane because Jilfidân always wanted to be holy, and that means being accepting and tolerant. But how she hated haughty old Azziz. I didn't ever meet the other legal wives but there were a lot of stories about Schazadi Scheherazade Kanum. She was the daughter of a Persian noble. She was very extravagant. It is said she dropped pearls as she walked and the slaves chased after her, harvesting the pearls to sew back on her trousers and slippers at the end of the day. The Sultan took so much of her demands and then no more. He sent her back to Persia to her father. Can you imagine the shame? Only no one in the harem had any sympathy.'

'Was she beautiful like the other Scheherazade?'

'Who knows? She did have beautiful baths at her palace so I imagine her fresh and lazy in the steam. Which is funny because that wasn't the end of it. My father had to return to Oman because the Persians were harrying the borders. They went to war, and we heard Schazadi Scheherazade Kanum was fighting at her father's side. Really fighting. Riding on a horse – can you imagine – brandishing a long sword. Nothing clean and lazy there, just her galloping down on my father.'

Her lover opened his eyes and squinted a little in the lamplight. 'Is this true?'

'It is what we heard in the letters that came back. But letters – who knows the truth?' She paused. So he still did not fully believe the violence in her family. She watched him sit up. He was white, but it was always a shock to see just how white his chest and back were. It was as if they had never seen the sun. His neck came out of the milky flesh like a dark stalk.

'Was that when the Sultan died?'

'Yes, on the way back from Oman.'

'And then your brothers fought? Marseilles and all that.'

This was the opening she needed to talk about the letter. But she didn't want to think about it. Go away Majid, she shouted in her head. She bounced toward Ruete and pushed her modesty pillow onto the crown of his head.

'Look now you have a turban too,' she crowed.

He grabbed her around the waist and they wrestled. Mock-exhausted, he fell back. His face was made for the contented look, his features benign in repose. Optimistic.

'It'll all be fine you know. You'll miss Zanzibar though.'

'We'll have to go soon,' she finally told him. 'Majid knows.'

'Soon,' he agreed, 'if you say.' She kissed him long and hard. For agreeing so simply.

'Did you know that our first point of landfall in Europe will be Marseilles?' he asked.

'So my path will be from Marseilles to Marseilles.' It sounded like a song when she whispered it.

Salmé had one of the younger eunuchs act as scribe. There was no point antagonising Majid with any further proof of her own writing abilities. She worded the letter carefully, to *His Highness, the noble lord Sayyid Majid ibn Sa'id ibn Sultan, my beloved brother*. She'd rehearsed it in her head in the dark, then cut and polished it until it shone with sisterly duty and gratitude. She thanked him for this opportunity to travel to the Holy City, and begged him time to make all the preparations for the journey.

His next letter gave her a date of departure: he did not give her much time. And then he asked why she was selling her possessions. Her reply was even more pious; she even recited verses from the Qur'an. She owned the weight of wealth onerous and expressed a desire to be closer to Allah in all ways. She was selling her possessions so she could take the gold to Mecca and do good deeds.

Salmé was rather pleased with the formality and solemnity of her voice but she saw Abdah fidgeting with the pen when she made him write these words in the return letter. She couldn't reassure him: she was letting the slaves think the sentiments in her letters were genuine. It was safer that way. She knew Abdah would be straight out to Johar to discuss her madness before getting a couple of tougher Abyssinians to carry the letter to Bet il Sahel. 'Doesn't she realise what they really intend to do to her?' he'd say. 'Cluck, cluck, cluck,' they'd mutter to each other, fat old mother ducks.

Majid could challenge her of course, and let the whole messy business come out of the shadow of gossip. But if he did, he'd have to openly acknowledge the supposed pilgrimage was an execution order. Until he did this, she was going to continue to use his threat to her own advantage.

'If he's plotting to kill me, I'm well within my rights to lie a bit too,' she told Ruete when they were working on their own plans. She imagined she sounded defiant. He wouldn't have seen the shiver in the dark of his bedroom.

The word about the sale of her property had spread as quickly as any market gossip. Johar hardly slept. He sat in the reception room with all manner of buyer, circling her property like carrion birds waiting for the wounded animal to die.

'They are offering too little. Your estate on Pemba is worth more. There are a thousand trees in the north, all ready to harvest. They think they can get it cheap.'

She knew he was trying to act in her best interests. 'Just sell,' she told him.

Amidst all the activity, every day – every minute – behind her defiance, she waited for Majid to get sick of playing the game. His troops could be at her gate at any moment. She lay in bed in the early hours of the morning imagining the noise they would make clattered down the street with their swords drawn. Would they lead her away to the six-foot-four-inch tall executioner under cover of dark or in full daylight? Every stray noise drifting up from the street and insinuated itself between her shutters was evidence of their coming. After one sleepless night she sat at *sefra* in such a state that she sobbed herself into thinking it would be a relief to hear a captain's fist banging at her gate. She convinced herself that all she wanted was time for Ruete to get home from his trading house so they could reach across roof to roof to say a last pathetic goodbye before her execution.

As soon as she'd eaten she was able to laugh at herself for being so melodramatic. She wasn't going to lie to herself: all she wanted to do was live.

When the date of the ship's departure for Mecca was a week away, more news arrived. It wasn't in an official letter. The content wasn't really a surprise, though the source of the message was. Salmé sat on Ruete's bed as she told him about it, trying to look as imposing as she could while half-naked.

'I haven't got a week,' she told Ruete. 'He'll come for me in three days.'

'You mustn't work yourself up. It's all planned,' he said, voice calm. 'You'll be away from Zanzibar in a week. Don't listen to gossip.'

'But I trust this source.' She didn't think she had to explain why. 'The letter came from my sister, Sayyida Khole. She hasn't contacted me since I tried to make peace with Majid. Even though the rebellion failed, she is still Barghash's ally. She has no reason to love me still, to her I am a betrayer – I schemed with her against our Sultan – but then I betrayed the rebellion and my loyalties shifted again. I am the worst of the worst in her eyes. So she must really believe I am about to die to send this letter. She has heard of Majid's change of plans and warns me to flee.' She paused. She wasn't going to say how she felt about the last part of her sister's letter. 'And she has offered me a hiding place in her harem.'

He paused in his gentle massaging of her right foot and looked up. He didn't say: *you wouldn't.* But it was in his eyes.

'She says the harbour is watched. It is dangerous to run that way. She knows you have a berth for me on the *Mathilde*.'

The name galvanised him. The German ship was their secret. How that detail got all the way to Khole's country estate was beyond him.

'We'll have to hurry,' she whispered. 'Another ship. Sooner.'

'I will miss these nights,' he said pulling at her foot and then her ankle and then her calf until she slid across the sheets toward him.

'You will follow soon.'

Neither of them believed the Sultan was stupid enough to kill a foreign merchant; he relied on trade as much as the Europeans did. So they would leave separately and meet up later, like they had at Marseilles. He had friends in Aden who were also willing to offer her a hiding place while she waited.

'Are they nice people?' she asked, pushing his hands away.

'They are nice people.'

Khole's letter didn't change any of the times Salmé went back to reread it. In three days time, on *Siku a mwaka*, the first day of the New Year when the festivities were at their height, Salmé would be quietly taken away. Everyone would be more concerned about which clothes to wear and how many fireworks to set off: there'd be no family around to protest and plead her cause. And then it would be too late.

The method of execution was not alluded to this time. Through the slaves Salmé had heard speculation about stoning, though that sounded too barbaric. Majid was a refined, educated man. But there were a lot of animals sacrificed to see the New Year in and she *could* see herself becoming just one more amongst the bullocks and sheep, and goats, gazelles, fowls and ducks.

Metle had more to say on the matter. She came on her donkey this time, now too big with the child in her belly to carry herself for ten minutes through the streets. Salmé heard the distant sound of the hoofs against cobbles and felt fear leap again like a fish on a hook. Majid has sent his guards! She'd got to such a state, she cowered at any change in the din in her own courtyard or even the restlessness of the pigeons in their coop on the second floor. She hid in her room when she heard her gates opening. She didn't even dare to look out to see what was clattering into the courtyard – which was a donkey, a horse carrying a eunuch who carried Metle's son, various other bodies of distant relatives, and Metle demanding someone get her down off the beast.

'I can't wait to get this thing born so the wet-nurse can carry him around,' she shouted up to her when Salmé felt safe to poke her head over the rail.

She hurried down the steps; it was clear Metle would not be getting up them without a lot of complaint. She ignored the entrance near the gate, suddenly made small with the shifting hind legs and colliding rumps of Metle's mounts. It was unclear if they would be taken to the stables or if this was a short visit. Salmé kissed Metle before they sat in the far corner of the reception room and let the others get on with coffee and sweet things.

'They say the executioner has been brought to Zanzibar especially,' Metle told her without preamble. 'He has to be paid more – because it is royal blood.'

She tried to forgive Metle her insensitivity as Metle rubbed her throat. She knew Metle was taking a risk coming to openly visit the tainted sister.

'He is from Egypt and six-foot-eight-inches tall.'

The axeman in Salmé's mind immediately sprouted another head in height.

'Well he'd have to bend quite a bit to get my neck,' she said lightly.

'Salmé, how can you joke?' Metle gasped.

'Because this is all rumour.' Salmé even smiled. 'Because I am going to Mecca.'

Moisture welled in Metle's eyes. The kohl that defined her eyes so darkly against her already dark cheeks smeared a little and looked like black tears hanging on her lashes.

'You don't really believe that?'

She didn't know if Metle believed her assurances or simply decided they should leave their brave faces on. She started a 're-member' game. Remember, remember, funny, lovely, exciting moments – but they were all stories from when their father was alive. That was a long time ago, Salmé reminded herself as she tottered on the brink of nostalgia. That past had long felt like another world entirely. All she could let herself remember were the eight years of loneliness since Barghash's rebellion.

She could not get as close as she wanted to Metle when she left. The unborn child stood between them.

'I'm like a hippopotamus,' Metle whispered. 'Remember when our father had the hippopotamus and the giraffe and the zebra brought over from the mainland for us to see.' They hugged around the bulge, long and hard. Their necklaces be-came entangled so a slave had to come and take Salmé's off.

'I have been to the British Consul's residence,' Ruete told Salmé only minutes later after a rush up the stairs, one flight, another, the roof. She almost ran across the waiting plank.

'But the British will not help,' she said between panted breaths. She felt all hope drain away. She felt so weak she couldn't imagine being able to walk back to her roof. 'The British are Majid's allies,' she whispered. 'It was their guns that defeated the rebellion.'

'But they are civilised people,' he assured her. 'Besides it is not the Consul I went to see. No, he is at your estate at Bububu. Only Mrs Seward is in town and she is to be our saviour.'

'The Consul's wife? Is she one of your bosomy friends?'

He paused. She could see him trying to bring himself back from the forward gallop of his explanation. 'Who?'

'One of the women at your dinner party that night.'

'No. Not that it's relevant, Salmé, where is your mind? They were French.'

'French.' She had heard stories about the French. He'd called that kiss a French kiss.

'You really are the cat now – a little green eyed monster.' Ruete reached for her but she kept herself straight. She would not fold into his arms.

'I am not jealous,' she sniffed in perfect imitation of someone who is jealous. 'It's this baby. My emotions are no longer mine. If I cry it is nothing.' She held back the tears that had no rational reason to be there.

'She won't tell her husband,' he said.

'Mrs Seward? About you visiting her?'

'No. About her helping. She has organised a ship. The Sultan can't accuse the Consul of interfering in affairs of state if she doesn't tell him.' He stopped. He was holding both her hands in his and followed her eyes with his own until he caught them too. 'The HMS *Highflyer* sails tomorrow. They will wait until evening so you can get on board.'

'Tomorrow?'

'Are you ready?'

She contemplated the word. Ignored it. 'We can bring the rest of the gold across now,' she said, all organisation and activity to hide that she was not ready. She'd already decided she'd have to dress as a slave to avoid Majid's spies when she left her palace. She got Ruete to call for tea and put off what had to come by entertaining him with the story this disguise brought to mind: about the time they dressed Barghash as a slave to get him out of his palace. She talked too much because silence was too difficult.

'He was like a sulky child, you'd hardly think he was the leader of a rebellion and fancied himself a Sultan,' she told him. 'But Majid had three hundred siege-soldiers at his gate. Three hundred. Can you imagine the noise they made?' Salmé imagined that many coming to take her away, then realised she was not so important. Majid would only need to send a handful to get her.

'Khole came up with the idea. Dress him as a female slave, swathe him in a shawl and get him past the soldiers as part of our procession. He had no other choice. We had to put a mask over his face, and then mask all the slaves too. I made the mistake of saying he looked pretty behind the black silk, though it was a lie. His beard made the mask sit very oddly. He wouldn't have fetched much at the slave market.'

Ruete laughed. That was good. That was what they needed.

'He tottered in the *kosch* and was so tall we were sure he'd be spotted. So we put him next to a huge Nubian.'

'So he got past the guards?'

'Yes, and fled to Marseilles.' And all that came after.

There was that silence that kept threatening them.

'Maybe he's never forgiven me for seeing him like that?'

'If it ever came to it, I would dress as a woman for you.' He put his teacup down and bowed from his waist while sitting in his chair, as if this was a gallant thing to offer. She let herself laugh. Tomorrow their farewells would have to be brief, though not quite as brief and melodramatic as a hasty goodbye roof to roof with soldiers smashing down her gate. She hoped. She prayed.

The next morning she leaned out of the window of the first floor sewing room to catch the last echo of Sultan Majid's troops on the palace parade ground. It was only on the most still days sounds travelled that far. It was a still day. She lost the high notes of the fife first; she felt the low notes of the drums continue to resonate through the stone. The last notes. Everything today was the last. The last sketch of the street below her palace window: a coffee seller, his livelihood like a set of scales balancing the brass coffee pot on one side, his patron's cups on the other; a slave balancing an earthenware water jug on her left shoulder, making her as tall as a giraffe. Everyone balancing something. Everything balanced, an equilibrium that looked so easy from above. A group of Arab men in white robes and turbans turned the corner. The one on the end looked like Hamdan, her brother who shared the teaching mat and the boring lessons, and was her accomplice in their childhood. He died young. She didn't want to think of him now.

Returning to her embroidery was out of the question. It would never be finished now. No last silk cushion with slipshod, drunken footsteps of stitches tracing the tail of a peacock in gold thread. She looked over at where she'd dumped it. It was slack across a pillow, needle and thread sticking out. It looked as if she'd be back any minute to pick it up again.

Nashwa kept sewing, along with four other slaves in the room. Salmé wanted to say goodbye but the ship bound for Mecca was supposedly days away. This bent old woman fed her as a baby, chastised her as a child, and was with her when her mother died. She owed her honesty.

'I'm going soon,' she said from the window. Then she stopped herself. This had to be a secret if it was to succeed. 'I'm going to Metle's for the night. I will sleep there. With New Year tomorrow that will be good.'

She went down to the courtyard and told Johar the same lie. 'I'll be back tomorrow.' His hunched shoulders and the collapsed fat of his cheeks told her he did not believe her. But she was Sayyida Salmé, daughter of the Great Sultan Sa'id of Zanzibar and Oman and no one would call her a liar.

'And is there anything else you want for the *Siku a mwaka* feast tomorrow?' he asked.

So she had to tell more lies and go through a menu. She could see the cooks already at work and she could smell the honey, tubs and tubs of honey to make everything sweet. Johar did not take his eyes off her face. She began to flush with shame.

I trust you, she wanted to tell him. But we both know the palace has ears. Majid's spies are not only outside the gate.

'I'll take Zada and Zafrani with me,' she said instead.

'And your guards.'

'No, just Zada and Zefrani.' She tried to make it into a joke. 'I'll frighten Sayyida Metle. She will be so surprised when I rap on the gate without the warning of a princess's procession.' He didn't even pretend to laugh.

'A New Year's joke,' she babbled.

She hadn't forgotten Johar in her planning. He'd watched her selling off many of her slaves along with the other property, but his freedom was amongst the letters she'd be leaving behind. Though he was worth a good amount, he'd been faithful. She couldn't tell him that, not amongst all the lies. He'd simply find himself a free man on the first day of the year. He might even think that auspicious.

'Remember what the soothsayer said,' she told him softly and turned away because the Faithful were being called to Prayer. She had to make her ablutions and prostrate herself as the sun set. Then there was too little time. Ruete was waiting on her roof. It was the first time he'd come across to her side of the street.

'You have to go now,' he insisted. 'I'll be with you before you know.' The moon made him silver. He stood on her roof and it was she who left.

Salmé called the two slaves, told one to carry a carpetbag, the other her ebony jewel box. At the last minute she saw Sinbad, her fluffy, senseless cat stalking a pair of ricebirds along the gallery. He'd come all the way from Persia, he'd be a good traveller.

She called for a basket and trapped him with tidbits of cooked chicken. Strapped to Zada's back he had no way out.

Johar came to the gate holding a lantern. His face in the firefly ball of light was too disconsolate to look at.

'We'll go without light,' she insisted. 'To scare Metle.' She wrapped her *schele* tightly around her, including her face, and made the slaves do the same so they looked identical. They would be silent shadows: she'd slipped her chattering bangles and anklets into the ebony box with her other jewellery. The catch was fastened, the lock secure, the bells silent.

On the streets they were shadows in the shadows. At the third corner, Salmé didn't take the turn to Metle's palace. The slaves hesitated. 'A detour,' she hissed. They followed. She kept going despite every instinct telling her to run home. There were people on the streets and as they got closer to the shoreline there were more and more. They did not give way to her. She was jostled twice. She cringed from the pushes and accidental shoves. This was what it was like without guards then? She wished Ruete had been able to come at least this far, but Majid's spies were watching him too and it was best they watched him doing nothing in his home.

The stench announced the harbour before they walked out of the narrow streets onto the shore. Salmé pulled her *schele* tighter over her face. Even the two layers, mask and shawl, both impregnated with all the armoury of a princess's perfumery, could not disguise the smell of rotting flesh. She cursed the slavers. They were inconsiderate to the good people of Zanzibar; they left the weak and dying on the shore rather than pay the two-dollar tax for each to pass through the Custom House. Indistinct clots of black dotted the white sands of the beach.

Salmé paused. The bay was full of *dhows* at anchor and bristled with the masts of European merchant ships, while small row boats and cutters used to transport people and provisions from ship to shore and back were pulled up along the long curve of the beach. The crowds were not down here though. It was quiet. No noise above the growling and snarling. The movement amongst the corpses was wild dogs gorging themselves.

Ruete had described where the British Consulate was, not far along the shore. She could see a small cutter pulled up in front of the squat building and headed towards it. The slaves trailed. She ignored their sniffing. A man stepped out and spoke. Salmé turned and would have run if there'd been anywhere to run to.

'Princess,' called the man, softly. 'Sayyida?' He was not an Arab. Salmé stood as still as a wild animal assessing its predators. 'I am the doctor. The British doctor. Mrs Seward has asked me to meet you.'

His arm stretched towards her and touched her. There were no eunuchs around to protest and drag a foreign doctor's hand from their princess this time. She had to ignore the breach of etiquette now the world had been turned on its head.

'We must hurry,' Dr Kirk said in Swahili, as if she needed to be told this.

He held her elbow as she felt her way onto the sand in the dark. Dr Kirk had the same comforting smell of whiskey on his breath as Ruete. Salmé wondered if all white men smelled like this. The doctor lifted her as another man's arms from within the cutter picked her up. The boat tipped, half on the sand, half in water.

Zada and Zafrani couldn't ignore their own fears any longer. They began to cry in unison. Whether it was because they thought they were being left behind or about to be kidnapped wasn't clear to Salmé who was trying to balance herself on the rocking boat. A sailor in the rough blue jacket of the British navy lifted wailing Zada and dumped her unceremoniously beside Salmé. The box and bag were thrown aboard. Zafrani was more agile once she'd dropped the carpetbag; she was not burdened with a cat basket on her back. Despite her uncontrolled screaming she had the wherewithal to break free and kick off her shoes and stumble loudly up the beach, bellowing like a cow at the slaughterhouse all the while.

'You have to go now,' the doctor said.

The sailors rowed swiftly away from the shore. Salmé picked up her ebony box and cradled it on her lap. She tried to ignore the sobbing slave at her side. If I can keep it in, so can you, she thought.

It had all happened too fast in the end. Her heart was beating so wildly it could only stop completely next. But her heart did not stop. It slowed, caught on the rhythm of the oars slapping the water. She began to breathe normally again. Her slave wept loudly on.

She hissed, 'Shut up Zada. It's not the end of the world.' She stared back through the dark for any movement of pursuers. The town looked closed off, a blank wall of stone. Majid's palace, Bet il Sahel, four storeys of white stone, was a shimmer. Yellow lights shone in windows. She strained but couldn't see any shapes in the light. Later there would be *fetâk*, fireworks to light up the sky. She imagined Majid on a balcony watching the display not knowing his plans were thwarted and his sister was gone.

She looked back at the Custom House. There was no move-ment there either. In fact, there were far fewer people on the shore than she would have expected, even in normal circum-stances. The escape had been too easy. It struck her that the Sultan Majid might be planning to kill her, but that her brother Majid wanted her to get away.

She was calm when the cutter hove to the HMS *Highflyer*. She had new strength and was able to climb unassisted onto the British man-o-war. The captain stood at the top of the rope lad-der. She was struck by the abundance of buttons on his jacket and vest; and the Europeans said the Sultans wore too much jewellery. As the captain lifted his cap to welcome her, two locks of hair poked themselves out over his ears like wings. Men's hair, let loose of turbans, was so unpredictable. Salmé was momen-tarily able to give a genuinely light and cheerful smile that even reached her eyes.

'Only three weeks to twenty-four days to Aden,' Captain Pasley said. If he was curious about his unexpected cargo it was not to be satisfied that night. The nausea had started without any period of grace: it was as if the sea awoke a snake in her belly. Salmé lurched back to the rail.

The bluejackets raced around the deck. The anchor clashed against its chain as it slithered over the planks and she retched and did not see the solid buildings of Zanzibar, darker still against the dark night, disappear. She hung over the side of the British gunboat, her chest heaving against the solid rail, pitching down into the inky black of the harbour water. All her thoughts blacked out in the heaving. When her stomach could expel no more she watched the wash of the water. She saw flashes of movement beneath the surface. Her thoughts were dark now: she imagined the bones of countless slaves rattled on the shifting tide, being ground into sand until they were the same as their resting place. Men, women and children who hadn't survived the forced march into exile and would never go home. It wasn't what she expected to be thinking as she left her home.

Homesickness, seasickness, morning sickness – Salmé couldn't tell the difference.

She lay on her bunk and wanted to die. A seven-foot executioner would be a mercy. She was too sick to notice there was nothing to do. She didn't notice the boredom. She stared at the ceiling of Captain Pasley's small, dark cabin and wondered what the other cabins on the ship were like if this was the best of them. Zada slept on the floor beside her bunk, an exhausted mess. Sinbad added to the nightmare with his howling and scratching and the smell of his urine stinking the timber. And they had only been at sea three days.

Salmé drifted, half-asleep, half-dreaming. The *Highflyer* lunged into the waves, an unbroken donkey pulling at its halter. She was on her donkey. 'Slow down,' she shouted at it. She woke. Felt the sweat prickling on her chest. She kicked off the thin blanket and breathed in the thick air and drifted again. She had no strength to keep back the nostalgia that attacked her through layers of nausea. 'I'd rather be riding a mad donkey.'

'What?' Zada asked as if from a hundred miles away, from the shores of Zanzibar itself. 'Is there anything you need?'

Salmé was too far away to answer. She was bored in this half-waking dream. She remembered that feeling. What a wonderful feeling in comparison to everything in this cabin, if only she could own it now. She surrendered herself and didn't know if she dreamed or remembered, and didn't care.

She was under a tree. Why am I under a tree? Because I desperately want to be on dry land, the lucid corner of her mind told her.

But I am bored under the palm tree. The sun is coming through the fronds and striping my legs, she noticed. It wasn't an interesting observation. The fact that her legs were short and skinny made no sense. I am a child, she decided. A bored child. Not that there was anyone who'd listen. The dream was empty of people. How could that be? She was never alone in childhood. Where were the sisters and cousins, the slaves? She had to assemble the dream so it made sense. I am not at home, she decided. Ah, I remember. It was the day I got my crooked arm.

The mothers were gone. They'd retired *en masse* to the courtyard of the *shamba's* villa, saying they were exhausted by the whole excursion. Salmé thought this silly. They'd come in boats so it'd hardly been taxing.

'So wearying,' she mimicked as she sat alone in the shade of the palm tree.

The mothers blamed the sun. But they'd all sat under shade on the trip down the coast, under parasols and umbrellas and near-tents spread across the boats. Salmé knew if anything had wearied the mothers it was the effort they'd put into getting ready to parade in front of each other. Are my diamonds too small, is my *derrière* too broad for this print, where is that scent from Paris? She didn't want to grow up to be a woman if they had to talk like that all the time. Even her sainted mother Jilfidân had been speaking gibberish about shoes back in Bet il Mtoni. Salmé had sat in a corner reduced to catching the light coming through the fretwork in stars. A trip away from the harem was a big thing. She'd been ready to go for ages. Since first prayers. Since the sun came up.

Finally the gong sounded downstairs. Bibi Azziz declared only then that she wasn't coming. 'Due to ill-health,' she told the assembled women.

Medine lent into Salmé's mother. Salmé heard the whispered words, 'Hangover more likely.' Jilfidân, who Salmé knew was scandalised by any mention of alcohol, protested as expected.

'Sshh, you shouldn't,' she shushed. Loud enough so it was she who got Bibi Azziz's dark look.

But then, without the Sultan's official wife along, the trip had taken on the air of a party. The further they sailed from Bet il Mtoni, the more the palace etiquette was left behind. Still, there hadn't been an interesting moment since for Salmé, and all her anticipation and expectation was reduced to a pool of boredom. With the mothers taking sherbet and then pretending not to go to sleep on the cushions along the shady side of the courtyard, she was left with only her little brothers and sisters; as if she'd hang around with them for long.

The men were riding down to the Sultan's *shamba* – his plantation closest to the oracle spring – and joining the women there. She'd heard even Hamdan was included in that party, the real party, though he was close to her in age.

'Oh go away,' she told a little girl with tiny plaits. She turned her back, and then, that boredom driving her like a whip, she stalked to the beach. The boats bobbed, a flotilla, parasols gay and obsolete flapping over each. Then she sat under the palm tree until she couldn't sit still a second longer. If the mothers weren't going to be fun she'd have to find fun elsewhere. She got up and drifted back over to the bustle of the slaves busy unpacking the food and setting up fires. At least they were doing something.

'Do you want me to saddle you a donkey?' asked one of the eunuchs after she'd hovered and made herself a nuisance trying to direct the waterboys. Salmé recognised the eunuch as the new one from her mother's apartments. He was young and soft looking. 'We brought a number of donkeys down with us in case any of the Sayyida wanted to ride,' he said.

Horses for the boys, white donkeys for the girls. She wanted to throw herself onto one of her brother's stallions and really race, but an ass would have to do, as it always had.

The donkey was a pretty thing with long eyelashes, made prettier by a tail henna-painted and a bridle bristling with jewels. It was bigger than the one she had at the palace in Mtoni. The bells around her ankles and the donkey's neck chimed in unison as the eunuch helped her mount. Now I can find fun, she thought. But the eunuch was telling her to ride carefully. Carefully, carefully, carefully, she chanted under her breath. Her mother would have recognised the tone. And, while she was in sight of the camp, she did pretend to be careful. At a sedate – princess-like – pace, she and her donkey plodded through the villa's groves down to the beach where the young kids were in the water squealing. Female slaves hovered around them, and one of the younger male slaves scuttled up a tree to collect coconuts for fresh milk. Salmé didn't like coconut milk. She hoped it wasn't for the children. If some slave tried to foist it on her she'd tell him to take it up to the mothers. It could take away the taste of the midday napping they were pretending not to have.

Once on the beach, she went right to the edge, in and out of the little lapping waves. The sun insinuated itself. One of the young Nubians ran over and started to walk alongside her with a parasol. Salmé pulled on the reins and slowed her pace, and he slowed, then she went faster and he started to run, and then she slowed. She watched her shadow moving in and out of the golden shade of the orange umbrella. She did the slowing-and-gaining-pace game a few more times, and sure enough, the slave couldn't keep up and never quite sheltered the Sultan's daughter. Then that too was boring. The hooves of the donkey on the tight sand squeaked like a little toy from France. It was irritating. And the sand went on and on. The stretch of beach looked endless with endlessness and not endless with possibility. She wondered if she could head inland and look for the oracle spring where the Magicians of Pemba had come to speak. Maybe they would tell her about an exciting future. Something better than this.

Before she could lead the slave off the beach, she heard a commotion behind her. At last something was happening. The donkey's bridle jangled as she turned its head back the way they'd come. The men were there, finally, a long line of them snaking along the edge of the foreshore. Now there'd be someone to talk to. Even Hamdan might have something more interesting to say than a running commentary on silks and embroideries and who had the heaviest bracelets and the biggest rubies. The commotion was moving closer. Most of the horses stopped at the villa orchard but four raced down the beach at Salmé.

'A race, a race,' Hamdan shouted. He was a little behind the front-runners, their brothers Majid and Barghash and their cousin who had the contest by a neck.

Hooves hammered the sand in a slave-drum rhythm, kicking up blinding spurts of the stuff. She watched, excited as they galloped down on her. The boys' shouting ripped up the peace of the *shamba,* tore down that fortress of boredom. She knew she should get out of the way. She could almost hear her mother telling her: all that *be careful* nonsense. Instead she wheeled her donkey back around and set off at a gallop. The Nubian beside her skittered over into the water. For just one moment in the race she was in the lead.

The bigger boys thundered past. The dropped orange parasol was trampled and lay with its spines sticking into the air like a dead rooster. Hamdan's horse crushed it last.

'You can't Salmé,' he screamed as he gained on her. Hamdan's face was close, his eyes squinting in a warning glare as he overtook her too. 'You're too young.'

Salmé didn't listen. Too young. Too small. But soon, before she knew it, she'd be too old. Her older sisters wore their veils and soon it would be her turn. She dug her naked heels into the donkey's surprisingly muscular belly. She hurtled through the sand spray being gouged and kicked up by the leaders in the race. The blood in her ears drummed as loud as the hoof-falls. The coins tied at the bottom of her plaits slapped her neck and shoulders. She was keeping up, like a small boat buffeted in the wake of a *dhow*. Then she passed Hamdan who screamed even louder.

'No Salmé, you're not allowed.'

Up ahead their cousin's mare stumbled and he dropped back, which left the beach to Majid and Barghash. That was until the beach's endless length ran out in a tangle of mangrove roots. Salmé expected this to be the finish line. She thought Barghash was going to win. But at the last second, the horses swerved into the clove plantation that ran alongside the beach, Barghash leaning into Majid on the turn. Horseflesh kissed sinewy horseflesh. She saw her brothers lock arms, struggling, slowing them down. She took her chance. As they fought, she streaked ahead. There was no one in front of her now. Her heart raced, her donkey raced. They were chasing her now.

'You can't catch me,' she shouted into the air that rushed past her like a typhoon and carried the words away. Then she couldn't resist turning to see how much ground she'd gained.

The boys had straightened, but abreast were almost too wide for the corridor between the trees. They looked like arrows shot from the same bow. Shot straight at her. Salmé whipped her head to face forward again. Just in time to see the branch. She threw her head back moments before the tree could strike her full across the forehead. Where the top of her mask would sit. The force of her movement lifted her off her saddle and she was left without the sturdy certainty of her donkey beneath her. For a moment, before the fall, she flew.

In the cabin of the *Highflyer*, Salmé did not hit the ground. She opened her eyes briefly. Her arm ached in a dull, remote way, a far-off echo of the pain the day she fell off her donkey and broke it. She wondered why she'd remembered that day, and wondered if her brothers had really raced like that or if she'd imagined it. There was no certainty except scars on a crooked arm.

She was only awake for a moment before the nausea ambushed her again and she fell back into her half-sleep. She was riding the donkey again, pushing her pelvis into the saddle as her mount stepped lightly on the sand, only when she looked down it was not a donkey, it was Ruete and his head was thrown back on his cotton pillows, his mouth open and his breath rasping, and the palms of his hands were hard up against her hip bones and she could feel the rocking deep inside her and she began to moan.

'Sayyida, Sayyida.' The words broke through the spell. There was a hand on her forehead. 'Bibi Mistress, you need to drink. I have water.'

Zada's hand left Salmé's forehead. Something hard came to her lips. Salmé shook the cup away. The warmth in her lower body subsided and she blushed. How can I have imagined that? She'd never be able to tell Ruete.

1866–1867
Aden

The dark line on the horizon that had confidently suggested land to the crew the day before was suddenly coastline across the entire view, left to right. She'd probably have loved any speck of land in the world, just to be off the ship, but this first fresh, early-morning image of Aden immediately made her think of all the stories the older women at Bet il Mtoni told about Muscat. Muscat, the Great Sultan's capital in Oman, that fabled land they talked about with a boundless yearning for home in their voices.

Aden's huge harbour hugged the sea in a circular embrace at the bottom of Arabia. The backdrop of mountains was not very far back: the foothills stretched their feet almost to the water's edge. Salmé had never seen mountains before, not one, let alone a mountain range. The towering height was astonishing, yet it was the buildings that kept her attention. The shore was lined with solid white blocks, their flat roofs reflecting the morning sun. They were reassuringly familiar, like the buildings of Stone Town – not so far from home after all. However, as they sailed closer to shore she realised everything was bigger, whiter, grander.

The harbour was congested with ships, far more than Stone Town could boast. So Zanzibar really was a backwater? She had to shake all the old Omani women's voices from her head. The ones that said the tiles were shinier, the brass lamps bigger, the Turkish delight sweeter and the clothes more fashionable by yards and years, once you got away from Stone Town. We are not uncivilised Africans from the end of the world, she told the chorus in her head. Luckily she had Zada to boss about and get together her possessions – what little she had with her – ready to disembark. Sinbad objected to going back in the basket.

'Oh do shut up cat, not you too,' Salmé told him through the weave. 'You wait till you see what's out there.'

As she left the cabin for the last time, she decided it was time to do one final thing. She took off her veil. Zada unlocked the ebony box to put it inside. As she handed it over, Salmé could feel the side of the ship nudging up against the dock. She had to hold onto the wall for a moment. She wanted to say something to Zada, something solemn about a new life but there was then so much shouting on deck and from the dock that mere words had no space to form.

His basket in the arms of one of the bluejackets, Sinbad continued to add his voice to the general caterwauling as the party crossed a real gangplank to solid land. The crowds surged around her. People doing things Salmé couldn't even imagine. She could feel Zada's hand clinging to the end of the silk scarf falling down her back, pulling a little too tightly, and then another face was thrust at her.

'Princess, Sayyida? I am Signor Mass.'

She looked up at a tall man with hair grey around the temples. He spoke in Swahili, his accent indicating he was fluent, so he knew their ways, but this man made no comment about her naked face. She felt exposed and wanted to hide behind her mask again but she forced a smile.

'You are Herr Ruete's friend.' His nice friend, she remembered.

'We had a message from the captain as soon as you docked. You can imagine our surprise that you are here earlier than expected.' He turned and shouted something to a group of dark men. 'They will bring your luggage later, I have a carriage waiting to take you home.' He said something in another language then translated it into Swahili. 'It's a Spanish saying, my language. It means, my house is your house. You are welcome, very welcome Princess.' He hurried her through the crowds and handed her into a carriage. 'Signora Mass is there waiting, go, go.'

'My first mountains, my first carriage. Roads!' she sang once she was alone.

The carriage, smaller than the one Queen Victoria had given her father – but with far fewer cobwebs and rats nesting in the upholstery – travelled joltingly over the hard, pebbly surfaces along Front Bay. They passed many other carriages and traps and carts doing the same. Salmé lent so far out she could feel the wind on her naked cheeks. She could see Zada up next to the coachman. She was hunched forward; the ebony box containing her wealth clutched so tight on her lap it was like she was sheltering a pregnant stomach. Salmé looked beyond her and could see women swaying toward them with jugs on their heads and little boys leading donkeys and a man peeing into the verge, his piss a yellow rainbow in the slanting sun. She was travelling in a town *in the daylight* and she could see whatever she wanted to. She wanted to write it all down for Metle.

'You won't believe it, I don't believe it,' she said over and over as they drove around Steamer Point then started the slower climb into the foothills.

The house was at the end of a short driveway. It was of the curious colonial design she came to recognise. Unlike Arab houses it insisted on looking outward. The verandah was on the outside, skirting the ground floor, while small balconies jutted out from under each of the upstairs windows. There was no courtyard. Once inside, there was only inside.

She stood in the entrance hall near the stairs. She didn't have to wait long. A woman swept down the stairs at a run. She'd expected Signora Mass to be as old and grey as her husband but she was half his age and not much older than Salmé herself. She came bouncing toward her, clearly unable to contain her excitement.

'I never lived in Zanzibar,' she confided immediately in Arabic. 'I married the Signor after he made his fortune. But Bonaventura has told me so many stories. I can't believe I have one of the Sultan's family in my home. Let me look at you.' Maria Mass twirled Salmé around in the block of light falling through the open front door. 'Those clothes, my goodness, trousers on a woman! We must get you into a dress.'

She tottered a little when Maria Mass let go of her hands. 'Ah, you'll need to find your land legs,' Maria diagnosed. She was smiling as she talked; the smile never left her face. 'First we shall take care of your body, and then we will have a look at your soul,' she said confidently.

There was a dress in a plain blue fabric lying on the bed when Salmé was finally shown upstairs after two cups of tea. She had a headache from a conversation that lurched between languages when the Spanish woman's Arabic was not enough and sentences had to be gummed together with bits of English and Swahili.

The room was a palace compared to Captain Pasley's cabin but it looked sadly bare when she let herself think about her home. The walls were pale – no painted tiles, no hung brocades. Her few possessions, oddly, made the room look even more foreign. Zada had been busy. She'd put bits and pieces from the old life out on surfaces. A brush, a small mirror on a shelf, some shoes on the floor. The ebony jewel box sat on the corner of a table that was backed by a large mirror, while the cat's basket balanced the other side. Zada was over by the bed half under some contraption when Salmé came in.

'What are you doing?'

'This has something to do with the dress,' Zada said. She looked distressed. The cat sounded distressed.

'Let the poor cat out. We're here now.'

Zada left the bed and the contraption and untied the rope that held the basket top together. Sinbad leapt out, and in one white movement was through the window. Salmé rushed after him and found him on a small balcony stretching his body into the shape of a swan's neck, front paws, belly, tail, all one sinuous line. Bougainvillea with flowers as purple as the flowers on Salmé's trousers cascaded down from the balcony into the shady garden.

'Here puss,' she called. Sinbad turned to look at her then strode along the outside ledge of the balcony beyond the wrought-iron rail. Salmé looked down into the garden, at the frangipani, the hibiscus, all the bright, happy colours. It was too far for a cat to jump. But when she looked back he was gone. The thorns of the bougainvillea were not going to deter his descent.

'A great lot of good that was,' she said between gritted teeth. 'I might as well have left you behind.'

'He'll come back,' offered Zada from beside the table. 'When he's hungry.'

Perhaps she was right, but a feeling of being jilted lingered as Zada coaxed her into the idea of the dress. Zada handed the garment to Salmé who turned it over. There seemed an awful lot of it.

'Well I can't help you,' Salmé said. Of course they'd both seen women in these cloth bells but this offered no insight into the secrets beneath them. The contraption that acted as some kind of undergarment was worse.

'If this goes around my waist, where's the top and where's the bottom?' Salmé protested as Zada thrust it toward her head. The crinoline snapped back at the slave and fell between them, looking like a bit of the *Highflyer's* rigging. Zada tried to pick it up, and fumbled, and it bounced like a spring. Salmé nursed her breasts, newly tender from all the changes in her body, while she laughed.

Zada scowled, her habitual face, Salmé was coming to appreciate now they were so much in each other's company. She waited while the slave sifting out the rings of tape and whalebone. When the crinoline was sitting on the floor in a rough circle, Zada suggested Salmé step into it.

'I'm not trying to get it over your head again,' she muttered under her breath.

That worked better. Salmé stood patiently and Zada pulled the rigging up and secured the pliant cage around her waist with the ribbons. Zada stepped back and tripped on the corset lying like a dead bird by the mirror-table.

'And where does this go?' She was almost in tears. It was all too much.

Salmé grabbed the silky corset off her and draped it over her own face. 'The latest Spanish mask, more sturdy than the veil I'm used to for sure.'

Zada's lips didn't even hint at a smile on her ebony face. So Salmé shimmied the corset back and forth, the ribbony tapes dancing to a point below her nipples. Zada's teeth remained firmly masked by those grim lips and her eyes accused: Allah will not forgive you. Salmé refused to get cross. She threw the corset on the bed. It felt like a device to crush her baby anyway.

'Did you know this is all whalebone? From real whales? Herr Ruete told me. He traded in them too,' she said as Zada was shuffling around with the dress. 'Do you remember the whales – those old humpbacks we'd watch migrate down the coast in the middle of the year?' Zada looked even more sour. 'They were such blubbery soft looking creatures, like a huge *meddes*, the biggest of the big pillows, floating above the waves. You could imagine just throwing yourself on one like a *meddes*, better than this silly bed here.'

Zada was blubbering now. It seemed odd that she'd feel homesick, Salmé thought. Zanzibar wasn't home for Zada. She'd been sold into slavery somewhere inland from Mombassa by the look of her. I'm the one who should be sobbing with homesickness, Salmé knew. She choked down the thought.

'They don't look like they have bones at all. Whales.' She watched the slave. 'And where is your backbone Zada?' she asked. The slave snuffled up tears.

She was not, simply was not, going to cry too. 'Dress. Now.' She pointed to the thing sitting like a ghost on the bed.

If they were to have any chance at success, the blue cotton did have to go over Salmé's head. Zada climbed up and teetered on the soft edge of the bed to drop it down. Salmé felt a lurch of claustrophobia. She was momentarily blind beneath the dress

– and then the world came back in hazy blue through the cloth, as if she was underwater. She heard Zada jump off the bed and thud on the parquetry floor. Then there was tugging. The oceans of cloth shifted. Her head popped out and the cage of the crinoline disappeared under a couple of blue waves. Salmé gulped air.

'Now that wasn't too hard.'

'Not finished, your bum is hanging out at the back,' Zada said. With maybe a hint of spite in her voice. Salmé got the feeling she hadn't been fully forgiven for dragging Zada onto the cutter instead of Zefrani.

Zada disappeared behind her back and there was more tugging. The cloth in the skirt finally fell over the more dramatically proportioned back bustle. Salmé walked to the mirror above the dressing table. She felt as if she was wading through water; pushing all the cloth in front of her. The dress was too big. The skirt rippled into wavy motifs on the floor, the shoulders slipped off her shoulders, the sleeves hung like two huge bananas, completely hiding her clinking bracelets and her hands.

'Thank Allah, Ruete cannot see me in this.' She turned slightly and patted the frame over her belly. The crinoline could almost have been designed to hide a pregnancy.

Zada was her shadow in the mirror. She was darker in every way, and still wearing a modest set of trousers and long shirt. Salmé tried to ignore her.

'I'll have to get a seamstress in,' she said, to herself. She imagined a dress in red and green, another in purple and yellow. She imagined how lovely she'd look then. She couldn't quite convince herself, so she picked up her skirt and spun around the room, her land legs pirouetting faster and faster, her bells drumming and chiming, the cloth twirling and lifting, the spinning-top of her body knocking Zada before falling, laughing again onto the wonderfully soft bed.

The seamstress was not the only visitor Salmé had in the early days in Aden. Maria Mass was serious about clothing her little princess's body and soul.

'You have to be a Christian to marry Herr Ruete,' she explained. 'And for the sake of your soul, Sayyida Salmé, it's no use pretending. You have to take the Faith wholeheartedly, earnestly, truthfully.'

God, Salmé discovered, could see as directly into her mind as Allah.

Spanish Maria Mass, with hair so black that in full sun it was, paradoxically, midnight blue, wanted to invite her Catholic priest to the house above Steamer Point, but Ruete, without telling Salmé, had been adamant in his letter to the Signor. So it was the Anglican Rev. Wishart who brought the mysteries of the Christian life to Salmé.

The minister wore a solar topee as he climbed the steps of Steamer Point. Salmé saw him coming from her bedroom window, the button on the top of his hat like a beacon in the sea of red fez and pure-white turbans. She came down the stairs in her new green dress, kicking the front of the whalebone and tape frame so it wobbled. She got there in time to receive the visitor in the drawing room. He'd been relieved of his hat at the door. The hair of men continued to surprise her. His was a sparse pale offering spread like slippery seaweed across his rocky scalp. His moustache was a sandy outcrop lodged on his upper lip.

He said 'good day' in a voice too deep for his scrawny frame. Maria translated the words into Arabic, although Salmé recognised them. He was a son of the British Empire it seemed. He sniffed audibly when he shook Maria Mass' hand and then he captured Salmé's right hand. Being handled by Maria was one thing, but she was still taken aback by the physical familiarity of this gesture. It felt less like a greeting and more like an assault every time a strange man did it. Her first instinct was to run back upstairs and hide her big, exposed, unmasked features in her pillow. She couldn't – because he held her hand tight. His sweat peeled off onto her skin.

'Now we must find you a name fitting for God's congregation,' he said in accented Arabic before he let go. She swung her arms behind her back to better flex and wriggle her fingers until they felt like hers again.

He listed names: Faith. Hope. Charity. He fired them off his darting pink tongue. He translated the meaning of the names into Arabic, making her understand that the English version would be the name she'd be known by. Patience. Grace.

'Sit, sit,' Signora Mass insisted as Salmé pretended to consider each name in turn. All excellent qualities; her mother would approve. Only Salmé liked the name her mother had given her. It meant peace, and surely that was a sacred quality too.

The British reverend, of course, accepted the offer of tea. Maria Mass served them at a low table and then went to the window to sit out of the way.

Grace, Salmé thought as the Rev. Wishart siphoned the tea from the china and slurped it through his sandy moustache. Grace Ruete. But she could not see herself as a Grace. The name had a grating sound compared to the soft plumpness of Salmé. She tried to imagine Ruete whispering it into her ear as he nibbled the lobe and walked his fingers down the hollow of her neck, *Grace my love, Grace take my…* These were not good thoughts to be having in a drawing room in the presence of a representative of a new God. She composed her hands on her green silk lap, stroking the material occasionally for reassurance.

'We must teach you the sacraments,' the Rev. Wishart said.

She watched the man as he talked. He kept his eyes anywhere but on her. He didn't seem comfortable with her presence so close. *I wonder if he has ever nibbled the earlobe of a woman?* Salmé reached for a cup and gulped down hot tea to stop her thoughts flitting down this particular road. Her body thought about it all the time: sex. Now she wasn't seasick and morning sick she missed that a lot. Ruete's body. She wanted to ask someone if this was normal. If she'd been in a harem she'd have no end of advice, but here the counsel was all about her spiritual needs.

'You shall partake of the body of Christ and drink his blood.'

Salmé looked across at Maria Mass, who stayed sitting by the window like a good chaperone, quiet but obviously there. Her needlework was on her lap and she was looking at the canvas of the Indian Ocean through the window. She had a curious little mouth, the lips always open, even in repose like now. Salmé could not catch her eye to ask what the man was going on about. She'd heard the Christians had odd rituals but this Christian's Arabic was execrable. He could have been saying anything.

'Can you repeat that?' she asked.

So it was the Rev. Wishart who interrupted Maria Mass's revere. In English, he said loudly, 'She's not a true Arabic speaker is she, being from Zanzibar.'

Maria rolled her eyes at Salmé when she thought the minister wasn't looking. For one second she was a white version of teasing, gleeful Metle. Salmé wanted to laugh, but at the same time, it almost broke her heart.

The morning didn't get any better. After too many interruptions of 'What?' and 'Pardon?' and Salmé's scrupulously polite, 'Can you repeat that please?' Maria ended up coming over to sit between them at the low table to act as translator. The Rev. Wishart slipped back into English and Maria picked out the meaning and sewed it back up into slightly more recognisable Arabic for Salmé. For an hour he told stories from the Old Testament. She did not concentrate as much as those around her wanted.

'But I know the stories already,' she said after Moses had parted the Red Sea. 'Islam is not ignorant of the Prophets who came before Muhammad. There is the Qur'an.'

Before she could say that Abraham and Moses were not a revelation as he seemed to suppose, Wishart held up his freckled hand and said, 'You must put all that behind you, child.'

It was an incantation she heard often in coming weeks as they moved from the Old Testament to the New. In the long afternoons between visits Maria taught her English, another language to add to her mothers' tongues, so she began to understand him with fewer translations. He kept calling her child; she could not fix on a new name. And he never was able to look her full in the face.

'He thinks I am unclean,' Salmé told Maria Mass after he retrieved his hard hat and left one day. 'I'm sure he does not look away out of politeness and sensitivity because I no longer wear my veil. He thinks perhaps that I will tempt him.'

Maria laughed. Then apologised. 'I'm sure your face would tempt any man.' Salmé knew she was referring to Herr Ruete. 'But,' Maria went on, 'our silly Reverend simply finds it too uncomfortable to be in this house. I have had to promise that my husband will never be home during his visits.'

'They are enemies?'

'He does not like Bonaventura's trade. The British drove him out of Zanzibar with their proscriptions on the slave trade. It is a wonder we can still make money.'

'Yes, my father had to sign their trade agreements.' Salmé remembered vague talk of it when she was living in Khole's palace. Something about bullying and restrictions over the slaves. They were still allowed to own slaves themselves so it hadn't affected her beyond coffee conversation. She could see it affected Maria.

'You would have liked living in Zanzibar. It is very beautiful.'

'But we would never have met there. I would not have been allowed into a harem.'

'Unless you married one of my brothers,' Salmé joked. 'I have some good looking ones.' Maria laughed with her. 'But it is good I am here,' she smiled.

'And the Rev. Wishart will continue to come because he is intent on saving one more soul for God.'

She didn't laugh at that. She could see Maria was with the Christian minister in that aim no matter what else they disputed.

Then one day, when he had bored Salmé for more than a few weeks, the Rev. Wishart swept into the house bursting with something important. Sweat beaded around his head where the solar topee rubbed. He stood in front of her and wiped it from his naked forehead with a big, floppy handkerchief which he then re-stuffed into a pocket that pouched somewhere near his genitals. He patted her hand with the same hand that touched the handkerchief and told her not to stand. He went over and relieved Maria Mass's hand of her embroidery to pat it too. Salmé looked down so she wouldn't see the look in Maria's eyes.

'I should have thought of this before,' the Rev. Wishart said as he sat himself down in a great shuffling of legs, chair and human. 'I know I have been a great advocate of the name Charity, and it would have done you well.' This was all addressed directly to Salmé while Maria was trying to keep up the translation. Then Wishart turned to Maria to add, 'Her life as a princess is a stumbling block, a rich man into Heaven and so on, and I had thoughts of a certain humility in her baptismal name. Charity suited. You need not translate.'

Salmé understood most of it anyway. She straightened her back. A ship had arrived from Zanzibar the day before, with a letter from Ruete but not Ruete himself. She did not understand. He said he was *tying up* business in Stone Town. There was no mention of the Sultan hounding him off the island. It was as if the complication of the errant princess was dealt with. Which left her, the errant princess, a guest in a stranger's house, with child to a man who had not arrived. How much more humility do I need? she wanted to demand of the man in front of her.

'But now,' Wishart gabbled over the top of any possible objections, 'the perfect name has emerged.' He had his black leather Bible open on his trousered lap, the sweat-soaked handkerchief under there somewhere.

'Ruth,' he said in his sonorous pulpit voice. He paused for effect, of which there was none. '*Wither thou goest, I will go; and where thou lodgest, I will lodge; thy people shall be my people, and thy God my God,*' he read.

Maria finally nodded appreciatively.

Salmé waited for an explanation and got an edited version of a foreign woman who followed her mother-in-law back to the Lord's Promised Land.

'Not with her husband?' she asked Maria.

'No,' Maria clarified. 'He was dead already. I don't think that's the point. It's the steadfast and loyal part of the story. He,' Maria tilted her head slightly in the direction of the impatient clergyman, 'likes the *thy God will be my God bit.*'

'Well I don't like the dead husband bit,' she said.

The Rev. Wishart was talking again. He didn't like them chattering in Arabic.

'She lived happily ever after,' Maria interpreted.

'Ruth,' Salmé said, turning the word on her tongue. Another rough word. But the Rev. Wishart seemed to think his arguments unassailable.

'Ruth,' tested Maria, and Salmé looked around.

'Wither thou goest, I go,' she whispered to herself that night. 'So why am I here alone?'

She started to spend the days at her bedroom window looking

out over the coal station into the ocean. A thin thread joined the blue of the water to the blue of the sky. Some mornings the horizon disappeared completely, then something as small as a housefly would appear. Salmé waved her hand to swat it away, and if it was a good day the speck did not fly off but grew into a ship and arrived to clutter up the harbour and she'd listen out for the gravel spitting out under carriage wheels in the drive. When no one came she'd go back to the horizon. One night as she tried to sleep she realised the tiny traces she saw against the blue weren't flies and they weren't ships. They were hope. And she could not avoid the truth: hope was not there every day.

She read Ruete's letter again in her bedroom, the one small sheet, scarcely enough words to fill it even with generous margins and expanses of white around his signature. She read it and reread it until the single page came apart at the creases and became four letters. She'd put it back together like a child's jigsaw puzzle, and still there was no clear picture. He sent words of love, but he had promised to be here with her, not to send mere messages across the entire Indian Ocean. He should be here; her stomach was unmistakably large. If it was a race to get to Aden, the child might win.

She started to write several letters back, but did not finish them. What was the point – they would pass him on the ocean as he came this way. That was the only hope. That he was even now on his way, his business all tied up tight with ribbons and bows like the ridiculous crinoline.

On the nights she could not sleep at all, the hours after midnight were worst. Far too dark for anyone to sight hope of the horizon. Had he lied to her, she asked herself. The idea once out would not go back, like Scheherazade's *jinni* with his copper jar. There was no certainty. When he'd asked her how she'd come by her crooked arm she'd told him a tale about an incompetent midwife and nothing about a donkey race with her brothers. She hadn't wanted him to think she was wild. If she could lie to him – why not him to her? Doubt became the great betrayer. It took all her might to deny it a voice. But it grew and began to whisper anyway, in those hours between midnight and dawn. *What will you do if he does not arrive?* it asked. *Who will you be then?*

She stopped going down to Crater City with Bonaventura and Maria Mass. All the stories Johar had told her about his trips to the market in Zanzibar to buy her trinkets had come alive there in Aden's main bazaar, in front of her, and behind her, and out of the corner of her eye. The people. The noise. The smells. The unpleasantness. The excitement. But she didn't want any of it anymore. She did not leave the house. Then she went downstairs only for meals, and then not even for those. She crawled into her bed and slept. She'd watched the mothers and her sisters and countless slaves through pregnancy and seen a dozy haze settle on them for the most part. Maybe they'd been feeling this utter exhaustion too. On bad days she felt anger stirring, fighting back at the fear and doubt. She beat her fists uselessly into the one solitary, measly pillow on the bed that these people thought was adequate. Signor Mass had lived in Zanzibar for years and managed to have no idea how the Zanzibari truly lived. They'd clung to their chairs and tables and beds and 'superior' customs.

After she'd beaten the pillow into her own exhausted state, she forgave Bonaventura and Maria Mass for their kindness to her. She watched her anger shrivel to a tiny poisonous ball that she swallowed, swearing she wouldn't let it engorge and vomit itself up again. She recognised the consequences: bitter old Bibi Azziz, legal wife to the Sultan, but childless; her sister Nanu born blind, who hated anything named as perfect and was caught trying to snip, by feel and with very sharp scissors, the eyelashes off their brother Majid when he was a flawless newborn.

Only the return of the cat was any comfort. Sinbad took several weeks to decide the compensation of regular food was worth the loss of freedom on the streets of Aden. Zada earned deep scratches attempting to wash him and divest him of his crawling parasites. From the first return he rustled his way up through the bougainvillea and announced himself with wild hellos at dusk each evening. He joined Salmé on the bed and sniffed at the scraps on her dinner tray and kneaded the bedclothes into a nest. When the house went quiet she could hear his soft purring. On the cold nights he moved in, resting up against her body, stealing her warmth.

The baby started to come in the middle of the night.

'Don't call anyone,' Salmé told Zada after the first wave of contractions subsided and she was able to speak. Then the pain ripped across her stomach and punched her in the small of her back and she sobbed, 'Bibi, Bibi, mother,' wanting more than anything for her mother Jilfidân to come and help her now.

It felt like a miracle when that pain let go again. It was a false promise of course, one of many through the night. Zada helped her turn onto one side and then the other but the pain found her whichever way she moved. 'I want to go home,' she sobbed. The cat deserted her and time broke into fragments and then light began to creep across the floorboards toward the bed and she grunted until Zada was able to pull the baby free.

'A boy,' she called up the bed. 'A tiny little boy.'

Zada appeared beside Salmé's head. Her own hair had come free in the night and stood in unruly tufts all over her skull. She held the baby while Salmé struggled into a half-sitting position. She wasn't sure about the thing held out to her. It looked like it would bruise at the slightest touch, would break easily. The head lolled against Zada's hand, overlarge and heavy. The naked skin was a waxy white and streaked with blood. Zada took no notice of her hesitation and placed him firmly on Salmé's chest. Salmé had to reach up so he didn't slip off. As she touched him, his eyes opened. He stared at her. No one had told her about this. All the births in the harems of her childhood and yet this mystery was kept secret. It was like she held the whole world in her arms. She could only look away when he let go of the gaze, when he looked down and mewed like the cat.

She could look at him properly then. 'His fingers are so small,' she whispered. 'And his skull, look it's soft.' A dent the size of a thumb breathed at the top of his head. She scanned down from his head to his toes, complete with long toenails needing to be cut. Her eyes came back to the umbilical cord, a bluish tied off stump sticking from his protruding belly. It was unsightly and unsettling. 'What is that?' she asked, pointing.

Zada appeared again beside her. 'That was where he was joined to you. I had to cut it. Your sewing scissors will need to be cleaned.'

'I never knew,' Salmé said. She'd imagined he was in there like Sinbad in his basket, ready to leap free, not like an orange that needed to be cut from the bough.

'I have to go and get warm water to wash him and you.' Zada lent in and chucked the baby under its chin. 'Definitely a boy,' she laughed. 'Look.'

Salmé looked. His genitals were swollen, too big for such a tiny body.

'His father will be so proud,' Zada said with a familiarity Salmé did not expect, though she suspected she should have after what they'd just been through together.

Then Zada was gone. Salmé tried out the words, 'My son.' He turned his brown eyes to her and began crying. She thought she knew what to do: she'd seen this part often enough. She held the baby to her breast. He snuffled around and she directed him and suggested what he should do and he cried and she finally pushed his sobbing mouth onto her nipple. The first tentative tugs were unconvinced. And then his sobs subsided. Above the moon curve of her breast his two unblinking eyes, awash with tears, arrested hers again. She knew she'd forget the pain of childbirth but not this. Love. Overwhelming, uncomplicated, unconditional; all the weight of pure emotion poured on something as light as a sheaf of peacock feathers.

He continued to suckle half-heartedly and she sang encouragement, forgotten lullabies in Circassian, her mother's tongue. His tiny fingers reached and she put her hand toward them.

They could not make a complete grasp around her smallest finger. He gave up his hold and spread his hand like a starfish on her veined flesh.

Time refused to return to a steady pace. Some days disappeared without her realising. Minutes listening to the baby's struggling breath seemed to take days to pass. Maria Mass insisted on calling the British doctor to the house. Salmé refused to have him in the room she slept in so she brought the baby downstairs for the first time.

The doctor wanted to look in his eyes. She understood his words before Maria translated; all the hours listening to her Bible lessons had improved her English if not her relationship with God.

The baby's eyes flickered open under the butterfly touch of her lips on his cheek. The doctor took him and he cried, a small, careworn cry. Salmé stood at the window and looked out over the garden because it was difficult to see her baby prodded and turned. She could hear the doctor and Maria talking. She could hear Maria calling to her. She heard the word 'thriving.' Salmé watched frangipani flowers float off the spreading branches of the tree outside. They danced on the slight breeze until they came to settle on the piles of rotting petals dropped the day before.

Maria translated the English in case she had not understood. Salmé heard the 'not' in front of the word. Let it float past her. She heard Maria asking what she, Salmé, should be asking. 'What is wrong?'

'His heart,' said the doctor whose name had been lost in the thrum of her blood being pumped too fast by her own heart. 'A hole most probably.'

Maria tried to get Salmé to go to church to celebrate Christmas. It would mean leaving the baby.

'You have to go out sometime,' she told her. She seemed not to mind that her guest had put herself outside all convention. An unmarried mother, yes, but still a princess. The balance was still in her favour.

Salmé knew Maria was right about leaving the child though. She had the seamstress come back to sew her dresses small again but in the end the symbolism of the Christian feast was too much to confront. She remembered the Rev. Wishart's stories. Mary and Joseph, the couple, together, beside the cow's feeding trough, the baby Jesus wrapped in swaddling clothes amongst the straw. The Nativity. Salmé's nativity lacked a father. She stayed in her room.

Her life was once again confined to an island. This island was the size of her bed. On it she dreamed of Zanzibar and wore her old clothes – crinolines were useless for lounging on a bed – and listened for the baby's heartbeat. Waiting for the skips in the rhythm. Holding her breath each time.

It was the end of the year for these people outside her door. In a week, a different new year would begin, not *Siku a mwaka* but the one on the Christian calendar. Salmé prayed to both her gods. 'Allah, that which happens is the will of the Lord. Allah Akbar. What is written, is written. Gentle Jesus, suffer the little children to come unto thee, but leave my child yet awhile.' She could not hear any answers. The baby struggled to feed. She spoke to him in Swahili, Arabic, Circassian, fishing for a response in his eyes. She tried Spanish. '*Tu eres bellosa, bella bella, bonita,*' she crooned. His eyes slipped off hers. Only a mother could call him beautiful; she was not so besotted she did not know this, but she was not lying either. To her he was more beautiful than life.

She closeted herself at first because she wanted only to be with her child, now it was fear that kept her secluded. Zada acted as intermediary with the world. She brought up food, she opened the curtains and brought light. Salmé closed them again.

Maria knocked lightly on the first morning of the New Year. 'I brought a present,' she said. 'The Rev. Wishart would not approve. You are right, he does not really like women, I think.' Maria held a small statue out to Salmé. She had to juggle the baby against her crooked arm to take it.

'This is the Virgin Mary, the Mother of God,' Maria said. 'The Protestants have pushed her out but we Catholics pray to her. You can pray to her too. She will intercede.'

Mary Mother of God was wrapped in a blue china cloak, her hair hooded. Her painted eyes were clear and kind, but when Salmé touched her she could tell this was a heathen thing.

'I pray to her,' Maria confessed. 'She brings me comfort.'

Salmé tried to sound grateful. There was no way to explain that she could not blaspheme so blatantly. This was pure idolatry: she could not risk Allah's anger. She hid the statue under the bed with the chamber pot once Maria was gone.

As if to reward her for this act of faith, a letter arrived the next morning. Zada thrust it at her in bed. Ruete did not know he had a son. He was in Bombay now, he wrote, with the last of his assets to sell up there. So he had finally left Zanzibar and was on his way.

'I love you. I am coming soon. I have had no letter from you. You must tell me any news.'

She believed him. She asked Zada to bring her writing equipment and she immediately wrote, sitting in bed, her writing sprawling over four pages.

'I call him Heinerle,' she wrote, 'when I sing to him and when I rock him to ease his aches and pains. Remember, you told me this was what your nanny called you until you were too old and embarrassed by shows of affection? The baby version of Heinrich, for Heinrich's baby.'

She remembered the night he told her about his baby name and how young and innocent he'd looked drowsing on the pillow next to her, his moustache lopsided and his lips raw pink from their work on her flesh. How could I have doubted him, she asked herself. She picked up the baby and tickled him at the corner of his mouth to induce a smile.

'Your father is coming,' she told him. 'He is going to take us to Hamburg and you are going to grow up to be a proper Christian boy.' He stared back this time, with unblinking eyes. 'Soon,' she told him. She pushed the perfidious Sinbad off the bed. Time to get up.

Easter was the next grand celebration in the Christian calendar. It commemorated the death of Jesus. The doctor came again and said the baby would not last that long. It was hard to fall from hopefulness. On the first day of April Salmé finally agreed to bring him to the church to be baptised so he would be safe with God. She stood at the font of Christ Church and handed him to the Rev. Wishart. He tipped the baby's head precariously toward the brass basin set on a tall marble plinth. The water took on the golden colour of the bowl, colour that broke as the minister's broad hand scooped in and picked up diamond droplets. Salmé had stopped wearing all her jewels after the birth. They sat, fists-full of gold and gems, on the dressing table at Steamer Point. Today, to come out in public, she'd taken her nose stud out for the first time. This would have to be treasure enough, she thought as she watched the Rev. Wishart dipping the baby forward toward the font, this golden water, the diamond droplets. Baby Heinrich didn't cry as the water hit his forehead. He'd stopped crying days before. The minister made the sign of the cross with his thumb on the child's damp skin.

'Heinrich Ruete, son of Heinrich Ruete,' he intoned in the cavernous interior of the brick church.

Maria Mass held him next. All her sewing during the Bible lessons had come to this: while translating she'd conjured up a christening gown and a bonnet of silk, with lace and ribbons. The dress hung like a cascade, three times the child's length. He was lost in all the white, the colour of ghosts.

Salmé heard only part of what passed between the Rev. Wishart and the godmother, questions, all answered with, 'I will, with God's help.' Her new friend promised to help baby Heinrich grow with God. Salmé could not get past the word grow. That's all he needed to do after all.

It was cool in the church. Dark and near empty like the Rev. Wishart's description of the tomb the women came to at Easter. The women stood in the cave, where Jesus had been entombed, but the body of Jesus was gone. Salmé did not like this Easter story. You had to look after your dead, not lose them.

Maria handed back her child. He was cold. It was not just the temperature of the church. After too many fevers his heat was leaving him.

'I must get him home,' she said to hurry the reverend as he started his last prayers. He looked up, startled by the interruption. He said quite a number more prayers.

In the carriage Salmé held Heinrich close to her heart and stared intently into his tiny wizened face to see if there was any change now he was God's child. Her own eyes smarted: she'd started to cry the day he had stopped. Maria's bonnet put two pretty layers of lace around his face. He was bald underneath it. On his fortieth day of life she and Zada had shaved all his hair – not that there had been much – completely off. As was tradition. It should have been Johar's role, as chief eunuch, but it was the best Salmé could manage. Her hands had trembled as she negotiated the indented nape of his neck, as she hesitated over the soft vulnerability of his fontanel. The skin had pulsed under the razor like a heartbeat. Now, framed by the bonnet, he looked not older but old. He reminded her of the description of one of the many *jinni* from the *Thousand and One Nights*, with wrinkles across the forehead where the wet cross had dried, the pointy nose, and the leatheriness of his skin. And the wise eyes.

'Grant me one wish my little *jinni*,' Salmé whispered. He blinked. A quiet, almost imperceptible assent. 'I wish you to stay with me a while longer.'

She was woken in the night. Not by movement. When movement stopped.

The invitation sat on the dressing table in front of Salmé. It was printed on silk. She'd thumbed it many times to feel the hard, raised strokes of paint that formed the words on something so soft. She'd read it with her fingertips: To her Royal Highness Princess of Zanzibar. Invited to a Public Concert. An orchestra from England on its way to Bombay. It would play in Aden, for one night only.

Zada brushed her hair. In the past, she'd had a tendency to tug just a little too hard, to attack a knot just a little too vigorously. Now she was as gentle as a mother with a child. Salmé noticed the change. She was beginning to resent it.

Maria Mass's maid had taught Zada how to put a lady's hair up in the European style, but she didn't quite have the knack. It was supposed to pile on the head leaving the neck as naked as a boy's. Salmé watched Zada haul up clumps and pin them and then reach for more. The whole point was to restrain every strand and yet tendrils sneaked out and tumbled back to her shoulder. Zada grimaced in the mirror, the line of pins in her mouth like an extra row of teeth.

'Can't I just wear a scarf?'

Zada didn't say anything. Whether this was because it was a stupid question or the pins in her mouth made it impossible, was up to Salmé to determine. Another hank of hair ascended to crown her head.

She had agreed to go to listen to the orchestra after a long campaign by Maria. She didn't know if her final *yes* was a moment of strength or weakness. She hadn't left the house above Steamer Point since her child had a second chance to wear his baptismal bonnet and gown. The doctor carried him out of her bedroom in the end. She didn't know who put him in the coffin. He was buried in the sandy earth in Christian silence; and now there was a public concert.

My first public engagement, and, she told herself, defeated on all fronts, probably my last. Because there was also a letter on the dressing table, almost hidden under the silk invitation. The Sultan had not written the letter himself even at this grave juncture. Salmé recognised the practiced hand of his scribe. She imagined Majid in his assembly room, striding from window to window and looking out over his harbour as he formed the proposal. In the scene she created, she wanted to put him in his private apartments – he would surely have wanted this matter kept private – but she'd never seen any of the men's private rooms to recreate in her imagination. So she made this a public display. She imagined the Sultan's advisors sticking to their opinions. She tried to imagine the subject of the letter upset Majid so much he trembled on the verge of one of his fits.

None of this was actually anywhere between the lines of the letter delivered by the Sultan's political agent in Aden that morning. The message was completely business-like in tone. The agent, Colonel Goodfellow, was British so maybe he did not realise what he was asking of the princess. It sounded magnanimous. Sultan Majid gave permission for his sister Sayyida Salmé to return to Zanzibar. The princess was to desist from appearing in public and was to return on the first available of the Sultan's *dhow*. The Sultan sent his sister Allah's love.

Salmé was drained. Emotions had become a burden. With nothing but time to reflect, and to regret, the past was returning with a silent ferocity. Metle's words: if it had been a British trader or a French monsieur next door, would she have made the same choices? She'd been in a storm cloud too thunderous to think through, but now she tried to put herself at a distance from her situation. As if she was the woman over there in the mirror not the woman on the chair in front of it.

It was clear there were no secrets in Aden. Majid's spies knew everything that had happened. It was almost two months since the death of her child and now everyone in Stone Town knew of it too. In the Sultan's eyes, the baby would have been the biggest impediment to her return. The impediment was rotting in a Christian graveyard. The episode was over. She was one of the family again. They would deal with her. Lock her away; or introduce her to a nine-foot tall axe-man.

From this distance she considered the generosity of her brother's offer. She pondered the sincerity. Where else could she go? She weighed the flimsy silk invitation to a Public Concert against the heavy royal paper. No letter had arrived from Ruete to put on the scales.

Zada clasped Salmé's ruby necklace behind her neck and straightened the rays of gems along the swell of her breasts.

'*Tu eres bellosa,*' Zada said. It was one of the few phrases she'd picked up in Spanish. It was what Salmé had said to the baby over and over.

Salmé didn't look up. Zada repeated herself in Swahili.

'Do you want to go home?' was all the reply Zada got. Their eyes met in the mirror.

Zada lowered her gaze. 'I am a slave. I go with you.'

Salmé was reminded of the Rev. Wishart's steadfast Ruth. *Wither thou goest.* Stupid woman.

Maria Mass was making efforts to subdue her own excitement in the hallway as they waited for the carriage, another kindness to Salmé's bereavement that she was beginning to resent.

'We have good seats. I hope they'll be comfortable enough. The riff-raff will be there as well. It's inevitable. But hopefully it won't spoil our enjoyment.'

So I'm supposed to go *and* enjoy it as well? She kept the thought to herself.

The carriage took the women and the resigned Bonaventura – resplendent in an almost mocking way in a crimson cravat – along the same route toward Christ Church. She looked out the opposite window as they passed the church. Then they continued to rattle along Front Bay, beside the water. The district was called Crater City because the bay was formed within an extinct volcano. They were travelling along the volcano's top edge. She could see the ocean swelling darkly in the erstwhile crater. All the fire had gone out of the earth long ago.

Set back from the seafront, Aden's concert hall sparkled with lights. The gas roared under the flames. Bonaventura Mass offered Salmé his left arm while his wife took his right. European independence for a woman included the convention of having a man on your arm, she noted, as she was led up the marble steps to wide double doors.

The concert hall was like one of the hives at Bet il Mtoni: an evening hive when all the bees had returned with the tattle of their day in the fields. The noise was almost physical. It was like walking into a wall, and she wanted to bounce off it and leave. It was worse when she started to recognise individual words emerging from the general hum. The words were in different languages, some she understood, and others she understood from tone. *Princess. Zanzibar. Scandal.* Heads turned. A pathway of silence hushed in front of her.

'I'll take us straight to the seats,' Signor Mass said loudly.

They had privileged places, the good seats Maria had boasted of. They were at the centre of the front row, the best seats in the house to see the orchestra and later the dances, but also the best seats in which to be seen by the rest of the audience. Her naked neck was exposed to the eyes of men she'd never met and never would. She'd be safe from this sort of thing if she accepted Majid's offer. The pressure built up and up: I have to run out of here; this is too much; they all know my shame. Her heart galloped in her chest, but just when the claustrophobia of the stares became too much to endure, it felt as if the whole concert hall – from the velvet chairs to the gilded ceiling to the high roaring gaslights – was rushing away. She fell from being a huge centre for all the attention of the world, to a tiny point in the vast cavern of the universe.

One day the Great Sultan played a joke and turned the telescope mounted in the Bendjle, the tower at Bet il Mtoni, the wrong way around. He called the children and let them look through it one by one. Salmé was so small she had to climb a ladder to reach the viewfinder. She'd been watching some slave boys on the beach while she waited her turn. Through the reversed telescope they looked so small they could be ants. The audience in the Aden concert hall felt as far away and unreachable as this. A *safe* distance. Salmé's breathing stopped its race and returned to a clippity-clop pace.

Finally, the London players came onto the stage, drawing some attention away from the back of Salmé's neck. She became one of the watchers, not the watched and the world was able to snap back to its usual proportions. The musicians sat on the chairs arranged on the stage. They shuffled into more comfortable positions. They hefted violins under their chins and double basses between their legs and flutes into the air from pursed lips. The instruments spat catcalls to each other. She was able to be shocked, even after everything else.

'I don't think I like your music,' she whispered to Maria.

She heard a suppressed giggle above the catcalls. 'They are tuning up,' Maria explained, her hand on Salmé's crooked arm. She thought Maria was laughing at her, but if she was she covered herself by naming all the instruments, the violins, cello, double bass, clarinets and flutes. Maria pointed out the kettle drum that looked like something out of the kitchen corner of the courtyard at Bet il Mtoni where there were so many mouths to feed. By the time Maria finished the list, the notes from the instruments, so named, were in harmony. Cat noises still, but now a contented murmuring purr, like Sinbad now he was allowed back on her bed after a big feed. Salmé tried to concentrate. She wanted to tell Maria later that she'd enjoyed the concert. She wanted to repay her friend for her constant small and large kindnesses, even that small suppressed giggle. But her mind drifted away and she failed again.

As I've failed in everything in life, she admitted. The kettledrum was rolling out thunder like artillery fire. The rebellion. A failure. Her passion. A failure. The flight. A failure. The list grew. The baby. She pushed her fingernails into the palms of her hands to stop her eyes filling with more tears. Failure. There was nothing to hold her here. The decision was very simple in the end. The music was foreign, the eyes boring into her back were strange and frightening, and Salmé simply wanted to go home. And the Sultan had sent his permission.

'It was lovely,' she lied.

Maria flung herself against the horsehair stuffed bench at the back of the carriage and sighed melodramatically. 'Yes, yes, it was heavenly,' she upped Salmé.

Maria unconsciously patted the front of her crinoline down onto a lump that would soon quicken and kick back. Salmé hadn't failed to notice the changes though Maria was being painfully discreet. It was part of the pity thing she hated. Or maybe it was superstition that held Maria's tongue about her pregnancy. I am now bad luck around pregnancies, Salmé realised.

Bonaventura was silent in the far corner. He'd slept through most of the concert. There'd been a small undertow of rhythmic breathing in Salmé's right ear. In the shadowy dark of the carriage she watched Maria's diamonds, the clues to her movements. Her hand never reached for her husband. Salmé wondered how they'd ever come to be married; and how she'd ever imagined it could happen for her. She'd tell them her decision later. Maria first, maybe at breakfast. Then Maria could break it to her husband. Salmé hadn't wasted her time at the concert after making her decision. As her first and last public concert played in the background, she'd composed a letter to Majid. His spies would know about tonight, but they would be able to report on her sincerity when she returned to complete seclusion from tomorrow.

There was something else she'd do now. While she waited for Sultan Majid's orders and his *dhow*, she'd finally finish a letter to Metle. Metle would love the stories about the dresses and the violins. Salmé let herself feel how much she missed Metle, and even Khole; and even Johar.

The lights around the front door of the Mass's house drew the carriage in like a moth. The horses fidgeted as Salmé climbed down onto the path, their hooves kicking up chips of gravel, grinding them down into the drive again. She was too tired to be up and willingly took the support of Bonaventura Mass's arm.

'Thank you, thank you,' she said sincerely. 'Now I must retire for the night.' She wouldn't be able to talk to Signor Mass after she started wearing her mask again but she couldn't bring herself to say goodbye.

Maria was looking at her with that kind smile she put on to try and make everything better. Salmé was sure she'd understand when she told her about Majid's letter. In the morning.

Bonaventura flung open the door to the drawing room and let out a rare laugh. The sort of laugh to ripple the belly and wag his cravat like a butterfly taking flight. A silhouetted figure moved away from the window, moving in the haze of gaslight. The man had the smell of the sea. She turned toward the stairs. It was rare that Signor Mass's associates in the trade came to the house. She could not be seen by one. Majid could still withdraw his permission for her to come home.

'Bibi?' the man called after her.

She stopped. Could not turn back. It could not be. Maria was clapping.

'We made it a good surprise didn't we,' she laughed.

The man was behind her. The heavy, briny stink enveloped her.

'I have missed you,' he said quietly so only she could hear.

S almé was surprised to discover she was furious. Forget extinct volcanoes and calm harbours, she seethed and boiled and could not speak. Let Ruete take it for grief. She wasn't about to tell him anything.

They were all politeness in front of the Spanish couple.

'I was so sorry to hear,' Ruete said when they were in the drawing room taking those endless, pointless cups of tea. 'I wrote a letter but it seems not to have arrived. The ship carrying it will no doubt come after we've gone.' Salmé sipped her tea. 'It was lucky,' he said. She choked on the tea. In no light could her last nine months since she saw him be called lucky. 'In the letter I suggested we baptise him Rudolf. Now we have the name for our next son.'

She excused herself then. Murmurs about needing bed.

'The grief, the mourning, she'll get over it,' eddied about in her wake. Bed but not sleep. How dare he simply turn up? Now. How dare he do exactly what she'd been praying for – but too late for there to be any gladness in it for her.

In the morning she made another discovery: they'd organised everything without consulting her. The plans were all for Sayyida Salmé, just not for her to have a say in. Even the Rev. Wishart knew the plans before she did. He greeted the party, Salmé, her groom – finally – and the Mass couple. He gave his usual overt sniff at the whiff of the slave trade before he let them through the church door, and then he led them down the aisle between the hard, comfortless pews, stopping the parade first at the font. Salmé's anger began to crack at that moment. It broke along with her heart, overwhelmed to be back in front of the shimmering bowl of God's blessed water. The same words she'd heard two months before were recited around her.

'Hallelujah Christ is Risen,' the Rev. Wishart sang, as she was invited into the family of God. They used English as their common language; if she'd learnt nothing else, it was that God was an English speaker too.

'I present Ruth, to receive the Sacrament of Baptism,' Maria said, as her elected godmother.

Wither thou goest Ruth? Salmé finally found her voice when she should have been silent. She felt she'd been treated like a slave, do this, do that, come here, go there. But she wasn't a slave or a child. For one moment longer she was still Princess Salmé.

'No,' she said loudly.

There was consternation around the font. Maria froze, Ruete stepped forward, Bonaventura back, and the Rev. Wishart reached for his handkerchief under his surplice to mop his anxious brow. Or maybe he flourished the thing simply because it was hot and muggy in the church with the sun streaming through the high windows picking out the dust that the sacred candles normally obscured. Salmé watched the progress of the handkerchief, mesmerised by its breadth and purpose again. Then she saw Ruete's face. It would take time to see her lover in this face, the cheeks plumper, well fed, the beard thicker, less kempt. All his features sagged above his beard. Did he think she was saying no to everything? She liked the fact that this upset him. This was however only a small rebellion.

She finished her protest: 'No, not Ruth. I want a different name.'

The disquiet left the group like an uneasy ghost laid to rest. Maria moved toward her husband while the men realigned themselves, stepping forward and back and re-depositing handkerchiefs in reverse to their previous movements. They all looked at Salmé. She hadn't thought this through. She only knew she wasn't going to be the steadfast and obedient Ruth of the Bible; the widow Ruth. Faith, Hope, Charity jostled in her mouth. Chastity was out of the question; obviously, though no one would ever mention this. She couldn't choose. It was too sudden, which was ridiculous after all the waiting, the storm-lurch of emotions. It was nine months since she'd fled Zanzibar.

'Ruete, what was Mrs Seward's name?'

He thought for a moment. 'Mrs Emily Seward?'

'Yes, she helped me. Organised the *Highflyer*. Without her I wouldn't be here.'

Ruete smiled. His features lifted from their slump. 'Emily,' he said.

'Emily,' the Rev. Wishart intoned, and before she could change her mind, he scooped the golden water and dribbled diamond drops onto her upright forehead. Gravity sluiced them off so the cross he drew on her skin was dry.

'Do you turn to Jesus Christ and accept him as your Saviour?' the Rev. Wishart asked, holding her eyes with his.

Emily quickly said 'I do.' Salmé took a step back and waited still and quiet in Emily's mind as she mouthed a litany of 'I believes.'

She'd entered the church as Salmé, and now as Emily she walked from the font up the aisle to the high altar. Ruete walked at her side. The aisle was narrow but they did not touch. They both stared straight ahead until it was his turn to say 'I do.'

'Until death us do part,' the vows ordained. Emily repeated the words after the Rev. Wishart. Ruete took her hand and slipped a plain band of gold on her naked finger.

'Frau Emily Ruete,' he whispered. 'You are too thin,' he breathed into her cheek after a brief kiss. It did not sound like a criticism. He sounded shy, unsure. It was as if he needed to learn her again as she needed to learn him.

There were tears back in her bedroom. Ruete had a ship arranged to take them to Marseilles, the real Marseille, the French Marseilles. It left that very night. The news put urgency into the packing and obviously unsettled Zada who cried and dropped as much as she was able to safely stow.

Salmé bent over her ebony chest rearranging her jewellery securely and wondering how offended Maria Mass would be if she left the plaster idol of the Virgin behind. She ran her fingers up the folds of its blue cloak and tapped the tear on its pale cheek. It seemed wrong to leave a gift. So she moved some of her gold coins and stood the statue upright in one corner of the box. She brought the lid down to make sure it wouldn't decapitate her. As it dropped and exposed the mirror behind, Zada's reflection came into view. Her eyes were puffy and bloodshot and sunk deep.

'Don't worry, you're not coming,' she told her. 'No slaves are allowed in Europe, Zada. Can you imagine?'

Zada dropped the runaway-night *schele* she'd been folding. It fell on the hard floor where it pooled and settled and looked like the entrance to an underground tunnel. Salmé turned to look at the real Zada and not her reflection. Signor Mass had offered to negotiate her sale but Ruete had also said they were rich. His business ventures in Zanzibar had gone well. 'Remarkably well' were his words. Zada would fetch a good price but as Salmé watched her crawling on the floor collecting up all the yards of black cloth she considered the Rev. Wishart's lessons. Charity was a tenet of Christianity as well as Islam.

'You have been faithful,' she said slowly. She didn't want to conjure up all the moments of faithfulness during her baby's short life; she had to look to the future now. 'You have been faithful and...' She searched for the right word and was surprised when she found it. 'And kind.'

Zada stood as immobile as the statue of Mary Mother of God.

Salmé realised she should have thought of this earlier. 'You deserve your freedom.' There was paper and ink amongst the brushes and perfumes on the dressing table, all waiting to be packed. 'I'll write out your freedom now,' she said and turned so she didn't have to look at the pathetic gratefulness of her slave's face. It made her uncomfortable. She was already thinking of her as a free person.

She checked the sharpness of the nib against the cushion of her index finger, flexed her ringed finger and saw the plain gold band that was momentarily more fascinating than all her golden bells and gemstones. She'd felt light-headed, almost light-hearted since leaving the church. The Rev. Wishart would have diagnosed this as a symptom of her rebirth and renewal as Emily

Ruete. Cleansed by the water from the font, remade by her marriage vows. It was easy to be generous.

'Signora Mass can find you a position here in Aden, Zada,' she said as she wrote.

'I want to go back to Zanzibar,' Zada said softly, a whisper above inaudible.

She put down the pen. 'I can arrange that if you really want.' They were looking at each other in the mirror.

'Yes, I want to go home to my son.'

'You have a son?' Salmé was astonished. She'd never imagined Zada had a life of her own. 'And how old is your son?'

'Five.'

Emily saw a five-year-old boy in her mind, but knew he was from one of her hopeful daydreams during her pregnancy. The image was of *her* baby as a boy, not Zada's child. The image tugged too deeply.

'Do you know where he is?'

'He was sold to your niece Sayyida Zemzem. Along with the other children in your household.'

Salmé had thought nothing of separated children from their mothers. She stopped herself from crying otherwise she'd not be able to see the gold coins in her box clearly. She counted out enough coins to buy passage to Zanzibar, and another pile to buy a five-year-old boy. She walked over to Zada and put the coins into her dry, cold hand. She pressed Zada's fingers over the palm and the coins to make a safe pouch of flesh and bone.

'You will buy his freedom too,' she commanded. 'I will write to my niece so she will know to accept your money.'

Zada tried to speak. 'No, no, hush up,' she told her. 'You still have to finish packing for me. Why my husband wants us to leave on the ship tonight I don't know. All this waiting and now all this hurrying up.' Please, please stop crying. I don't want to cry too, she hushed in her mind.

Back at the dressing table, she wrote to Zemzem about the child. 'But make sure he learns a trade Zada. Freedom is not easy.' Salmé wasn't sure this was true – but it sounded true.

Zada was still crying. She wrapped shoes in brown paper and piled them on the soft bouncy bed. She snuffled and her shoulders heaved up and down as she worked.

'Where is that cat?' Salmé asked loudly over the top of the sobbing. 'I'll just have to leave that silly thing too.' Now I am going to cry.

Emily Ruete did not recognise the harbour from the day she arrived. By night it was a canvas of flaming lights and falling shadows. The noise swelled and didn't fall back. Men shouted and called and bellowed and didn't listen to each other and yet the steamship *Himalaya* was somehow made ready for its journey to Egypt.

The embarkation whistle interrupted Ruete and Mass discussing the new canal the British were building. They stood on the wharf, shaking their heads.

'Then,' Mass said, 'ships will sail directly into the Mediterranean Sea.'

Emily tried to remember the map they'd had as children, the one that was formed by a British jigsaw puzzle so in fact had spent most of its life in pieces on the floor. Africa was large and on the bottom half of the map, Europe was above it, Arabia wedged between. Aden, when the jigsaw was complete, sat half-way to many places. Now she wondered how they were going to get from one landmass to the next without this canal to let them through. Passengers walked up the gangplank to the ship and the men kept talking earthworks and tons of rubble so she asked Maria. She asked with gestures because of the noise. A raised eyebrow, spreading hands, a mouthed, 'How then?'

'You disembark at the top of the Red Sea and travel across Egypt by train, then board another ship,' Maria leaned in to tell her, pitching her voice so it didn't compete but travelled below the noise. Emily thought she'd have spent her childhood better if she'd taken note of the seas and not the land. 'The heat along the Red Sea is *unbearable*,' Maria confided. 'Whatever is at the end of it, land or manmade canal. Particularly so at this time of year. Last time we went home to Spain there was no breeze and the cabins were as stifling as tombs,' she said, or something that sounded like that. The part Emily was sure about were the last words, 'I would rather have been dead the first horrid night.'

They had moved so close to talk that it was natural to hug when Ruete shouted it was time to embark.

'Thank you,' Emily whispered in her ear. 'Your baby will be lucky to have you as his mother.'

'You will be a good mother too,' Maria whispered. 'Write?'

'Oh yes, I can write.' She laughed. Her first laugh since her baby died. 'I can write, I taught myself, and look where it has got me.' She knew Maria couldn't hear any of it.

Ruete held her hand to pull her along the steep incline of the gangplank. They waved from the deck and then, before the ship left the quay, she followed him in search of their cabin. Maria's comments should have prepared her for the sleeping arrangements. The cabin *was* a tomb when they got there. She backed out of the wall of heat and bumped into a strange man.

'Captain,' Ruete greeted him.

'Welcome aboard, Sir, Princess.' So he knew. 'I am suggesting we all sleep in the public saloon tonight. Passengers find the cabins inhospitable.' She could feel the slick film of sweat starting to trickle down her neck and between her breasts as they stood there. 'The saloon is up there,' he pointed. Up there: up a steep ladder back into the night. 'I know it's not private but at least there's a chance of a breeze.' He moved down the corridor repeating the same offer to other passengers.

'Up?' Ruete asked. She cringed at the thought of sleeping with strangers. She stepped into the cabin and immediately retreated.

'Yes. Up.'

They touched briefly on the ladder to the open deck. His hand on Emily's naked ankle. And then they had to part to make the best of the situation, women to one side of the saloon, men to the other. There was a French woman from Mauritius sleeping on the mattress next to her. She seemed friendly; and then ground her teeth deep into the night. Emily lay there listening to the squeaky, granulate grinding, wondering what on this earth would happen next. She already missed Zada. There was no one to fan her, or massage her into sleep. She counted the moonlit panels along the saloon wall, then the number of men snoring on the opposite side of the saloon. It was like a cacophony of frogs beside the pond at Bububu. The other exhalations and eructations sounded even more fit for the animal kingdom. Metle would believe this scene as soon as she'd believe her sister was flying to the moon.

My wedding night, she reminded herself. She wept as silently as she could: she didn't want the strange teeth-grinding woman from Mauritius waking and thinking badly of her.

The next morning she kept her head on her pillow and watched a man rise in his nightshirt and creep out of the saloon, his legs, hairy, knobbly-kneed. Emily glanced at his face, and was astonished to see there was nothing furtive in his look. A British woman, also rising, didn't know her nightdress was hitched up and her thigh was revealed, blotched and covered in mosquito bites. Another woman, to the right of where Emily slept, rubbed her cheek but it remained rumpled like crushed pages from where it had lain on the pillowcase.

Now I am a civilised wife, she laughed to herself; and finally, thankfully, at herself.

Before she could steel herself to get up, Ruete came into the saloon by a far door. With the sun behind him through the open door, he was briefly a shimmering angel, haloed like the saints in the windows of the Christ Church. Then he stepped in and she could see he was already dressed, his short hair smoothed over his skull and a cigar smoking between his lips. His eyes searched through the women's side immodestly. She watched his face as he searched and as he found her in the crowd. He looked happy. She sat up, clutching a thin sheet around her. She smiled. Then he pursed his lips. She could imagine the sound: the smack of a pantomime kiss. While performing the funny gesture he looked like a fish. My fish, she tested the idea. She felt a hesitancy, the same as she'd felt on the earliest days across the roof from her palace to his home. *My husband?*

There was so much to say to him, but there was no privacy at breakfast either. Emily was sure the eggs and toast were cooked in with the bacon and were unclean. She didn't care what the Rev. Wishart had said. It seemed wrong. *Go away Salmé*, she cautioned herself.

'Eat something,' Ruete coaxed through a mouthful of pig.

'I think it's a bit of seasickness,' she apologised. 'I had it badly on the way to Aden.'

'Do you want to lie down again?'

He didn't wait for an answer. He stood, took her elbow and pulled her up from her full plate and led her back to their claustrophobic cabin. Inside the thin door they had to creep and nudge aside obstacles. Ruete's trunks cluttered the floor between the low bunk and the table bolted to the ship's side. He hadn't let go of her arm, even on the slipping descent on the ladder. She'd had to follow him: she was his Ruth after all.

He closed the door onto the corridor. They were alone. The claustrophobia was not just a result of the overcrowded cabin. The heat was almost as bad as the evening before. He was mad. He was so close she could feel the heat of him combusting. His lips were against her neck. She stiffened, and he must have felt it too under his searching hands. He hesitated.

'I'm scared,' she whispered.

'Scared?' He pulled away slightly. She could still feel the imprint of his hands on her back. They were two large, sweaty patches through her cotton dress. The cloth prickled against her skin.

'My Sayyida is never scared.'

'The birth,' she began. But she didn't know what to say. Did women discuss such things with men? She had no mothers to tell her so she stumbled on as best she could. 'It hurt. Down there.'

He looked puzzled. He wasn't touching her at all now. 'I thought you'd want this, as much as I do.'

She took his left hand and pulled it slowly down, deep into the folds of the dress, through the webbing of the crinoline, to the spot he'd wanted all along.

'It might not be the same. I don't know.'

'Oh my poor Bibi,' he cried. He was really crying. Tears in his eyes, lips quivering. He pulled her down onto the bunk. Her head knocked against the higher bunk and her hair fell out of its knot. He kissed her bruised crown before undressing her, negotiating all the ridiculous undergarments, kissing each new inch of flesh to emerge into the mote-dusted light. His tongue smoothed over past wrongs, and enveloped what felt like the very core of her being. The central need of the sex blocked out all the other sensations. Sweat trickled and pooled in the dip between her breasts and her underarms and behind her knees but the perception of it evaporated. The convulsions that shook her, rather than breaking her apart, started putting her back together.

'What was he like?' Ruete asked. They were seated on the upper starboard deck with icy water in tumblers nursed in their hands at matching angles. 'Our little Heinrich?'

It was the kindest thing anyone had said to her since the baby died and everyone started to pretend he'd never existed.

'He had eyes like my father,' she whispered. Ruete dragged his cane chair closer, leaned toward her, to hear, to protect her from the other passengers strolling on the deck with its great attraction of a determined breeze and its minor attraction of a foreign princess. Word had spread and she drew eyes. They could not stay in the cabin, so he appointed himself as her shield. 'And his toes. You should have seen his toes. They were so tiny. But the one next to his big toe was the longest. Just like yours.' Her hands trembled around her glass.

The one vast funnel of the *Himalaya* pumped new clouds into the bold, blue sky above their heads. The smoke was caught in the upper currents and teased out. She watched the movement rather than look at his sympathy. She couldn't cry in public. She let her anger come to her aid.

'You were so insensitive about his name. That night when you suddenly appeared.'

'I'm sorry,' he said softly. 'But you weren't helping. Your haughty silence. You were a terrifying princess again, not my love.'

'Why weren't you there when he was born? You should have been there.' She was hissing and crying at the same time.

'But what could I have done, it is women's business, not men's.'

'If you'd been there you wouldn't have to ask what he was like. You'd have memories of your own.'

'But I wasn't.'

They sat, together, but a world apart. She looked up. He had cried in her arms that morning. There were tears in his eyelashes again now. She felt cruel.

'He had brown eyes and stubby eyelashes. He would never have been pretty.' A memory of her mother and Medine gossiping came back to her with her words. *She'll never be pretty.* It had been like an on-going joke between her two mothers.

'He was more like me than you.'

The wind blew across the land before it got to the Red Sea. It picked up the sand of the desert and threw it over the steamer. Red grit settled in her hair as they talked, filmed the meniscus of the water in her glass, rusted her new white dress.

'What can I do to make it right?' he asked.

She wondered as she watched the balletic flight of a gull. The French woman from Mauritius passed by. She called her walk constitutional. 'You should join me,' she called in French and then English without breaking her stride. The silence settled again. A bit more grit settled on her dress.

'You didn't come,' Emily said eventually. She addressed the handrail in front of them.

'I am here.'

'It took so long.' She held herself back and didn't say it took *too* long but it meant almost the same thing.

He was sitting as far forward as was safe on the chair. He searched across the space between them for her hands, which she kept resolutely around her glass, now empty of water, but dirty with a small residue of wet red dust.

'Did you *doubt* I'd come?'

Her answer was a congested sob. Holding the misery in burned the back of her throat and the insides of her nostrils.

He sounded hurt. 'But I said I was coming when you left, and then in my letters.'

'Those were only words on a page. Written words can be erased, burned, thrown out.'

'But I am here,' her husband repeated.

She looked at him. His brown eyes, the soft lashes – unlike their son's – the large physical presence of him in the chair. The glass he'd clumsily shifted at his feet so he could get closer.

'I will never leave you,' he whispered as three fellow passengers stopped to watch the gull return for another matinee of aerial ballet. The silence hummed until the impromptu audience moved aft. Who knew who could speak Swahili and overhear.

'I can't think of any reason I would leave you,' he said.

She let him touch her left hand, let him turn the gold band around her finger. She had no other family now. The Sultan couldn't let her go home after this. Ruete was all she had. His eyes didn't falter from hers. He was here.

'Till death us do part remember,' he said.

She felt a huge swell of gratitude. She couldn't say if she'd truly loved him when she left Zanzibar, but she knew she did now.

'*Ich liebe dich*,' he told her.

'What does that mean?'

'You'll have to learn German to find out.'

French Customs was pandemonium. The first class passengers stood in an orderly queue, to be sure – the Rev. Wishart had been at pains to tell her she was going to civilised countries – but this queue was the only quiet point in the vast, grubby space of the warehouse. She could see the lie in any assertion of civilisation at all other points around her. The clearinghouse for the slaves in Stone Town could not have been more calamitous in its noisiness and the crush of bodies. Tugs hooted impatiently in the harbour and stevedores screamed as if this was their only register and she watched men with blue hats pushing the passengers from steerage into another snaking line which bulged like a python after a good meal before getting hustled back in line to bulge at another point. There were possessions everywhere. Boxes, crates, trunks, misshapen bags holding all the stuff of life. Everything and everyone was alive with anticipation and insisting on this at the top of their lungs.

Their orderly first-class queue moved a few feet as the teeth-grinding enthusiast from Mauritius cleared customs. She turned and waved to Emily, mouthed a hopeful 'Good luck.' The passengers had turned into nice people once out of their nightclothes and especially once they were out of the heat. Emily pulled Maria Mass's gift of her second best coat around her. The customs hall was open at the shore end and she couldn't believe how cold it was. This was supposed to be the European summer.

'You are not impressed, Bibi.' Ruete leaned down to tell her this as his two menservants hauled their luggage up the queue. He was a new man again, this time transformed by a bowler hat. It had become slightly dented from its place in a trunk and he'd spent the last five minutes in their cabin punching it back into shape.

'By your hat? No of course I'm not, it is too funny.'

'You'll get used to the different hats. Think about how odd I found your turbans when I got to Zanzibar.' He laughed but was not distracted. 'But what I meant was, you're not impressed by anything and everything. I can tell by the top of your lip. The way it is pulled tight and quivers when you think no one is looking.'

'Your Marseilles is not as beautiful as our Marseilles.'

'Our Marseilles is not in ruins.'

Her upper lip really did quiver. She'd peered out the porthole of their cabin at the patchwork of red roofs jammed over and stacked up beside each other, all under a grey haze of a sky whose dirty light turned the roof tiles the shade of dried blood. Blood – the name made her think of her Marseilles, as was inevitable. She'd tried hard not to let that push her into the rush of homesickness that still ran alongside her at every step. She continued the battle now on land, about to be admitted onto the continent of Europe.

He placed a hand on her arm. 'Bibi, I'm sorry,' he said. 'And you are right as you are in everything. Marseilles is nothing. You wait till you see Hamburg, the Venice of the north.'

Words were never quite adequate as usual. 'Venice?'

'An Italian city. They have no roads, canals instead. Hamburg's canals are more lovely. *And* we have roads!'

A city with canals instead of roads, and a city with canals and roads? It was as silly as his hat to tell her these things.

'Ruete, honestly, what if I said Hamdan had more lice than Barghash when they were children?'

'What are you talking about?'

'Exactly, it makes no sense without explaining the bushy quality of Hamdan's hair and the naughtiness of Barghash when the eunuchs tried to approach him with the lice comb. If you have no knowledge of brothers or lice it means nothing.'

The European cities with canals had to remain a mystery a while longer because then the man behind them in their civilised queue monopolised Ruete's attention with a question. He was a French businessman with a professed interest in the Middle East and Ruete had taken to avoiding him on deck. She raised her eyebrows at Ruete now to see if he'd laugh but he deliberately avoided her face and composed politeness on his own.

She didn't understand anything of what they said. Some of the passengers across the Mediterranean on the *Aleppo* had come all the way from Aden with them; many others, like this bore, had boarded in Alexandria. She'd lost count of the languages on the ship. Her native Swahili, Arabic, Circassian and her functional Turkish, Nubian, the Farsi she'd used with her Persian relatives and three of the languages of Ethiopia including Amharic, were nowhere near enough to span the new Babel Tower. She could not join in the conversations on board so she'd had to play the docile wife as much as she would have in a harem. As she did now.

Her eyes slipped from her husband. At the back of the custom's house a coffin was being carried into the hall. The crowds parted by some miracle within the chaos to let it through. She had an image of the Red Sea, the Rev. Wishart's, not the one they'd recently sailed up. The coffin came to rest in front of a pair of officials. Whether the coffin had been their companion across the Mediterranean, or from halfway across due to some misfortune, she could not tell from the pantomime across its polished wooden lid. The gestures indicated that the customs officials wanted the top off. It was not a good omen. Emily started instinctively praying to Allah and then stopped herself. She had to remember what she'd learned and who she was now. She was not that docile daughter in the harem at all.

'Our father who art in heaven,' she said, quiet words under her breath so only God would hear.

She knew she was failing to be the Christian Maria Mass wanted her to be. She was confused and forgetful. They'd stopped in Cairo on the overland leg of the journey, and there Ruete organised a tour of the city with some other passengers. They ended the morning at the great Mohammad Ali mosque on the Citadel. They gained permission to go into the mosque itself, only the guards stopped her taking off her shoes and sent her over to line up with the Christian Unbelievers. The infidels weren't allowed to enter until they'd donned felt slippers over their shoes. She'd wanted to protest, to call Allah down as her witness, until she'd remembered who she was now. She'd quietly slipped her shoes into the communal slippers and said nothing to Ruete, who pretended not to notice. He acted as if religion was a private thing between you and your God. He had his own problem: he could not call her 'Emily' yet. He slipped often into Salmé, settled on Bibi, meaning sweetheart, my love, and not only my lady.

Emily turned away from the coffin as a weeping man helped to unbolt the lid. Her lips continued the Lord's Prayer, and in her mind she asked Allah to bless the man and the soul within the coffin, and her too. Then she was distracted by life going on: while the tragedy unfolded on the other side of the space as huge as the Mohammad Ali mosque, she and Ruete gained the front of their own queue.

'Almost there,' he told her. 'You are going to love the train.'

A French official stood on the other side of the counter. He had a long, white moustache that fell languidly onto his collar and was a false advertisement to his approach. He questioned Ruete with vigour in a rapid flow of French. His particular interest was Emily's personal box, which was now a slightly dulled black after the long journey. Ebony spoke of wealth nonetheless and the official demanded that it be opened. Ruete indicated she should hand over the key and then the bedlam fell away and the only performance worth watching was over her possessions. The custom's man snapped open the gold clasp and dipped into the rest of her gold. The bells on her bracelets and anklets didn't have a chance in the din but the shine could not be masked. His beefy hand sifted through the carefully arranged diamonds and pearls and then he pulled out her favourite ruby and rubbed it between his thumb and forefinger. She protested, instinctively in Arabic, and the man barked a question at Ruete. Suddenly she wasn't Frau Emily Ruete a civilised Christian lady any more. She heard her husband repeating her old name. 'Sayyida Salmé.' She heard 'Zanzibar' said over and over. 'Sayyid Sa'id Sultan.' 'Zanzibar.' Ruete's French was pedantic and laboured and the white-mustachioed man shook his head repeatedly.

'He will not believe these are your personal possessions,' Ruete explained quietly when the custom's man went to consult a superior.

'It's his ignorance,' she said angrily, though she was scared. She hadn't expected any challenges now she had Ruete by her side. 'Surely he can see, surely he knows this is the normal wardrobe of any Eastern woman?' She stood close to her box monitoring all the individual pieces and making sure the coins at the bottom stayed there.

'He thinks we are importing jewellery. To sell. He is demanding tax on every piece.'

The superior came over and the same arguments were repeated. The new official was embraided with epaulets of woven, false gold and was clearly impressed by the real stuff at his finger-tips. Even Emily could interpret his gestures. A little something for him and the problem would go away. She felt Ruete's posture change. He had weight and he moved in close, using his body not only as a shield for her but as a threat to the officials. His tone was black. He was being a bully. She had never seen him like this before and she suddenly understood his success in business. His voice grew louder. The official had the statue of Mary out and was poking it at him. She could feel many eyes on them. She glanced around to confirm that they were not only the eyes of the customs' men. The people in their queue, held up and impatient, were also curious. As were the closest mass of passengers in the other line who hadn't a diamond necklace between them for sale or ornamentation. She wanted to telescope herself out of this high customs hall as she'd done in the concert hall in Aden.

The official stepped back after a long pregnant silence. He gave a deep wave: an invitation for them to move into the city of Marseilles. Emily could not ask what Ruete had said to sway the argument. He laid the Catholic statue on a bed of gold and carried the ebony box himself, leaving the rest of the luggage to the servants.

So here we are, she thought as they walked into the grey air.

'Herr Ruete and his wife, born Sayyida Salmé of Zanzibar and Oman, are on European soil with their wealth intact,' she joked.

'We'll have a photograph taken of you,' he told her in the street. 'In your Arab clothes. With your jewellery. A kind of proof.' He sounded buoyant, enthusiastic about this next step.

He'd won the argument after all. 'As soon as we get to Hamburg,' he said. 'The photograph.'

Emily stepped into the waiting carriage. Her body felt like it was rocking so she reached out and held onto the window frame. Either the carriage was very well sprung or she'd have to look for her land legs again.

'You looked a bit worried back there,' he said from behind her.

She felt immensely tired. As their trunks and crates were loaded she watched the coffin from the *Aleppo* being slipped into the back of a long low carriage with nothing but glass down each side so there was no disguising what it carried. A woman in black wept on the road beside it, oblivious to the traffic. Emily pushed herself away from the profundity of this image as quickly as she could. Her recent lessons in religion told her to pay no heed to omens.

'Maybe we can get a decent coffee here in France?' she asked. 'I am sick of the stuff that tastes like coffee coloured water.'

'Ah my mercurial wife. Worry to thirst in a moment.' The only point of warmth was his hand moving along her thigh. His flesh was hot through the layers of petticoats and dress and coat.

'Soon we'll be home,' he said. There was a slight rising in-flection in his voice on the last word, making it sound like a question.

1868–1870

Hamburg

The thing wouldn't look at her. After almost two weeks in the Hamburg house it had given up responding to Emily's face peering over the lip of the bath. Winzig and Babette skittered on the bathroom tiles beside her. Winzig, being tiny like her name, couldn't reach, but Babette's claws slipped on the porcelain a few times then she too peered at the turtle with the liquid eyes that looked staunchly away.

Ruete had thought it a good idea and sent the turtle in a hackney carriage so it had arrived unannounced the Tuesday before. Straight from Zanzibar, like Emily. This coming Saturday, for their first Hamburg dinner party, there'd be turtle soup. She hadn't known this when Lene came rushing in with garbled news of the arrival.

'Not a package from the master,' the maid tried to clarify. 'Come and see for yourself.'

There were always misunderstandings. Two hours of German lessons in the afternoons had equipped Emily for polite conversations but not news of green turtles in hackney carriages. It was doubtful Lene knew what a turtle was in the first place; mistranslations on misapprehensions. Emily followed Lene to the front door that previous Tuesday morning and they contemplated the turtle, on its back, rocking on the top step. Looking not unlike a large soup dish. Two weeks later, she reached into the bath to grab hold of the same shell now turned the right way up. She'd made Lene carry it into the house that first day but today Lene had made herself scarce, a trick she'd developed on all the bath days since.

'Come, come,' Emily crooned in Swahili, as if the animal would respond more to a native language. As if it had spent a good long life beaching itself on the white sands of Zanzibar picking up harem gossip. She stretched her arms to either side of the mossy shell. Judging by its girth, the turtle *had* spent a good long life. Somewhere. His eyes, staring implacably at the plughole, were old. Old meant wise.

Somehow Lene had got him into the bath – his watery habitat in miniature – and somehow each bath day since, Emily had to get him out. It was gamble each time. She could never remember how it'd worked the time before. It was a deep bath, with two taps on the side, fixed to the water pipes in the wall. She remembered her initial fascination with the gaslights in the streets and the water pipes in the house. Hamburg had to have something good to offer when they finally arrived. The trains were less exciting than Ruete made out and Europe was far bigger than a children's jigsaw puzzle on a palace floor could possibly represent. Travelling from the south to the far north of the continent had been a trial. She'd thought arriving in Marseilles meant they were close.

'Straight from Zanzibar,' the newspaper announced when they finally arrived in the city. Ruete got her to translate the headline.

'I'd hardly call those months as a direct line from there to here,' she'd complained. Though she was more surprised that she was in the *Hamburgischer Correspondent* at all.

'Of course a princess makes it into the news in Hamburg,' he'd said. 'I believe there is a place in Hamburg's Republican heart for an envy of Prussia's kings and crown princes.'

'Well, I don't look like a princess now,' she said as she leant over the bathtub. With a helping grunt, she lifted. Her grasp wasn't secure. The turtle fell back into the murky water. Bits of muck splattered her bodice and skirt. She stood upright and contemplated her scratched palms.

Winzig had pushed herself under the bath at a glimpse of the turtle's shadow. Her sweet poodle face popped out next to the claw foot. Babette lowered herself back onto four legs and briefly nuzzled Emily's bare toes. Her feet didn't feel secure on the slipperiness of the splashed tiles. On the second attempt she wedged her knees and her pregnant stomach against the high side of the bath, putting pressure on her back. The turtle remained stoic as she maneuvered him around in the water, hanging onto one flipper, a softer limb than it looked. Then she was able to get a hand tucked under each side of the shell again.

'Lift,' she told herself. 'You've done it before.' Before. Four times in the last couple of weeks. But with the baby coming and the dinner party even more imminent, she was tired. Her perpetual state since arriving, *straight from Zanzibar*. She wanted a gang of eunuchs to take over. But here there was only one cook and two useless maids pretending to be busy.

Her dress sleeves took this moment to drop from their rucked-up position. It was her favourite dress, with a fringe in mock suede along the tops of the sleeves and in a line across her breasts. The newspapers would have the fashionable women of Europe believe these were the type of tassels favoured by Native Indians. A matching handkerchief hung around her neck, like one, so the newspaper writers insisted, worn by General Custer, the hero of the American nation who was out fighting the savages. The sleeves of her Wild West dress soaked up enough bath water to make any marine animal happy and drowned out any stray thoughts of looking grand.

She steadied herself to lift again. '*Eins, zwei, drei,*' she recited, like she was back in the first weeks in Hamburg. She'd regressed to being like a five-year old learning numbers and letters and days of the week. 'Your days are numbered,' she told the turtle. 'This Saturday my lovely. *Samstag.*'

It was exactly like being flung back into childhood when she'd first arrived. She'd practiced her new words every day. One to ten, she counted the steps up the wide staircase of their Alster home. Then she counted the closed-up bedrooms, each with a window out to the lake. Four. The chandeliers in the dining room. Three. The pillows on the bed. Two. The wives in the house. One.

Then she learnt her A, B, C, wondering why these people had to have capital and lower case letters. And those alien sounds, the s, sch, t, tz like the twittering of birds, the bickering of ravens. Now she could say, in precise German, 'Get up here woman, there's a green turtle to be lifted.' But she didn't. She'd been a bit scared of Lene since stumbling across her intoxicated, *sternhagelvoll* – Ruete's description – on Christmas Eve. Drunk and defiant. She swore she'd never get used to all the alcohol in Hamburg from the top of society to the bottom. The Germanic peoples had such ideas of equality. When she asked Ruete why she couldn't slap her maid for being drunk, he'd been quite adamant. 'She can go and complain,' he'd told her. 'To the police. Each slap would cost us ten *thalers.*' Hamburg was taking all the fight out of her. 'It's only the pregnancy, it's only because I'm always tired.' A smaller voice said it was because she was anxious. Scared. Pregnancies didn't always end in beautiful babies and new nursery maids and lessons to teach them their A, B, C and one, two, three.

With an extra guttural grunt, a childbirth groan, she lifted the turtle clear, staggered backwards, and slipped. When she opened her eyes, the turtle's face was inches from her nose. The tassels on her bodice had flipped, giving the effect of a ruffled collar for the turtle. His eyes were mirrors, but his down-turned mouth, now upside down, was suddenly an upturned smile.

'No wonder you are smiling,' she spat at him: it was now Emily on her back struggling to flip herself over. Or at least to sidle out from under the animal lying on top of her like the shield of a Masai warrior from the continental part of the Sultan's empire. Babette started to lick her cheeks, her tail whipping around as if this was what named the breed. Whippet, thwack, whip it, against her belly and the turtle tottering on top of it. Winzig made a sortie from under the bath to nip at the turtle's rudder-like tail.

'All this for a bath.' She lay still for a while longer, feeling the weight of the turtle, catching her breath. 'All this so I can sit in water that does not flow, like a boiled chicken sitting in its own juices, like a turtle turning into turtle soup.' There'd be no slave to sponge soap onto her back either. No laughter competing with the tinkling of flowing water over jade tiles.

Lying there, she could hear the cloudy bath water sloshing itself back into stagnation in the tub. She was determined she'd get Lene in to empty it and clean the porcelain before she ran her own. There was a gurgle in the pipes, coming across from the kitchen. The turtle stank of piss and shit, sorrow and loneliness. She'd seen one once, when she was swimming at Bububu. The sun, when it caught the faceted shell, picked up rainbows and shimmered them across the surface.

Ruete left for work at half past nine each weekday morning. He came back from the offices of his reestablished trading firm, Ruete and Company, at four, already searching the rooms for her as he took off his coat and hat. All except Sundays, when they could go for a walk after church. This time they spent together emphasised what a lot of time she spent alone on the other days with only Winzig and Babette as companions; and the occasional turtle. A lot of time for one day – even a bright, cloudless Sunday like this one – to make up for.

The breeze always picked inordinate amounts of cold off the lake and draped it across them as they walked.

'Do you think it is very cold out there?' she asked Ruete who looked pink and fresh on Sundays. Funny how Lena and Gert were always around and willing when the master wanted a turtle out of a bathtub, she thought as the master looked speculatively out the window. Instead of opening the window or a door, he went out to the hall to check the thermometer and the barometer. It was a tick of his, to look to machines. From these instruments he judged the umbrella's worth; from what they told him he would or would not recommend a scarf – the thick, horrid thing that felt like it was intent on strangling her. She knew she'd have to put on the disgusting coat; and that she'd feel cold anyway.

He'd bought her the new coat the week before, a travesty in ermine.

'I can't wear that,' she'd told him when he brought it home.

'Why on earth not?'

'The fur looks like something a Nubian would wear. It's no better than cat's skin.'

She'd seen he was hurt. He was trying hard to help her fit into life as a German wife. She was Frau Ruete, but she'd known very quickly she'd never be anything like her mother-in-law, *the real Frau Ruete*, as she came to think of her.

He brought the coat to her now. 'The thermometer is low,' he said. 'But it seems we will be spared rain,' he added cheerfully. He helped her into the coat. The pure whiteness of the ermine, between the black of the creatures' tails, reminded her of Sinbad, though Maria Mass' latest letter said his fate was not so dire and he was still enjoying his life in Aden.

'It would have been cheaper to get cat fur,' she told him as she shrugged the coat over her shoulders. He'd told her exactly how much the coat cost but she still only wore it to humour him. And to avoid those icy claws of winter outside.

They took the carriage to the docks, across the bridges and along the fleete canals – 'Ah this is what you mean by canals!' 'Yes, and I will take you to Venice one day too' – until they got to the inland port that dominated the banks of the Elbe. It always struck her as odd and eccentric that Hamburg had made its fortune as a port and yet was on a river and not the coast. The harbour was their frequent destination. They liked the St. Pauli Landungsbrücken, the jetty between the Fischmarkt and the lower harbour. From the pier they could watch the ships coming down the river's wide canals from the north, bringing the world to them, then taking bits of Hamburg away again, including most Sundays, their hearts.

Ruete walked briskly along the jetty that day. Emily struggled to keep up for a while, the cold burning her cheeks. She knew if she looked in a mirror they'd be pomegranate red. She pulled her hat more firmly over her ears, and looked down at her feet to let her crown take the direct wind. The dogs milled in and out of view. Winzig would have to be carried if they went too far – his little poodle legs were all eagerness but no grit. Babette fared better, but Emily decided to use the dogs as an excuse to sit. He noticed the absence at his arm and turned and came back.

'Why do we keep coming here?' she asked as he sat down beside her.

'You can walk along the Alster any day while I am at work, this is special.'

'No, you know what I mean. Why do we needle ourselves by watching the ships we can't go on? Dreams are such heavy things to carry on a walk.'

The ships, steam and sail, wood and ironclad, waited on God's day of rest, slumbering until they could leave for China, India, Persia, the Americas, Australia. Zanzibar. They sat looking outwards, their shoulders touching, in silence, in the cold, in their own worlds.

In the early days, new from Zanzibar, they would get to the harbour by first taking the ferry from the Walhalla Steamer Station near the Alster house, simply to be on the water again, amongst the colonies of bobbing coots, and then, from the lake, they'd hike across the city – you saw so little from a carriage – Ruete as eager as her to explore. 'Look, look, look,' he'd say, sounding like one of the seagulls squabbling for scraps in front of them. It wasn't only that he wanted her to share his world in those first days. 'It's not at all like I remember,' he'd told her, amazed. So much had changed since he'd left, and not only because he had changed and his way of seeing had changed. The old quarter of the city, called the Altstadt, was now not so *alt*, old. Fires devastated its heart while he was a boy; the streets he led her through were fresh and clean looking because they were built new while he was away in Zanzibar.

'It has grown from the fires, phoenix-like,' he told her. Then he'd had to explain the phoenix was known in Europe too, not just in Persia.

They'd be amazed together at the differences between Hamburg and Stone Town. 'I only have two eyes and two ears,' was her maxim, 'I'd need ten to see and hear everything new and different.'

She'd watch him looking as if he too needed all ten of those new eyes. He looked with his eyes and also with his lips slightly agape as if to drink it in too. She had to remember he was only sixteen when he sailed out of the lower harbour, new in the position of junior clerk for an enterprise he had no way of imagining. That he'd spent more years over there than here. It took longer to realise that his biggest wish was to go back to Zanzibar. He said it was for business. He threw in phrases about 'trading interests' and 'good rates of return' in case she thought him a nostalgic fool, not a hard-nosed businessman. When he started to talk about going to Chile, she knew Hamburg did not feel like home for him at all and that his homesickness was his alone and not a contagion from her.

'We can't go back,' she told him again as they sat watching Sunday-lazy sailors on the deck of the closest steamer. They were playing a game; it looked like *Schafkopf* or *Skat* from this distance. Their ship nudged against the dock again and again. 'You know as well as I do that the Sultan wouldn't consent to it.'

'You are my wife now.'

'But I will always be his sister.' No matter how much I have changed. No matter that no one would recognise me now. Naughty Salmé, the family's tomboy, was never this anxious woman in Hamburg. She kept all her doubts out of her letters home. She wondered how Metle pictured her as she read them. Emily could see her stretched out across a *meddes* in her palace, shouting for more coffee and to come here, listen to what naughty, darling Salmé has to say. But what could Metle really imagine from the details in the letters?

Each return letter from the harem with its new births and petty squabbles was a lifeline and a heartbreaker. She picked up the shivering Winzig and nestled her inside her coat, tight with her growing belly.

As they drove back through the tall buildings – fresh and clean – Ruete pointed out the foundations of the new Rathaus, and tried to sound enthusiastic. She squeezed his hand through two layers of gloves. The idea of going to Chile had fallen through. She knew he was trying to convince them both how wonderful his hometown was.

Emily prayed in the rhythm of the carriage across the cobblestones. She tried her hardest in St Michaelis's on Sunday mornings, joining two hundred other Christian voices, but habit tricked her into addressing her prayers to Allah.

Oh Allah, make light in my heart, and make light in my tongue.
Oh Allah make light in my ear, and make light in my eye.
Make light behind me, and light before me.

And make light above me and make light beneath me.
Oh Allah, bestow upon me light.

They came along the Alster toward their tall house on the lake's edge. He saw first that the upper windows were open. Again.

'Close the windows Bibi, the neighbours want to know if we are heating the street.' He sounded cross. 'And now I think of it, close the curtains too, the neighbours can see in.'

In this country where God was already parsimonious with the sun, she was expected to close everything up, shut herself inside, shut out the fresh air, shut out the light. Of course the rules made her angry. And also cross at him for being cross at her. She held her tongue though. She knew the melancholia of watching the ships had battered both their defenses.

'You are only cross because you miss Zanzibar's air too,' she said, tears in her lower lashes. 'But if you'd rather have a good German *hausfrau*, I can go.'

'And I'll come with you,' he said, all his irritability gone.

And so they were back to where they started – in the endless, mostly unspoken conversation about leaving.

T he house was flooded with light the night of the dinner party. The three chandeliers in the dining room glowed like floating fires. Winzig and Babette had to be locked in the master bedroom because the lights scared them and made them bark at every new noise.

A second cook and the two male servants in tail-coats, specially hired for the night, turned to Emily for instructions and she realised just how insolent Lene and the old cook had become while she'd been trying to learn their language. The extra new cook followed Emily's recipe for the turtle soup and the curry without turning up her nose. Lene made a snide comment about foreign food, but was ignored. Emily decided Lene was not going to last and felt almost brisk when the guests arrived.

They were all friends, Ruete's friends, his parents and their friends. A few had lived outside the confines of a Germanic town and two spoke Swahili.

'It's a bit much being told you are looking lovely in two different languages when you know you are not,' she whispered to Ruete in the front *salle*, and he said the right thing – that of course she did – before looking after Herr and Frau Raabe and offering them a drink.

She knew it was the diamonds everyone was really complimenting. She'd chosen the largest ones to compete with the chandeliers. A string of diamonds tugged at each ear lobe. Though she'd stopped wearing the six gold rings on each, her lobes sometimes itched with the memory and she resisted scratching her left ear as Herr Ruete and the real Frau Ruete were shown in with their second son, Hermann. The diamond around her neck was the size of a turtle egg. Ruete winked at her as he went to welcome his parents and brother, and the diamond winked back.

'Can you ask that tall maid to help with the coats?' he asked her in their private Swahili.

'Why can't you speak in a proper language?' Frau Ruete complained as a greeting. She was a large woman, and like her oldest son, well upholstered. She had softened slightly in her reaction to her Heinrich's wife. He'd protected Emily at first, only much later translating his mother's first concession, which was as hurtful as the initial prejudice it implied. 'I thought she'd be black. Darker at least.' In her relief at having her son home safe, the real Frau Ruete moved from this concession to almost forgiving him for marrying a foreigner. Almost. In turn Emily tried her best to like her mother-in-law. After all, except for his moustache and beard, she looked very like the man she loved. 'It's just a mother's love,' Ruete mollified after the worst intrusions into the household. She dreaded, and knew, that her mother-in-law was going to be a fright when the baby was born.

If the real Frau Ruete was like the upholstered sofa, her husband, Ruete's father, was the stiff Biedermeier sideboard. He stood away from the other guests, his silence severe rather than helpful. Maybe he'd been as open-faced as Ruete when he was young. Maybe he'd grown into a headmaster face when he was promoted to the job.

Emily greeted each of the guests in turn as they arrived. She heard half of what was said. The house didn't know itself, leaping from the silence of the working week to the clanging of twenty voices. She didn't know it. Everyone was talking at once. The noise was like the market in Aden, like the cacophony of Judgment Day. She wanted to retreat into silence again. She went to stand by her father-in-law. It was too awkward to say nothing.

'I noticed something in the church,' she said in precise German. Inevitably she had to do all the work to start the conversation, rather regretting it even as she fished for his part, knowing she'd have to do all the work to stop it once the old man got going.

'St Michaelis,' she said. Their church, named for the archangel: above the door was a niche with a life-sized archangel Michael conquering a human-sized devil. Inside it was cold. Crypt cold, seeping through her shoes on Sunday mornings. 'There's a sculpture on the side wall. I thought St Michael was there to keep the devils out, but this figure has horns. It smiles.'

'And where is this devil, child?' At last Herr Ruete spoke.

'Near the side aisle,' she said quickly. Next he'd be asking why she was idling the service away looking at decoration. She could not explain her discomfort when the offering plate was thrust under the noses of the congregation and their *thalers* were inveigled out of their pockets. Charity was a given; here it was begged for. She tried to look anywhere than at the crass request coming into the pews.

'Yes, I know the one you mean,' Herr Ruete told her. 'You are being fanciful. You are speaking of Moses, in the scene that depicts the handing down of the Ten Commandments.'

'Moses has devil's horns?' She turned to look up at her father-in-law. He'd never said he'd expected her to be black. He never said anything personal, and he wasn't going to disappoint now. The lecture began. He was worse than Bibi Toad, her teacher in the long gallery at home.

'The Hebrew Bible,' he began, and went on and on. It seemed one word – which needed so very many other words for him to explain the situation – just one word caused the problem. Of the parts of the lecture she understood, it appeared that this Hebrew word could be translated as a ray of light, like a halo, or as horns. Moses, it said in the Scriptures, had one of this word. Moses had a halo or horns. Someone decided it was horns.

Ruete appeared to save her. 'Time to go in to dinner,' he said.

'Translation is a difficult thing,' concluded his father. Emily didn't need that translated.

'Was he boring you to death?' Ruete whispered. 'Do you think I'll become like my *Vati*?'

She laughed, and then lowered her voice. 'I'll never understand anything,' she whispered.

'You understand me,' he said, and then he wasn't at her side and there were twenty people sitting under their three chandeliers.

One of the male servants, in a thin bow tie as well as slick coat tails, appeared at Emily's elbow with the bowl of bouillon. She'd made the old cook prepare it especially. When it came time to slaughter the turtle in the kitchen, when those liquid eyes stopped roaming around, she couldn't stomach the idea of turtle soup. The baby kicked encouragement in her stomach as she raised her gold spoon of tepid, strong-smelling bouillon to her lips.

She marveled at her power. No one had started eating. Only at her raising her spoon – her signal it seemed – did the guests reach to lift their own spoons and follow suit. She glanced at Ruete's mother. The real Frau Ruete won't like that, she thought, just a little gleefully.

After a few minutes she looked around. So this was what Ruete's dinner parties were really like: not as she'd imagined when she'd watched from her palace rooftop. It was far louder in everything, and a relief when the guests had to hold their tongues and eat. And then they drank. The wine kept appearing at elbows, by the miracle of hired servants, and no one was putting their hands up to say no. Emily had an inch of dark red wine in the bottom of her glass for the sake of appearances. She sipped occasionally, feeling the sinfulness of it. The other women were not so careful. Four of them were blond; she was afraid she'd never be able to tell them apart. She eyed each in turn over the top of her crystal glass, noted their jewellery, scant amethysts, tiny rubies, and a string or two of jet, feeling enough superiority to sit still and not run away as the noise rose again. The banker's daughter, one of the women who were not so blond, and a bit younger, leant across the tablecloth and moved the flower arrangement slightly.

'Thank you for the strange soup,' she said slowly, enunciating every word as if Emily was herself a slow child. So the turtle had served its purpose. It had surprised and fed their guests. Then his fate was forgotten as more food took his place on the table.

'God take the French,' moaned one of the older, weathered, men as she murmured her own thanks back to the dutiful banker's daughter. 'God take them all to Hell.'

His words were like a signal as well. Once the politics started the women kept quiet. They smiled. Her veil was now upstairs in a cupboard, but here she noticed the women didn't need strips of black silk and tiny bells. They had a mask woven into every feature. Their muscles were the silken ties. Their endless smiles, perfect politeness and permanent affability, what were they but a mask? She wondered what was really going on behind the smiles. Did they want to speak up too, to say how nice they found the French? But this wasn't a women's realm, because the talk was of war. Even Frau Ruete held her tongue, and Emily knew she had very determined ideas about everything. Hurts and ills and provocations dominated the to and fro discussion across the table. From one end to the other the men were compelled into the same subject. The man who spoke Swahili, after a career in Mombassa, Herr Raabe, mentioned the word 'unification.' Emily bent toward Ruete and had it translated for her.

'All of the German states, united, together as one country,' he whispered.

'The Northern German Confederation is not enough,' the older Herr Ruete agreed. She tried to remember the history. The Hanseatic League town of Hamburg had joined in Confederation with other small states a couple of years before, but now it seemed the alliance was insufficient against the French.

'When we have a fully united Germany,' Herr Raabe talked over the top of everyone, 'we will be able to properly compete with France and England.'

'In terms of colonies?' questioned Hermann Ruete who seemed jealous of his brother's chance to go out into the world to make his fortune.

'Yes, exactly,' Ruete agreed with his brother. He was sitting forward on his chair, a fork pointed like a spear. 'Zanzibar a case in point,' he said with the air of some authority. Emily took her eyes off the devastated tureen of potato dregs then, and looked at her husband's wine-flushed face. He listed the advantages of Zanzibar becoming a colony of a united Germany. 'In terms of trade,' he said. He spoke of her home as if it were some fruit for the taking. As if the only impediment to the taking were the competing colonial ambitions of Britain.

In Stone Town Emily would push Ruete away after lovemaking to let the air cool her off. Here, tonight, she stayed in the cocoon of his warmth, her back hard up against his chest.

She really did try not to make endless comparisons between there and here, then and now, though there were too many hours to do so, listening for his walking stick on the step every after-noon as she waited for four to tick itself out on the clock on the hall table. The clock, the thermometer, the barometer, measur-ing each day, instead of glancing up from the verandah at the sun. Or using the smell of roasting goat wafting up from the courtyard as a dinner gong.

She listened to his breathing now in bed. Calibrated waking from sleep. He stirred, kissed the back of her neck, and moved her on his arm, letting his tongue run along her collarbone, 'your camel bone' he called it.

'Come back from your dreams Bibi,' he said. 'You're already away in Zanzibar,' he accused. 'Say hello to our friends there from me.'

'So you are awake.'

'No, not really,' he said. She reached back and punched his chest lightly. 'I can hear your mind galloping along like a donkey on the beach,' he said after a mock splutter.

'Can you?'

'No, but you want to tell me something?'

'The talk at dinner. About a united Germany and colonies. Is that likely?'

'If the Kaiser and Bismarck got their way and had us all in a confederation under Prussia, well of course the next step would be to compete with the other powers. And that means having other parts of the globe safely tucked under a colonial wing.'

She recalled her language lessons, a lot of which consisted of reading the newspapers. Learning from 'current affairs,' the teacher called it. Prussia: she placed the huge German state on the map in her head. The Kaiser: she translated him as the Sultan of Prussia.

'If Zanzibar belonged to Germany,' he added, 'you wouldn't need any Sultan's permission to return home.' The statement hung in the curtains around their bed. She thought he'd gone back to sleep it was so still. She wasn't going to let it rest though. She dreamed of home, but she felt a stirring of other loyalties.

'So you would watch the Kaiser take the throne from Majid?'

He was alert to her tone. 'Didn't you try?'

'But that's not what the rebellion was about. I wanted a Sultan on the throne still. Just a different one, not a German one.'

'He'd still be Sultan. But who should have quite so much power as your brother? Over life and death remember. A colonial power coming in would be good for everyone. No more slavery.'

The baby turned in her belly. Emily felt it, and Ruete gasped. 'The baby just kicked me,' he said in astonishment. He held her away so he could run his hands over her rounded stomach. A tiny heel-shape punched into the palm of his hand. He laughed. 'This child will have the Sultan's blood too,' he said. He sounded as if the idea was a surprise to him.

'So we'd be there with two faces,' she said slowly.

'Or two feet. We call what I think you mean, *having a foot in each camp*. Imagine it Bibi. Aren't you sick of having to translate everything in your head all the time?'

'We wouldn't be cold.'

'No,' he said, drawing her back against him so the baby nudged his slack belly. 'We wouldn't be cold.'

That spring brought the term of her second pregnancy to an end and Antonie Thawka Ruete entered their world. Emily held her too tight and the nursemaid had to prise the baby away to bathe the animal muckiness off her. When Emily took Antonie back, she was washed and dressed in a dress and bonnet, both presents from the older Frau Ruete – who Emily continued to think of as the real Frau Ruete. Like all Europeans it seemed, her mother-in-law wanted to dress this baby like a shade, a ghost. Emily looked at her baby done up in white and hankered after the colours of the harem. Her mother-in-law arrived in person the same day as the birth and wanted to hold the child. She felt her reluctance to let her daughter go like a call to battle. She wasn't going to let go ever, not this time. She couldn't forget that her other child died in her bed while she slept so she missed the moment of passing. If she'd been alert she believed she could have held Heinerle in this world.

There was no stopping it: the real Frau Ruete took the new child off her. It was as physical a wrench as when the midwife dragged her from the womb. Frau Ruete held the child up and examined her closely. She undid the ribbons and removed the bonnet.

'Not black either?' Emily mumbled under her breath, a small catty rebellion.

'Sleep now?' Ruete pleaded after his mother left. He was to say it many times in the coming days. Instead she shooed Winzig and

Babette from sleeping on the bed and replaced them with the pink intruder. Emily watched over the child, and should Antonie's sleep become profound, she leant over her and woke her. 'Are you still alive?' she'd ask the baby, who stared steadily out at the world, a little Ruete, with nothing of the Sa'id dynasty in her looks.

Antonie fed greedily, she slept, Emily woke her, she slept more, fed more. Emily woke her. Emily could hear her own mother in her head telling her to stop this silliness, to trust in Allah. It's any wonder you're not creating a fractious child, the voice of Jilfidân admonished.

Antonie burped lustily, happily, every time after the nursing was done.

'Beautiful, Tony, gorgeous Tony,' Ruete burbled like a madman when he heard it. As if it was the cleverest thing in the world.

Within weeks the baby grew into a ball of fat with squirming limbs and pink gums she smacked together when she was carried outside. Which the real Frau Ruete insisted be done daily.

'You shut up your houses and air your babies,' Emily told Ruete when he came home at four by the clock.

The dogs were allowed join them then, outside, yapping and straining at their silver leashes. Tony turned her head toward the barking. Tony kicked her legs free of the blanket and threw her fists out when Emily pushed her pram beside the Alster.

By mid-summer she didn't need a blanket anyway. Emily picked her up so she could see the lake and the steamers passing on their business.

'It is good to live by water,' she told her. The sun slipped out from behind a bank of cumulous clouds. She looked down at

Tony. There was light behind her, light before her, above and beneath her. She was made of light.

Their presence seemed to take up the whole room. Duha cradled Rudy as if he were an overlarge pawpaw. The eunuch brought the baby to his face and breathed deeply, for all the world like he was testing the baby's ripeness. He smiled hugely. Everything about him was large.

'Sa'id is the best of names,' he acknowledged. 'Like his grandfather the Great Sultan.'

Emily had instinctively introduced her children by their middle names: Sa'id the baby, Thawka the girl child. Antonie Thawka, her little Tony, sat on her nanny's lap by the window and bawled every time a black hand came near. The three eunuchs were in heavy naval uniforms against the climate. Bright sashes around their waists were the only concessions to their origins. Emily had forgotten how black Nubians were. She hadn't realised how white her children were.

'How did you find me?' she asked once the palaver of their appearance on the Alster doorstep had calmed, though poor Anna was still sobbing. Greeting a crowd of black men was not normally within a servant's daily duties. Emily half wished she'd kept on the recalcitrant Lene as maid and subjected her to the shock. Twenty slaves prostrate in the entrance *salle*, kissing the tiles and crying her mistress's name would have been a lesson to her. At least rude old Gert was getting her comeuppance with the slaves crowding the kitchen needing warming soup and more floor space.

Amara answered her question. 'We asked every white man who came on board once we were docked.' He was the most senior of the bookkeepers from the trading schooner the *Ilmedjidi* and he now sat cross-legged in the centre of the three eunuchs on Ruete's fine woollen carpet. Emily watched Faraji, the third, running his fingers through the pile as the sequence of discoveries was told.

'No one knew where you lived. But we knew you were in Hamburg.' The how of this knowledge hung unspoken. She had to consider just how much market gossip she'd left behind in her escape. 'We could only ask in English. Our German, none.' Amara, whose name meant 'urgent news' in Swahili, opened his hands flat to indicate a preponderance of nothing.

Duha murmured, '*Guten tag, klein, gross*, that is all.' His hands were full of Rudy Sa'id who had fallen back to sleep. No one in the room appeared to be ready to impart any urgent news, though she desperately wanted everything, anything, the slightest, most insignificant morsel of market gossip, from home. But the story of finding her must come first.

'Then this morning I asked the attendant at the Tabakhändler when we went for our tobacco. He took from his cupboard a book of names and found the section for R.'

As the eunuchs came closer to finding their princess in this story, she began to feel strange sitting on a chair with them on the carpet. She lowered herself down, her legs stiff, the new baby in her belly a weight to be shifted. None of the eunuchs looked at her as she made herself comfortable with cushions. They had been speaking to her feet. The shock of her unveiled face was as obvious as Anna's continued nerves. One of her sobs slipped into the room. The maid hovered just out of the door, unable to come in, unable to leave.

'The tobacconist wrote your address on a piece of paper,' Amara continued.

'Which we were unable to read,' interrupted the soft-fingered Faraji, speaking for the first time – to a point over Emily's left shoulder. 'The Germanic alphabet is complicated.'

'And not as beautiful as your writing I am sure,' she complimented him. She could see he was still very young.

'So we showed this piece of paper,' Amara took the same from his breast pocket and flourished it, 'to people in the street. Three, four, five, along the way through the canals, until,' he stopped. Paused. Finished. 'Here we are.'

Gert pushed into the room with a tray tottering with cups and *Streuselkuche*. She looked down at her mistress on the floor. Emily knew she'd never be forgiven for such barbarism.

'Have Anna come in and build up the fire,' she commanded in her precise German. 'Eat, eat,' she coaxed the eunuchs in a singsong Swahili. Gert was leaving, but Emily was not going to suffer her rude back. 'You have fed the crew of the *Ilmedjidi*?' she asked before the cook could escape.

The open doors between the front room and the entrance *salle* and the kitchen let through all the noises of a busy harem. She was overwhelmed by a tide of homesickness. She hoped Ruete would get her message and be home soon or she'd float away on it.

'Mama, *streusel*?' came a small cry from by the window.

'Come, come,' Emily beckoned her daughter as the eunuchs hung back from the plates of food. The two-year-old slipped off nanny's lap and negotiated her way around the room, clinging to furniture all the while, though normally she could walk confidently.

Amara leaned forward with a plate of cake and Tony cringed into her mother's arms. 'Scary men,' she cried and Emily was glad the eunuchs knew no German beyond hello, little, big.

'Not scary men. Visitors from home. The beautiful island of Zanzibar,' she whispered, sugaring her words with morsels of sweet apple from the cake.

'Do you know anything of my eunuch Johar?' she asked once her daughter was contentedly chewing. She had started to dream less of Zanzibar and more of her children and where they should go to kindergarten, but now she wanted to be back there.

Duha laughed, deep, resonate, bold. Rudy Sa'id mewed in his arms briefly, scratching his cheek up and down the rough canvas jacket. Duha appeared to have no jealousy of Johar's status as a free man.

'He is working for the Christian school. It is said he is very good at giving orders.'

'And how many Christian children can there be in Zanzibar?' she asked. 'Have the European consuls and merchants enough children to fill a school?' It did not sound to her like an onerous place to work. There was a pause. The eunuchs could have been taking time to decide on coffee from the tall pot or tea from the squat one. Amara answered for them all in the end.

'This school is not for white children. It is named after the saint called Andrew and is for freed slaves.'

'A school for freed slaves,' Emily repeated.

Amara added, 'They are going to open a school for freed slave *girls* too.'

She was astonished that her Zanzibar had changed so much

in such a short time. She shook her head and dragged her thoughts back to the Alster house. She insisted the eunuchs eat, though they would not until she allayed their fears about pork fat. Then they answered her next questions with full mouths. She asked about everyone, friend and slave: they knew nothing of Zada and her son save the stir it caused when she returned from Aden without her mistress. She asked about everyone except her brothers. Metle's letters said Majid ate too little and took more wives and Barghash ate too much and beat the wives he already had. The eunuchs would know this too, but it would be beyond barbarism to openly air any thoughts about the imperfections of the Great Sultan's children.

Light did not last long in Hamburg on the cold days. The fire was built up twice and the lamps lit to ward off the approaching evening, but they all knew the crew must return to the *Ilmedjidi*, anchored for one more day at the St. Pauli Landungsbrücken. Ruete arrived back in time to see the slaves properly loaded with foodstuffs and small presents to take away, every one of them down to the beardless boys.

Dohu held back. 'Let me stay,' he begged. 'Your children need a eunuch to undertake their care. I will be yours. Sa'id must have the proper care, he is of the Sultan's line. My owner would willingly sell me to you if he knew for what task.'

Emily wanted to take his plump, black, capable hands and thank him. She knew which room he could sleep in, but Ruete took Rudy from his arms instead.

'No, it cannot be. There can be no slaves in Hamburg,' he said. It was clear even in the lamp-lit dusk light how imperfectly her two worlds fitted together.

'Don't come out,' Ruete warned her after too many goodbyes and unshielded tears. She came to the front door anyway. Anna opened it and left it ajar and ran, jostling through the sailors and up the staircase, her redheaded energy back, fleeing up two steps at a time.

A crowd pulsed on the road outside, all the way back to the lake. Gawkers had gathered and followed the black men during their quest with the piece of paper containing the Hamburg address. This was a sight as strange as a trip to the circus. The eunuchs pushed through the crowd at the head of the crew, the rest of the slaves marching two by two behind. The crowd shouted and pointed at the departing black men and at the woman standing in the doorway. Emily's temples pulsed with pain. Ruete closed the door once the procession was out of sight.

Downstairs was in disarray. The cold had invaded through the long-open front door, so Rudy was taken to the kitchen and put near the stove to keep him warm, and Tony could be heard jumping up and down on the cushions left on the floor in the front room. Her shouts sounded distant and muted after all the noise.

'I'll just have a smoke,' Ruete said as he headed toward his study.

Emily climbed the stairs slowly. She too wanted to be alone. And quiet, so her life could rock itself back into place.

She hadn't thought she'd be able to sleep, then suddenly she woke up. Her skin was slick with sweat but her head was miraculously clear for the first time in a week. The fever had broken. Weaning baby Rosy was worse than it'd been for Tony and then Rudy; or maybe she'd forgotten the illness of it, like she had the birth pains until it was too late and she was being ripped apart by the unforgiving teeth of a lion again. In truth, with three children born almost exactly a year between each, she congratulated herself when she was able to remember anything at all.

Emily turned in the bed and judged the hour from the creep of light coming under the curtain and striping the floor. It was uncertain. She listened. There was no owl-hoot of a steamer along the Alster in front of the garden. No servants moving like rats below; or indeed, any rats. The Prussian officers they had billeted because of the war with France had been moved out to the guesthouse in the garden so it wasn't them making noise to wake her. The tick of the clock's pendulum downstairs expanded into the silence.

It had gone nine, she calculated from the quiet, but it was not quite midnight, she guessed from the dark. Ruete was not in the bed beside her. A shock of fear electrified her, running through her sweat to the roots of her hair, as if she'd been wired up to a machine in some 'electric kiss' parlour game. He'd said he'd be home by now. He was always punctual. He'd never do anything to deliberately frighten her.

The floorboards were cool under her feet when she swung out of bed. Her head spun a little. It's just from the fever, she told herself. Something is terribly wrong, she interrupted herself. He had come home at four as usual that day, thundered up the stairs, hat still in hand. He'd bounced the bed; a ricochet of pain shooting through Emily's headache as he plopped down.

'Are you feeling any better?' he'd asked and she'd told a small white lie, the type of assurance she always gave him and he sometimes accepted. He scanned his eyes across her clammy face, a fast-read of the symptoms of fever. He squinted slightly. His assessor's look.

'If you really are, I'll go and see Vati. He hasn't been out of the house since Antonie's birthday, and you know he only made an effort then because she's the favourite and we really should stop him spoiling her.' But who could not fail to love two-and-a-half year old Tony, so profligate with her smiles. 'I'm worried. I won't stay long. Just to check on him.' He sat on the side of the bed, or rather perched, because he'd obviously decided to accept her word on her own health and was already off to his parents' house in his brain. 'I'll look in on the nursery first.' He kissed her forehead.

Emily, despite her pain, had smiled up at him. He'd demonstrated in one swoop that he was a good son and a good father – and a good husband. So why wasn't he home in bed with her now? She lit the small candle beside the bed and padded to the nursery. She stood at the door to check on the sleeping children. Rudy snored gustily. He suffered from hay fever, but it didn't slow him down by day. Babette had sneaked onto Tony's bed then made herself more than comfortable, on her back, spindly legs akimbo across the eiderdown, pushing Tony up against the wall. In the light from the candle, the dog's exposed belly and the soft, hairless, naked skin down her inner thigh gleamed a human pink.

The dog and the children were quiet but as she turned to leave, the loose floorboard by the door creaked. Baby Rosalie shifted in the high-sided cot. Emily crept over. It was probably too early yet but she was determined to catch Rosy the first time she rolled over. She smiled down at the sleeping baby. Then remembered: something was terribly wrong.

She leaned over the railings on the landing. She stretched out to twist and catch a glimpse of the hallway below. Winzig appeared out of the shadows to join her. Winzig's head could fit between the railings. The poodle stared down, then up at Emily, and then down to confirm there was nothing to look at in the dark below.

If she hadn't been in her long nightgown she would have gone down. There wasn't enough strength on a normal day to get into the apparatus of European dressing without the maid's help, and none now in the dark. So she twisted and stretched to see a little further down the stairs, feeling the wood of the rail dig into her pelvic bones. There was a flash of memory. She was leaning out of the sitting room window in Aden, scanning the garden. Maria Mass was sitting behind her, talking about the cat. 'He'll come back,' she was assuring Salmé. The memory was from the first week after Sinbad leapt from his basket and over the balcony. 'And if he doesn't, well they are survivors, cats. He'll catch his own food. Canaries perhaps.'

Maria Mass was being fanciful. Rats more likely. But sure enough Sinbad did come back. And, Salmé's real fear was un-founded – Ruete did appear in Aden.

Emily stood back from the rail in the Alster house. She stood firmly on her feet, three years on. Three years of trust binding her to him. 'Come home,' she whispered. Though one of the Circassian 'cats' of the harem, she didn't know if she'd be a sur-vivor if left alone.

'Ruete?' she called. She couldn't believe she'd gone back to sleep. She struggled up out of bed again. She was sure she'd heard the bell, softly rung. It was close to dawn. He must have lost his key.

'Mistress,' the maid called a minute later. Anna was coming up the staircase. She climbed slowly as if this one flight was the highest peak of the Alps. Emily waited on the landing.

'There's a doctor below,' Anna whispered.

Emily felt no satisfaction that she'd been right to be fearful in the middle of the night. She wasn't allowing herself to feel anything.

'He's still alive, the doctor says.'

'Alive?' The word made no sense. Why would he not be alive? She followed Anna down the staircase, pushing the dogs away so she could get to the bottom before them. There was a large man in a long coat near the door.

'You do not know me,' the doctor said. 'Herr Doctor Klaus,' he added.

I know nothing, I know no one, Emily thought as he spoke some more words. Her grasp of German had slipped as she descended into the hall. She could understand only a few words: accident, hospital, alive.

'I have to go to him, I have to go to him,' she kept interrupting.

'Visiting hours are only on certain days Frau.'

'I'll go now.'

'I don't think you will be able to see him.'

'I have to get dressed,' she said, ignoring him.

'Anna hurry,' she barked over the corsets.

'Nanny,' she said to the children's nurse who came upstairs disheveled in a mop cap, 'don't tell the children anything until

I get home.' The doctor was waiting in the hall where she'd left him. 'I will take my carriage so I can bring him home,' she told him. 'The groom will know the way.'

'Your husband will not be coming home today,' Herr Doctor Klaus told her. 'Please, I have to go back there. Come with me.'

She couldn't fight him. She was too busy building defenses against her emotions.

'He's alive,' she told herself, the mortar to hold the bricks together.

'You are not well yourself,' the doctor observed as they turned off the road along the Alster and crossed the bridge. Emily could feel sweat beading across her hairline and upper lip. The fever was back. Ruete said the moustache was used by men to soak up sweat. He'd said it one steamy night in Zanzibar, across the rooftops, before they'd touched. When they were both caught in a different kind of fever.

'It is the fever,' she said. She was having trouble finding words to speak in German too. What was the word for weaning? 'The baby. Stopping to feed now.' The sweat dripped between her breasts, which had changed with each birth – were now like an old slave's she'd joked. Ruete had said he was glad he owned this old slave.

She looked across at the doctor. The sun was edging over the horizon, he was coming into focus. 'He'll think I'm stupid because I can't speak his language,' she thought.

The half hour journey seemed as long as the distance between Zanzibar and Aden. The hospital was in the labyrinth of streets of the Altstadt between the inner Alster Lake and the canals of the Elbe. It was a district she rarely came to, only passed through. The glimmers of early light revealed the bones of the older city showing behind the new and ornamental facades, those parts the fire had left untouched, left old. Here the streets were narrow, the buildings mean and pressed right up against the cobbles of the roadway. The hospital was of this world. Inside it stank of something that killed germs and burned nostril hair. The Supervisor in charge of the door protested at first.

'Routine is critical to the care of our patients,' he said. He pointed to the notice on the wall. 'These are the times you may come. Now it is still night when patients must sleep.' The Herr Doctor took him to one side, gesticulated in her direction. Emily slipped slowly toward the corridor that led off the reception. She held a handkerchief to her face like a mask, as much against the smells as to sop up her sweat and leaking nose; she regretted giving up her arsenal of pleasant scents when she left Zanzibar. The noises seeping down toward her didn't speak of sleep. She looked over at the men and took heart from the Supervisor's refusal. Time must not be critical. Ruete was not only alive; he would be around at the visiting times painted on the board. Silly man, she was going to tell him, you gave me such a fright. They'd be laughing by lunchtime.

'Fifteen minutes,' the Supervisor finally agreed. He said it loudly, folding her back into the conversation. 'And then I will request that you leave us and return at the permitted hours.'

Doctor Klaus came over and indicated the way. He put his hand on the small of her back. Emily did not protest the intimacy because he guided her through corridors to where she needed to be. She lost count of the doors they passed.

'This is Herr Ruete's room,' he said at last. 'Remember fifteen minutes only. Or he'll prevent you coming back in the morning. The Supervisor is of Prussian stock through and through.'

'*Danke.*' She was able to smile, her German language fully restored, her fear at bay. She no longer felt she had to close her eyes to make it all go away. This was merely one of any number of nightmares the fever had thrown at her, which she always woke up from. And when she woke up, Ruete was always there.

'Bibi?' In the half-light of dawn sifting through a high window, she saw a hand lift off one of the two beds in the room. It stretched out to her.

'You ass, what have you been doing with yourself?'

'Bibi. Thank the Lord. Bibi, *roho jangu*, you are my breath, the breath of my life, Bibi. Now you have come.'

She stopped halfway from the door. The sentimentality scared her more than Anna's appearance at the top of the stairs had. He stopped talking. The groan that filled the room seemed to come from another place inside the body where the voice had no access. It swept all words away as it fought its way out through his mouth.

'Does it hurt?' she asked, then cursed herself for such stupidity. 'Where does it hurt?' She knelt beside the bed. The floor was very cold and very hard. She took the proffered hand. 'What on earth happened?'

When he got his breath back, he tried to answer. It was a relief to hear Swahili. 'My father is not good, it does not look well for him.' She watched his face from where she knelt and saw him struggling against the pain. 'I caught the late horse-tram. At the terminal – I was in a rush – I was late – I knew you'd be worried.' Another rip of pain stopped him speaking. His hand squeezed hers unbearably. She put her other hand over his and took the pressure. He closed his eyes and she was able to wrench hers from his face, daring, finally, to look at the rest of him on the bed. From her kneeling position she could only see this one side. It was not so bad, she told herself. It was her Ruete.

'You'll be home soon,' she reassured him. 'Just not as soon as you wanted.' She attempted a laugh.

'I jumped from the front platform. The tram was still moving, and I slipped. The horse couldn't stop. I was dragged.' His breath was coming hard each step of his story.

A hand rested on her shoulder. 'It's not fifteen minutes,' she said without looking round.

A woman's voice answered. 'We need to give him something against the pain. You can stay. But maybe it is best you come back when the drug has taken effect.'

The house was stirring into life when Emily arrived home. The activity anesthetised her. Nanny and Anna and three babies made enough noise to drown out any accident except the splashing of bath water and the losing of soap. Rosy was grizzly when she smelled her mother so Emily left her to the nanny and dressed Rudy and Tony. When they were ready she held Tony's hand and they climbed down the stairs, one big step at a time for the two-year-olds' chubby legs. Rudy sat high on Emily's hips, squirming his nappy against her as he tried to get down and do what his sister was doing. Anna was in front of the parade like a lively pony with Rosy over her shoulder. Rosy's creased forehead and squinting eyes peered up at her, glazed.

None of them would remember their father if he went now, she realised. She pushed the thought away, told herself she was always imagining the worst, yet look at how lucky she was. The worry was easy to disguise under the battle of breakfast. For a while.

She'd brought home such a good report from the hospital that the servants were buoyant with relief. Cook, the new one after Gert was finally prised from her hold on the kitchen, boiled too many eggs and nanny cut the bread into long thin strips she called soldiers to dip into the runny yolks. The children always ate in the kitchen. It was a friendly room, full of life. Cook sang, Anna joined in. Rudy leaned deeply into his food, his jaw already chewing before food got near his mouth.

The sun was streaming through the back window. The kitchen was warm with activity. She was lulled. Then Rosy started to cry, neglected and hungry in Anna's arms and the noise gave Winzig permission to whine. She came out from under Rudy's highchair where she'd been waiting for crumbs from heaven and jumped up repeatedly like a jack-in-a-box. Tony and Rudy shouted encouragement to the dog. Babette was the only stoic one in the room. She simply added the metronome beat of her tail against the hearthrug.

Emily went over and sat on the chair furthest from the wood stove. The children needed her, but she watched from the distance of a continent. Tony lifted up her hands – fat with dimples around the knuckles – and slammed them together in one big clap. The child watched the air between her hands as if she could see the reverberations of sound. Another resounding, smacking slap tested the air. Tony held her hands apart, poised like cymbals, a look of the deepest concentration on her Ruete features.

Emily looked at what their father was missing out on. She felt she could hear his cries all the way across the Altstadt and into their kitchen. His pain was telling her something the doctor and the nurse had not. The Supervisor was just a stickler for rules, not a man who knew her husband was going to survive. She didn't cry. The tears were there, but wouldn't come. She worried about that. The tears were being stored in a huge reservoir.

She passed the tram terminal on the way back to the hospital. She hadn't noticed it on the dawn journey. The terminal: a place where things came to an end. Emily imagined every darkened patch on the cobbles was her husband's life pooled out in blood. She closed her eyes as the carriage jerked and trotted and pulled her past the vertigo of the place. She tried to ignore the existence of this point in the universe.

She stopped watching through the window of the closed carriage. Anna was opposite. Nanny had to deal with all the children at home on her own for now, because Anna was needed to take the message. They went over her instructions again. Anna was to stay in the carriage and continue to the house of Ruete's parents and deliver Emily's note. The words in it were reassuring, yet she recommended they come to the hospital as soon as they could. *To lift your son's spirits*, she'd written in her awkward roman script.

Emily was put down between the two pillars that flanked the main entrance of the hospital. Except for these pillars, the building was hardly distinguishable from one of the warehouses down along the dock. She didn't wait to see the carriage go. There was a new porter on the door; the officious Supervisor had gone home. Though it was a sanctioned visiting hour, this new man insisted she wait for a doctor to be called. She pleaded but he would not let her pass. This was the worst of the German people she decided: their regulations, the way they put rules before people.

'It is important work in there,' the porter said.

'It is my husband,' she argued back.

The porter cocked his head and pretended he didn't understand. 'You're a foreigner are you?'

She paced the wide reception hallway near the front doors, counting out the seconds – one elephant, two elephants, three – until the doctor arrived from within the belly of the building. Twenty minutes of trampling elephants later.

It was a different doctor too. Emily didn't catch his name and didn't ask for it to be repeated. She felt she'd wasted enough time already. Distance had been strangely distorted by candlelight. She didn't recognise the way she was taken and she didn't recognise the room she was led into. She wouldn't have been able to describe either from the night before, she simply felt she was in another hospital. So it *was* all a dream.

'He's been delirious,' the doctor warned as he ushered her into a small ward.

Full light fell through a high window, bouncing across an empty bed. Opposite, on the second bed was a seemingly sleeping man, his head tilted on the pillow exposing a bloody hash where his ear should be.

'This isn't Herr Ruete,' she told the nameless doctor.

The man in the bed turned his face on her voice. The half

that had rested on the pillow was perfect. This half was the husband she'd whispered to only hours before. The left side of the man was an unspeakable monster. Crushed cheek, no ear: a leper seen through the fretwork of a harem window at Bet il Watoro. The monster was talking to her.

'He's delirious,' repeated the doctor.

'No,' she corrected him. 'He is talking in another language.'

Swahili poured into the corners of the room. Recognisable words that she tried to catch as they sped past. Together they made no sense. She was about to tell the doctor he was right after all when he rudely pulled back the blanket covering Ruete, who stopped talking then and shuddered like a dying dog. Exposed, his left arm too was an inhuman shape under discoloured, blood coloured, bandages. His leg, hidden in pyjama bottoms that were not his – as if that mattered, but it did matter, everything mattered – was at an angle that could never be natural. And his chest, held together by swathes of bandages, was dented, crushed inward to the width of a tram wheel.

She stepped back. This was definitely not Ruete. *This* was the dream. In her real life, the one she should be living now, the children needed to be taken for their walk beside the lake. To the park with the exotic gingko tree. The children loved playing with the leaves; Tony picked one up last week and fanned it against her cheek as if it were a petite lady's fan, then tried to eat it. They should go back there. They'd take the big pram, a high-sprung affair with a canvas cover that looked like the wings of a bat; the one all the babies could fit in, for the long push home.

'You have to see,' the doctor explained. His voice was gentle if she could register such detail in the crush of her senses. 'You have to understand there is no hope. His limbs, well, the internal injuries are worse.' A nurse appeared carrying a chair. She blocked the door. Emily could not escape through it. 'Sit with him,' the doctor advised. 'It won't be long.'

'Long until what? You operate?'

'There is no operation to help this.' The doctor repeated himself. 'You need to understand.'

She didn't want to sit. She was terrified of this man who was talking about train stations and seagulls and twitching those leprous limbs.

'Can you pull up the blanket now? It's cold for him.'

The nurse positioned the hard chair beside the bed. She took Emily's crooked elbow and lowered her onto the seat. Emily did not hear her go, nor the doctor. They were simply no longer there. She was alone. With him. It was too fast for her to understand. There was nothing she could hold onto to steady herself. Slow down, she told the world. She breathed in the stench of rot and antiseptic and resisted the urge to hide behind her handkerchief again. There was blood through his beard. She had difficulty focusing on the undamaged half of her husband's face, her eyes straying back to the trauma. She told herself, this is the man you love.

'It's me, your Bibi-love. Emily. Salmé.' She tried all her selves to catch her husband's mind back into some coherence. Maybe he'd know his mother. Emily wished she'd written more urgency into her message. She wished none of this was happening.

'I want cherries,' he said. 'Today we will have a full moon. I'm happy to meet you.'

She took his good hand, the one that had made a fool of her in the half-light of the dawn. If she'd known the true state of his body she would have rebelled against the Supervisor and refused to leave his side. She would have been with him, holding his hand, holding him back so his mind couldn't slip away. She wouldn't have let any other person she loved slip away. She started to tell him a story. One of the Scheherazade stories he liked, the one where Sinbad was a sailor not a cat. It was a story about a man who travelled on seven voyages, but ended up at home. No wonder they both liked it.

He talked against her. Mumbling, singing, words in no order. 'I want cherries,' he said. She heard the request twice more in the soup of his statements. 'I want cherries.'

He'd always loved cherries. 'Cherry season,' he'd cried one day in their first summer in Hamburg. Sometimes he came home with pomegranates that had arrived on ships from afar, but that day he had a bag of local fruit. He made earrings from joined pairs and hung them from her ears. 'You do not need Zanzibar gold to be beautiful,' he told her. She wanted to give him all the cherries he desired in return.

She went to the door of the room and beckoned over a passing nurse.

'Please, can you help me? Are there any cherries in the hospital?'

The woman was polite. She didn't appear to be surprised by the question. She would be able to tell Emily's wealth by the cut of her dress and the gold on her ears, and wealth talked loudly in Hamburg.

'I'll ask the kitchen,' the nurse said.

She had to force herself back into the hospital room. She entered the one-sided conversation, giving up on Sinbad and reminding Ruete of the way they met.

'You know I watched you and your European friends. But did you watch me?' She should have asked earlier.

The nurse poked her head in the doorway. 'No cherries. Sorry.' Then she was gone.

'Cherries, yes cherries,' Ruete said, this time fully in German.

'I'll get you cherries,' she promised. She couldn't just sit there. She had to do something.

She left the hospital hatless, stood on the front step turning left then right, choosing right. The market on the Rathaus Square opened up around two more corners though she felt no triumph in finding her way through the labyrinth. The pretty awnings of the Rathausmarkt dipped in the breeze on the other side of the square. From here she could already hear the voices of the salesmen competing like squabbling seagulls.

It was an odd name, she thought, as she started to cross the square, because the market had no Rathaus on its flank. The Town Hall was one of the buildings lost in the fire, yet to do its phoenix impersonation. There were only the beginnings of foundations squatted there, low and waiting. But it wasn't just the absence of this building that left her feeling exposed as she crossed the echoing, empty space. It was because she was alone. She didn't go out alone.

He'd promised he'd never leave her, that she'd never have to go through the doubt and fear she'd felt in Aden as she waited for him to come. He'd said he would never abandon her. But she was abandoned now. She felt the size of an ant, struggling to cover the distance on aching legs in shoes that rubbed her ankles and skittered on the cobbles. She knew she should be sitting beside her husband's bed but she kept moving. She was running to find cherries for him, she told herself, but in truth she was being pushed further and further away from the hospital by his blank eyes, the way they slipped off her face without recognising her.

She talked to God, hoping He'd hear her above the din of the market. There were no set prayers she could think of, only the ones of her childhood invoking Allah. She chanted silently: *Nothing shall ever happen to us except what Allah has ordained for us. He is our Lord, Helper and Protector.* But not this, don't ordain this, anything, but not this, she interrupted herself, and then stopped. You do not question Allah. She prayed, 'I'm so sorry, Allah is the Almighty, the Noble, and for His servants He is forgiving, merciful, so Allah you will understand that I can't lose him too.' She was getting into the habit of the Christians. They were the ones who made up new words each time they prayed. 'Don't take him,' she said to this God, as she shouldn't to Allah. 'It would be cruel.'

She paused. She paused in her praying and in her walking. Humble. The word hung in front of her. She remembered the Rev. Wishart's injunctions to be contrite and meek in the presence of the Lord. The rules were the same for both her gods.

'Please God, please, grant me this mercy. Look at his children. What will they do without their father? Father of us all. Please.'

The calls of the market engulfed her then. 'Bushels and bags, potatoes and beets,' stallholders cried. The first stall had only potatoes and onions and turnips. Emily had to plunge into the heart of the market to find the more expensive wares. Cook would know where to look. She paid for two pounds of the fruit without pausing when she finally saw some. She handed over the money like an expert *hausfrau*, not a harem-bound princess. As she waited for her purchase to be wrapped, the vendor gave her a pair to taste. The cherries hung together like Ruete's earrings. She watched all the real *hausfrau* haggling and piling up bundles and wanted to scream at them: how dare you, someone is dying, and you go on with life as if nothing is happening.

She wanted to keep heading away from the hospital and be like them. She could take this Siamese twin pair of cherries home and drape them over Tony and Rosy's ears and make them pretty. The sun filtered between the awnings and glanced off the burnished skin of the little globes in her hand. She could see the sky reflected in tiny windows of light on the surface; windows rendered blood red by the cherry's colour. She ate one, leaving its pair alone on the stalk.

'Here you are Frau,' the vendor said, breaking into the silence she'd woven around herself. She took the parcel. He'd already moved onto the next good housewife by the time she said a polite *danke schön*, as she'd been taught.

The sun went behind a cloud. She had the overwhelming feeling she was late, so she hurried. She stopped addressing God, now too busy chastising herself. I shouldn't have left him. I should be there. It seemed further back across the square and over the two bridges and down the backstreets. She thought she was lost, then she could smell it. The antiseptic sting, overlaying a foundation of rot, brick and mortar and flesh. It leaked from the walls ahead.

Ruete's brother was standing between the pillars at the hospital entrance. Not in the middle, framed, but slightly off to one side. Watching her. When she was within hailing distance she could see he had red, raw hay fever eyes in his fat face. He didn't say anything until she was standing on the step below him.

'It's all over,' Hermann Ruete said.

'But I've got the cherries.' Emily handed him the bundle.

Emily sat in the front pew on the side of the church with the devil-Moses. The Ruete family were on the other side of the aisle. She couldn't talk to them, or anyone. Couldn't say it was all her fault. If Ruete hadn't been rushing to get home to her this would not have happened.

At first, when she arrived in Hamburg, she thought she'd never survive a thousand and one nights in such a strange place. Of course she plotted with Ruete, conjuring impossible dreams of getting back to Zanzibar, to leave again. Then she had to push back the dreams of going home to make enough room to create a home for the children. After the *Ilmedjidi* sank on its return voyage to Zanzibar just before Rosy was born, she could only think of the hazards and her hopes faded a little more. The whole crew perished. It was too sad. From then on, each day, each night, she pushed the dream of going home a little further away.

The two hundred and ninety-eight nights from her marriage until the birth of Antonie had miraculously passed despite her dreams of home. Antonie squirmed on the smooth bottom-polished wood of the pew beside her: her first daughter who brought the first moment of clarity that a thousand and one nights were not so long after all. There were three hundred and forty-four nights until Rudy joined them. He was fast asleep in Anna's arms closest to the side aisle, Rudolph Sa'id, his face scrunched up on the maid's breasts, all his looks inherited straight from his grandfather, the Arab one; a sleeping baby Sultan throughout the funeral. Then three hundred and sixty-eight nights until pretty little Rosalie took over the baby's cradle. She was up the back of St Michaelis, bawling over Nanny's shoulder as if all the grief of the family was channeled through her lungs.

She counted up again to check. That added up to one thousand and ten nights. She'd fallen over the finishing line she'd created in her mind. I've made it, she'd told herself after Rosy's birth. Like Scheherazade, it was her turn to live happily ever after.

There had been one thousand and eighty-seven nights until the end. Wife to widow. Now she didn't want to live if she couldn't live happily ever after.

In the three days since buying the cherries, she had spent her time fantasising about the ways she could be killed. How they could all die, because she couldn't bear to leave the children behind. Watching the cook put the coffee on that morning: a knock of flame onto the bench, igniting the lard too quickly to stop it. Flames to consume her. She took pity on the babies and suffocated them with smoke. Travelling to St Michaelis behind the hearse, the horses take fright and drive the carriage into the Alster. A peaceful way to go, she'd heard in Stone Town where many *dhows* faltered on their slave-trading routes. Drowning. Quietly. Going to sleep one last time. The church tower collapses now, on top of them. The bronze minute hand of the tower clock above them, piercing Emily's heart like an arrow. A solid block of granite for each child. Bang, bang, bang. Sitting on the pew, listening to an unknown minister talking about the goodness of Herr Heinrich Rudolph Ruete, she imagined she felt the fever creeping over her. Maybe it was something she'd harboured since the hospital. Not weaning fever. Scarlet fever perhaps. They'd all be burnt up in the night. Nanny would wail when she found their dead bodies in the morning, all bunched together on Emily's bed. Winzig and Babette would whimper and whine and succumb too.

She'd stopped eating. The one cherry at the Rathausmarkt was the last food she'd had. Three days before. She tortured herself that Ruete died at that moment, when she was sucking the heavy sweetness of it. How long did it take to starve to death? Not quickly enough. It had to be fast, so she wouldn't have to think about any of this anymore.

Emily had to endure a house full of strangers after the horrors of St Michaelis and the muddy graveyard were over. Relatives Ruete had never mentioned filled all the downstairs rooms. Her mother-in-law acted as though she had a monopoly on grief.

'I was waiting at the deathbed of my husband. It was him who was supposed to die, not my son,' she told anyone who came within her orbit. Insensitive to her husband, alive, off his deathbed and like a stoic model for a statue on the stuffed chair beside her. Perhaps he too thought it would have been better if he had died instead of his son. No one asked him.

Food was piled on the dining room table. The guests suffered themselves to demolish the dumplings, both bread *knödel* and potato *kartoffelkloesse*, the boiled eggs and the things made of pig, along with the cook's best *Streuselkuche*, full of apple and cherries. 'Not cherries,' she wanted to protest but it was too late. The buttery crumbles from the top of the cake dusted the busts of the matrons and joined the grey in the moustaches of the uncles. The billeted Prussian officers stood around the walls and made small speeches about the sadness of loss in a time of war. They would go off and defeat the French and unify Germany and she did not care.

She shaded her eyes against the headachy shine of every surface. The servants had scrubbed and burnished the place, lucky to have had something to do. She said nothing and allowed the throng of well-wishers to harbour old first impressions of the poor little princess who understood nothing. It was, in all, a relief when her brother-in-law dragged himself away from the table and asked her to come into Ruete's smoking room. Hermann, a man who'd grown to almost eunuch proportions since she'd met him, looked like he was also growing into the role of oldest son without any hesitations. Emily went to look over the garden rather than have to face the shape of his breasts, bulging above his waistcoat, and his thighs, thick tree trunks in tight black trousers, and his I-know-best eyes. It was still raining outside. Everything looked grey, because it was grey.

'You should sit down,' Hermann said. She heard it as an order and felt the first fire of self since widowhood put her in the grey world. She stayed by the window. Hermann sighed. A long-suffering gust of yeasty air, poor man.

'Heinrich did not leave a testament,' he said. 'He left no instructions.'

She watched a blackbird rooting in a berry tree outside. She thought, no instructions. So I can do whatever I want.

'His estate will come to you and the children of course.' Emily had not doubted it until he said it. 'But in Hamburg, here we have certain laws.' He continued, as to the child he thought she was. 'Widows are not allowed look after their own money.'

'I was perfectly able to look after my own inheritance when my father died,' she said too low for him to hear even if he'd been listening.

'My father, Heinrich's father, is far too ill to be concerned with this. I shall be managing your wealth.'

Emily moved away from the window and faced into Ruete's special room, the one he retired to when the house got too loud with children and maids and the feminine life he could have no part in. Hermann was at his desk – Ruete's desk, annexing it as his own.

'I do not have high hopes. The returns from Ruete and Company's agent in Zanzibar will be low this year – the Prussian war with the French is taking its toll on importation. But I shall be putting the bulk into Hungarian North-Eastern Railway bonds. I have heard they are sound.'

'What a quick worker you are.'

He seemed startled that she spoke. He did not hear the irony in her voice.

'Yes, I am taking my responsibilities seriously.'

'Your brother has been dead three days.'

'The devil does not wait.'

She moved closer. 'You can go now.' Her words were not a request.

Hermann hesitated, a huge German dumpling himself. A dumpling sporting the evidence of *Streuselkuche* scoffing.

'I need to be alone.'

He understood that. Women grieved and knew nothing of finances. 'I'll be…'

'Thank you.' She closed the door behind him.

Only then did she sit down. She went over to Ruete's smoking chair and stroked its high back as if to comfort it. It was leather like a cow. It creaked when she sat and pulled her legs up and curled into its wide arms. The windows were never opened in here and the smell of tobacco and cognac and her husband at the end of the day rose up like a fog around her. Unpleasant and heartbreaking. The world collapsed into a circle one foot around her. Ruete's tobacco table was a hand stretch away: a rack of pipes, a bowl of tobacco, thumb marks on the surfaces and an unforgivable white stain, a ring the diameter of a wine glass. She reached out and brought a small wooden box back into her circle. His Cuban cigars. She took one from the box and held it to her nose as she'd seen him do so many times. It was woody, a bit peppery; nothing there to make her want to do this every evening. The cigar's tiny strip of paper slipped as she put it back with its set. Everything here pierced her with memories. She was back in his Stone Town bed, the night he carefully pulled his evening cigar's wrapper off intact and asked for her hand, in those words – *can I have your hand* – and placed the gold and red paper strip on her left ring finger beside the sapphires, and laughed, and said *Now you are mine, till death us do part*. Or, she asked her memory, had the *together unto death* only come later in Aden?

Emily wanted to escape. She struggled out of the embrace of Ruete's chair. Staggered a little, disoriented, hungry and lost, and knocked against Ruete's desk. The pile of unopened letters there, scooped up and dumped from the hall table in the maids' frenzy to clean, toppled. Black framed envelopes with platitudes that stood for grief, condolences that stood for social etiquette and no more, spilled on the carpet. One letter was left fat and unmoved on the desktop. The pale Indian stamp announced the letter was from Zanzibar. It could have arrived any time in the last four days. No one had told her. Or she hadn't listened.

Faithful Metle. 'I have to go back now,' she said aloud, testing the idea. 'They are my family, not those strangers out there squabbling over dumplings like coots over dry bread.' She ripped the letter open as she stood. *Dearest Sister. It is with such grief.*

She did not understand. There was no way her sisters could know about Ruete. The news would not get to Zanzibar for weeks. She read, eating the words, the neat handwriting of Metle's scribe that covered three pages. He'd made sentences out of Metle's normal incoherence, a timeline out of her gossip and distress. It had every detail, everything Salmé missed by being Emily. The Sultan was dead. The fits had finally claimed beautiful Majid, her beloved brother; her emotion was pure in death as it could never be in life. Now there was a new Sultan.

Isn't it strange, the letter said. She could hear Metle's voice telling her scribe, *yes say that, yes strange, not sad, no we'll praise Allah in a minute.*

Emily felt how strange it was. Barghash had wanted to be Sultan so badly. He raised a rebellion, led men to their deaths, and lost, and then got to be Sultan after all in the most normal scheme of things. And strange now, strange for this to happen right at this moment, scuttling the ship on all hope of return. Barghash would never forgive her for trying to be Majid's friend after the rebellion.

She went to the window and drew the velvet curtains, twice as thick as a winter dress, against the grey of the garden, and walked to the smoking room door and turned the heavy key in the lock. She pressed her back up against the door and sank to the floor, and sat there, on the floor, in the way she had been taught not to from the moment she climbed up the ladder onto the *Highflyer*. The skirt of her black taffeta dress popped up in front of her and she slapped it down. In Zanzibar, when a husband died, his widows lived locked in darkness for four months and ten days. All her mothers obeyed this. Salmé visited Jilfidân on the first day after the Great Sultan died and sat beside her and thought grief had an acrid smell before she realised her mother's clothes had been quickly dyed black while she waited for new shirts and trousers to be made from black cloth. Around the wrists and ankles, the cloth was still wet. That was the smell. Dye, not death.

She'd thought her mother was old then. She held her hands up in front of her, still smooth and supple, bare of any rings or bangles. In the play of meagre light and shadow her flesh appeared to be painted with henna again. I am only twenty-six, she whispered, there is too much in front of me. *What is written, is written*, but not this, she prayed, make this all go away. Ruete did not deserve to die, a man who never did anyone harm. She wanted to pour a bottle of ink on the whole thing and write her life over.

There was a scratch against the far side of the door, the sound of small claws on wood. Winzig whined. It had always worked in the past. She'd be let in and push her wet nose into Emily's hand and lick her arm with her little pink tongue.

'I don't deserve to be comforted,' she told the dog through the locked door.

Emily knew then that she was being punished. Allah had turned His back because she had given him up. And God – was God angry because of the slaves?

The scratching continued, louder more insistent. Two sets of claws perhaps.

'Go away dogs,' she crooned.

The scratching stopped.

'Mama, Mama?' It was Tony's voice. A pause between each call. 'Mama?' A longer pause. 'Bibi?'

EPILOGUE

1875: LONDON

When Emily heard the Sultan of Zanzibar was going to the capital of Britain for a royal visit she knew he would never be closer. She had to get there. She would not let herself imagine reconciliation or a right of return, but she was in pursuit of recompense. And this was not begging, she told her advisor and friend, the Baroness von Tettau.

'This is my rightful inheritance, I'm only asking for my portion. It is not only Majid and now Khole who have passed on. Five brothers, five sisters, aunt Aashe, three nieces, four nephews and a step-mother have died since I left Zanzibar. I am entitled under the law to a proportion of their estates. Their *shamba*, their palaces, their slaves and the full attire of each.'

The Baroness told her to hold back on mentioning the slaves. But what was she to do – it was the truth.

The £500 the British diplomats were thrusting at her to keep her away was an insult, the tiniest part of what Sultan Barghash owed her. And their excuse: she could not see how her giving up Allah meant she had to give up a legal inheritance too. Barghash was simply hiding his pettiness behind her apostasy.

Emily did not tell anyone, friend, family or advisor, just how tempting Sir John Bartle Frere's £500 were. Pride would normally have prevented all of this begging. If the five years since Ruete's accident had been kinder she would not be in this position, but Hermann Ruete was an incompetent fool with his worthless railway bonds, and Herr Biggest-Thief-of-All, the Ruete & Company agent in Stone Town had been rather too free with his interpretation of *mine and thine* and had made off with all the money at that end. Living in a smaller, cheaper town, Dresden, in a smaller, cheaper house with one maid, herself rather small in fact, the jewellery and the ermine and the gold spoons sold, meant she could no longer afford pride either. She felt naked without her emeralds and diamonds, but she would now be truly naked if she'd tried to hold onto them.

In London she stayed with a man who was known as a friend of Zanzibar. Captain Rigby, while British Consul to Zanzibar, had learned about their ways.

'Hide the pigs from the farm-set,' he hissed at his young daughter when Frau Ruete came up to the nursery. Emily understood the words as well as why he thought he had to say them. She had worked hard improving her English before leaving Dresden, remembering Aden as she remembered the language she'd learned there.

Captain Rigby had been in Zanzibar during the rebellion and knew a thing or two. Dr Kirk, the current Consul, travelled with the Sultan as translator and knew, she was sure, nothing. For three weeks, in that indefatigable British way, he'd put off a meeting between sister and brother. She was to understand that they would do anything to avoid 'a scene' while the Sultan was signing the Anti-Slavery Treaty. She found she was immeasurably pleased when there was a scene anyway, or as Captain Rigby said in his perfect Swahili, 'There was a bit of a to-do at Ascot today.'

Rigby settled at the table under the elm tree in his own garden with a cup of tea on his lap and explained that Ascot was not just a place but a horseracing event of some importance. The Queen was at Ascot this year, 'Still in black,' he added as a translated aside to his wife who was looking quite drowsy in a patch of sun sneaking between the high branches. 'And your brother was there too,' he told Emily. 'But someone had got to Her Majesty so the Sultan was not invited to the Royal Enclosure.'

Captain Rigby seemed uncertain about this slight. He shifted on the garden chair, uncomfortable pieces of furniture that explained any shifting, yet she could see he was weighing his words during this manoeuvre.

'She'd heard about you.'

Emily felt a surge of satisfaction. Maybe Queen Victoria's namesake daughter, the daughter-in-law of the Kaiser – whom she'd been introduced to one bitterly cold afternoon in Dresden – had written from Germany after all. Being a citizen of the new united Germany might have its own compensations.

'Then to make the slight more obvious, two military gentlemen, the Duke of Cambridge and Count Gleichen no less, possibly inebriated, I would go so far as saying, definitely inebriated, accosted the Sultan beside the racetrack. Went right up to him and went on a bit about the disgraceful way he was treating you.'

'Can I thank the gentlemen?' she asked, sitting forward a little. She was happier than she'd been since arriving in London.

'Best not. Dr Kirk didn't translate what they were saying too closely but your brother is not stupid. He noticed. Enough people noticed for me to hear about it this afternoon.'

Emily must have looked too bright.

'Sorry Sayyida, you must see this does not help you. Not really. The Sultan won't see you because of this. He's likely to be angry you know. The politicians and diplomats will want to protect him.'

She tilted her head slightly and watched the flicker of the sun through the elm. It reminded her of the sparkle of her diamonds when she poured them out of the ebony box onto her bed. Before she sold them all. She accepted what the Captain said. It didn't seem to matter what happened, the British politicians controlled the Sultan. They were acting like Zanzibar was theirs. It was time to go back to the children. *Mutter dearest*, wrote Antonie, *I hope you are well. We are all well. Grossvater and Grossmutter send their greetings. That means hello.* Antonie's handwriting was improving, though her ability to chatter aimlessly was still muted in front of a blank white page.

Mrs Rigby got up. 'I'll call for a fresh pot,' she said to her husband. But he grabbed her hand and insisted she sit.

'I'll go,' he said. As he stood the Captain kissed her lightly on the top of her head. Emily remembered the feel of a kiss like that. The bump, the scrunching sound of hair compressed into the scalp. She felt stupid. Because it was as if her heart was breaking again. She missed Ruete every day. She loved him; and she hated him for leaving her. And she wanted one more tender kiss on the top of her head.

Widowhood had taught her many proficiencies: she could do her own household accounts, teach Arabic and Swahili to businessmen and colonists, and find her way on public transport. She had one thing to do before she left London. She left the Rigby house and walked to the omnibus stop in Portland Place. The green double-decker would take her to the Egyptian Hall, Piccadilly, which boasted all kinds of inducements, a mermaid from Feejee to a Circassian harem girl. The 'bus conductor banged the roof and called 'alight' and they were out from the curb cutting off a brougham.

'You'll have to change at the Circus,' the conductor told her as he picked amongst the coins she offered in her open hand. She had long decided not to be amazed or bemused by what Europe had to offer. Ruete had taken her to Circus Rentz when they were first in Hamburg; she'd loved the horses and remembered being shocked at the legs of the showgirls, and though it seemed nonsensical she imagined just such a circus in the middle of London. Piccadilly Circus, a large roundabout, but a part of the road system nevertheless, was necessarily a disappointment.

If she worried about finding the Egyptian Hall she needn't have been. The architecture was less a subtle hint and more a gay swagger. Pillars with lotus heads flanked the doors. Above the lintel near-naked Egyptians cavorted in stone. The façade was painted in garish colours, pinks and yellows, reds and blues, and only someone who had *not* visited a temple in Egypt would be fooled. Ruete had taken Emily's hand at the Temple of Karnak, on their trip from the Red Sea to the Mediterranean; she walked into the Egyptian Hall alone.

It was almost as crowded inside as it had been on the pavement despite the steep charge for entry. The people of London were manifestly interested in the Exotic Peoples of the World. Once in the hall, she automatically looked up with everyone else: the ceiling was high enough to suggest a theatre at the least, or a cathedral. The height did nothing for freshness and space, and the summer temperatures and human breath and sweat and the hum of excited voices, vibrated the air hot.

There was a display in the centre of the room, directly below the dome, and then others on every side, around the walls. She took off her hat but did not stop at any of the thick clusters of audience until she came to the banner announcing, in painted gold, the Marvel of Mecca. This had to be the Circassian Beauty. She felt her heart begin to beat faster. The heat she told herself, or the bee buzz of conversations making her anxious.

Emily hadn't come to look at the back of men's coat jackets or the trembling feathers of fashionable ladies. She slowly deployed her elbows to get through the people who were also there to marvel at the Marvel. They were well dressed Londoners, though the hygiene on the summer day was not all she could have wanted. She regretted her height as she sidled her way beneath the armpits of two bearded gentlemen. She could then read a small sign propped in front of the display. *Zobeide Luti. Circassian Beauty. Rescued from a Turkish Harem.* One last push and she was at the front, with a low rope barrier preventing her from stepping any further forward.

Behind the low rope that couldn't in reality stop anyone crossing, if they really cared, was the Circassian Beauty. Emily stared. Rudely stared. Astonished. Thinking, there is nothing left in the world to be astonished at. The presumed Zobeide Luti was definitely very pale, like the Circassians of Emily's youth, but her white face was surrounded by a storm cloud of dark hair, hair that belonged on an African head. She was not at all what Emily had expected.

She was seated, this woman who was acting as if she was alone and not trapped by twenty staring strangers. Emily vaguely recognised one piece of her wardrobe, namely the trousers, though they were fuller and puffier than anything she'd worn in the harem. The skimpy vest and little leather boots up to the ankle must be pure fancy, or Turkish harems were another thing altogether. Zobeide had one leg crossed over the other, and held in the opposite hand a water-pipe. When Emily looked closely, tearing her eyes off that hair, she could see it was a prop rather than a working hookah. The most bizarre element in the whole display, and there were too many to name, was the way the woman pretended to be alone. She looked steadily at a point just above the heads of the audience. Emily wanted to break through the invisible wall between her and the woman. She hadn't come to gawk like any Londoner. She'd come here to talk in her mother tongue one more time.

'*Wimafa shoo*,' she called softly.

The Circassian Beauty turned her head. Emily wondered what to say next. She should have been more prepared, but there was too much to say. Her lips stumbled and in the gap she saw that Zobeide Luti was not looking at her. With a bob of her amazing – astonishing – hair, the Circassian Beauty acknowledged a man who'd stepped over the rope. He had to be part of the show: his suit shouted out in bold yellow and the hooks of his moustache were stiff enough to hang a coat from.

'Ladies and Gentlemen,' the man called, his voice like a roll of thunder. Emily felt a shove from behind. Over her shoulder she could see more people pushing in to hear what the shouting was all about.

'Ladies and Gentlemen,' boomed the man. 'You see before you one of the most beautiful women living in the world today. Feast your eyes, ladies and gentlemen.' The man appeared to wink suggestively at a gentleman behind Emily's left shoulder. 'We are lucky to have Zobeide Luti here with us today. Extremely lucky. You will thrill and you will shudder at the life she has suffered, the world she has seen. Ladies, take a care, avert your eyes, block up your ears, turn away if you do not want to be shocked.'

There was an audible gasp from the crowd. Emily was certain not one woman averted not one eye nor blocked one ear.

'You will thrill,' he'd said and the thrill was there. She remembered her mothers; she prepared herself to take in the terrible story.

'Zobeide Luti is a pure example of womanhood, a daughter of the Caucuses, that captivating region on the Black Sea we know as the cradle of all the white peoples of this world.' A few murmurs behind her indicated that this particular cradle was not in fact well known. 'But this lovely daughter was cruelly stolen away from her family.'

Emily's heart had slowed down but it couldn't be still after this. It thudded blood up into the chambers of her ears. Shock more than thrill deafened her. This was indeed her mother's story. She stared back at the poor woman's face and wondered at her stoicism. Zobeide Luti's features were placid, tranquil, untroubled by what would seem to be the cruel and insensitive, and public retelling of her fate.

'This woman before you was sold. Sold as a slave, ladies, taken by the Turkish raiders to the white slave markets of Constantinople.'

Just like my mother, she wanted to shout.

'Her beauty commanded a huge price, one only a man of great wealth could afford. Yes, it is true. Zobeide was the new property of an evil Turk, a Midas of the Muslim world. He veiled her beauty from the world. Hid her away in a harem. Where she languished, ladies, where she yearned for freedom, gentlemen.' The loud man stopped. His sudden silence reverberated through the expectant crowd. 'Until,' he said more softly, more gently, 'until a daring rescue freed the woman from this evil Turk. Allowing her to appear before you today.'

Emily's English was not perfect. She'd recognised most of the words in the excited pitch, but she wondered if she'd truly understood. Rescued meant saved. She couldn't understand: saved from what, for what? If Zobeide Luti had stayed in the harem she'd be safe now, fed and housed and with her friends. There'd be no need for this shameful public display of her body to cater to the gratuitous curiosity of strangers. She could only imagine the woman sitting there with the plaything hookah was doing this for payment. She understood that. Now she had failed in London she'd have to display herself in her own way, teaching Arabic, Swahili – anything to bring in enough money to feed and house her children.

Zobeide Luti shifted in her chair as the yellow-suited man took a storyteller's delight in detailing the daring rescue and the prurient unveiling of the harem beauties. There were swords, there was running. There were heaving bosoms. Zobeide Luti uncrossed her legs, crossed the other over the top. The bare sole was gritty from the floor. Emily lifted her eyes from the crumbs of indented dirt and stared into her face again. She wanted to ask her how she felt when she first took off the veil and let strangers look at her. She wanted to ask if she was now really tranquil, or purposefully vacant. Were her lips set in equanimity or was it a stern stoicism? Her features gave nothing away, these features the man described as beautiful even though she was big-boned and obvious. And that hair. The Circassian Beauty gave an enigmatic smile to something the man said. Emily wondered how much she was paid. She wanted to ask her that as well.

The pitchman was coming to the end of his story, or more correctly, his Circassian Beauty's story. The thunder in his voice was turned up again.

'And now ladies and gentlemen,' he boomed. The crowd shifted. The gentlemen and the ladies were being shoved tighter at the appearance of a cage. It was on wheels, pulled in from the side: a painted, gilded cage. Zobeide Luti stood from her chair, shot the lock on the cage and bent into it. A visceral gasp went around the audience. Emily joined the involuntary exhalation. The Circassian had straightened – and she had a snake in her hands. Her cumulous hair hardly moving in the manoeuvre, but to a man and woman, and gentleman and lady, the hair of the audience stood on end. Emily instinctively put her hand to the back of her neck to calm the bristling.

'A python,' said a woman beside her, one with a pheasant feather in her hat. The woman was then no longer beside her, courage lost to retreat. Emily wavered but stood her ground. She hoped the python, if that was what it was, was well fed because the Beauty held it only lightly, one hand around a point close to its pointed head and the other a foot or so from the last segment of its tail. It looped like a rope between these points. It could surely reach her and the retreating pheasant-lover in one jolt.

To her horror, there was worse to come. Zobeide Luti proceeded to dress herself in the coils of the snake. Round and round her naked belly, her fragile neck. Ten foot of diamond-tessellated python glowed orange and black against her ivory skin. Thrills and shudders. The loud man was right. But for all the hands flying to mouths and the moans and the tiny squeals of fear, she could sense the crowd loved this. They were shuddering and applauding in turn. The snake's tail kicked and joggled when the clapping boomed; its tongue flicked.

'That's what they learn in the harem,' said a man up the back of the crowd.

Emily turned. He had the look of an ordinary man, indistinguishable from any on the street or in the omnibus. Other men were looking and laughing at what he said.

'All sorts of snakes,' added another wit.

She didn't understand, but there was something in the sniggering that told her they weren't actually talking about snakes. She blushed for Zobeide Luti – who wore the same imperturbable expression across her face.

She left the Egyptian Hall by the grand front doors. The Circassian had been ushered out of the main room into some region not meant for the audience. Emily had called after her but her voice was lost in the fire of conversations lighting up in the crowd now they could talk about the exotic woman freely.

From the front doors it wasn't hard to find an alleyway off Piccadilly. It was drizzling and must have been for some time. The lane was muddy, rural in tone and smell. Animal odours. She picked her way, trying not to look at her feet as she searched around the backs of the buildings. She hadn't put her hat on in the rush to get out and find Zobeide Luti. She'd thought it wouldn't take long. Her hair soon brushed damp against her lined forehead but then she was lucky, or it was written, because a door about where the back of the show hall should be was wide open. It took a moment for her eyes to adjust to the dim light within. After the stench of the alleyways, the long corridor smelled of human: human sweat, long stale; and human cooking, mostly cabbage, a smell she associated with Germany.

Many of the doors off the corridor were closed, others offered glimpses of people from dark regions of the globe. A man came out of one. He had beads entwined in his plaited hair and beads hanging from pendulous earlobes. The beads grazed the shoulders of a green suit. A Masai warrior nonetheless.

'*Jambo*,' Emily muttered. He echoed the hello as he passed. Did not look back. She wondered how she'd greet a Laplander, should one be about with his reindeer, or a South Sea Cannibal with his mermaid. Then she saw the corner of a gilded cage through one half-closed door on the opposite side of the corridor. Close up, the cage was an insubstantial pen, thin wood, daubed with flaking gold paint. She couldn't see a snake within. She didn't know if she was in the right place. She knocked lightly and pushed the door wide.

Zobeide Luti was sitting at a dressing table in front of a mirror. She was scrubbing make-up from her face. She was less pale, her eyes were not so big, without the paint. She had a homely brown robe pulled over her shoulders. With the damp cloth scouring up and down her face, she couldn't at first see Emily behind her. Emily hesitated, and then spoke.

'*Fasapshi, thamshaga sa* Sayyida Salmé bint Sa'id.'

The Circassian swung around, obviously startled and defensive. But there was no recognition in her eyes. 'Hello, please, my name is Salmé,' was all she'd said.

'*Wimafa shoo*,' she tried again. 'Hello' in another of the Circassian dialects.

'What's all this about?' the woman asked, in English but accented by a region far from Piccadilly or Portland Place.

'You've forgotten your mother tongue?' Emily was embarrassed. The poor thing must have been stolen away when she was very young and forgotten even the simplest words. It was unfeeling of her not to have foreseen this. 'I shouldn't have come, this is too hard for both of us.' But the woman was laughing.

'Oh, you think I'm Circassian. Was that Circassian lingo?'

'You are not Circassian?' Emily had not moved from the door. This was even worse than anything she'd imagined when she decided to find the Circassian Beauties.

The big balloon of frizzy hair was quivering like a bird's nest caught in the wind. 'You believe everything the ballytalker sprouts?'

Emily tried to make sense of the transformation from Zobeide Luti of the Egyptian Hall to this laughing woman in the backrooms.

'But *you* are not from these parts,' Zobeide said, 'not with an accent as thick as cream. Don't tell me, you are from the *cradle* of us all.' The woman who posed as a Circassian rose and took her hand, dragged her over to the mirror. They bent into it. The two faces in the powder-hazed mirror couldn't be more different.

Zobeide's features were large and generous and strong, her eyes round, that hair uncontainable. Emily's straight hair, plaited and wound on top of her head, was completely contained and constrained. Her nose was thin, her upper lip a line.

'My mother was Circassian, God rest her soul,' she told the stranger. She could see her own lips moving in the reflection. She wondered why she wasn't simply walking away from this fraud.

'You gotta be kidding me.' Zobeide turned to her. The mirror was full of her hair's reflection. 'I've never met a real one.'

'She was stolen, as a child, from beside the Black Sea. She was sold in the slave markets of Constantinople.'

The woman who was not Zobeide Luti kept mouthing 'bleeding heck' and 'blooming hell,' which Emily decided meant the same thing.

'You'd better sit. I don't believe... Yes, of course I believe you. Only it's pretty unbelievable, all that manure the ballytalker puts up. Like a script from a play.'

'Or my mother's life.'

'Sit, sit. We need a drink.'

Emily perched on the edge of a spongy velvet-covered sofa that felt like it'd gobble her up if she moved any further back.

'Gobsmacked,' the woman said.

'Gob?'

'Mouth.' The term fitted perfectly. Emily felt she too had been smacked across the mouth.

She was rummaging below the dressing table now, this strange woman. The room was very small: the sofa, the table, one wooden chair in front of it, the cage, a stand of mock-harem clothing.

'What is your name then?' Emily asked her.

'Call me Zoe. Everyone does,' she said without turning around. 'I've been Zobeide for so long it's easier. I was just out of being a kid myself when I hooked up with the moss-haired girl lark.'

When she stood up, Zoe had a bottle and two tooth glasses.

'Ta-da,' she waved them in front of Emily. 'I think we can dispense with the customary tea,' she said in a lady's accent. 'I can't speak Circassian but I can speak hoity-toity. Brandy?' She was pouring before Emily could demur.

There was too much to ask after this avalanche of information, so Emily latched onto just one of the unknowns.

'What are moss-haired girls?'

'All us Circassian Beauties, descended from the luscious Zalumma Agra, the Star of the East.' The descendent handed over the glass of brandy and plumped up her hair with her freed hand. 'Zula Zelik and Zoe Zolena and Zada Zuletta and the incomparable Madame Zenobia.' The names skipped playfully off her tongue. 'Showgirls every one. We get our hair like this by soaking it in beer. To look Circassian.'

'My mother's hair was nothing like that.' Emily held her brandy; she wasn't sure she should be drinking, let alone in the afternoon, with a strange woman.

'You're kidding?' the strange woman said again, becoming more familiar each time she said it. Zoe pulled the hard chair away from the dressing table and sat in front of Emily.

'Sit back, it's okay, Jake's under the sofa I think, not in the cushions.' For the first time since entering the room Emily looked into the false-gilded cage. The empty cage. 'He's not a biter,' Zoe reassured her.

Emily gulped down some of the alcohol. The taste scrunched up her face. She rarely took it, but then, she rarely sat in a room with a snake. She made no secrecy of pulling her legs up beside her on the sofa.

'So what was your mother's name?'

'Jilfidân.'

'Nothing with a Z? Bleeding hell, I always believed the hair and the z-thing.' Zoe sounded like she felt defrauded as well. There was one last thing she had to hang onto. 'And was she a Beauty then?'

Emily hesitated. Took another sip of the brandy. It slipped down easier this time. She decided to be honest, as her mother had taught her.

'Not by the standards of the harem.'

'She was in a harem?'

'As was I saying.'

Zoe was like the entire audience in the Egyptian Hall distilled into one human form. 'No!'

'She was beautiful on the inside,' Emily appeased. 'The time I drank a cup of water during Ramadan she didn't punish me. She sat me down, explained about fasting and about Allah's great love. *Forget not to be bountiful one towards another*, she told me. *Surely Allah sees the things you do.* She was being kind but it made me feel more guilty than if she had beaten me. The idea of Allah watching everything I did.' As Emily talked she could feel the gold of her small cross necklace burning her skin. Branding her like a runaway plantation slave.

Zoe's face was fully animated during all these disclosures. So, her previous serene composure was part of the public act too.

Her eyebrows twitched, her lips opened and closed, like those of a hungry child.

'We did use rosewater and saffron in our hair,' Emily added. 'But not beer.'

'I'd rather drink it myself. It's a long way from the East End to the Exotic Far East for one little Stepney woman.' Zoe's robe fell open as she lent forward. Her breasts were like melons, ripe and firm. Hardly a little woman, Emily thought as she dragged her eyes away from them.

'So why do you?'

'For the money, of course. You are sheltered aren't you?' Zoe leaned in even closer. Emily could smell the brandy on her breath. Or maybe it was on her own.

'What was it really like in the harem.' Zoe whispered. 'All that sex.'

Emily hadn't heard that English word before. 'Sex? What is that?'

Zoe put her brandy glass on the floor and held up her hands. She took the pointer finger of her right hand and thrust it in and out of the ring formed by the thumb and index finger of the left. Her lips smacked in wet kisses as she performed the mime.

'All that sex. Was the Sultan always there? How did he choose?'

Emily blushed, not a ladylike pink, but a red wine stain to the roots of her hair. Sex wasn't something you talked about openly to strangers; it was not something you imagined your father doing. And the Sultan was her father not some man who picked a girl for a night in bed, to do things like Ruete did to her. No, she couldn't think in that line any further. She tried to rise from the sofa. Zoe ignored her struggles. She took her glass and refilled it. Emily sank back into the cushions and didn't say no.

'Drink, drink. You're very innocent for a harem girl.'

'No I'm not. It's just that the harem,' she tried to explain. 'It wasn't about that.'

She saw Zoe's expectant face. Sex. Suddenly Emily laughed at the idea; a stream of brandy snorted the wrong way down her nose and she had to wipe it away. This only sobered her for a moment – because it was no use being coy; of course she remembered all the talk in the harem. Sex, whispered about, hinted at, details mysterious, was always a subject that caused laughter amongst the women. But she'd never imagined any of the wives actually doing it. Even more impossible an image than her turbaned father. Her mothers and sex? Pious Jilfidân, Medine with her fat leaping about under her skin like frogs when she giggled. Scary Bibi Azziz. Sex!

She tried to stop herself from laughing so much. She formed the word in her mouth first, felt it in her vulva, before she said it aloud.

'Sex. It wasn't about sex. It was our home.' She paused. Gathered her thoughts through the brandy fug. 'You can't see what's going on in a harem from the outside.'

Zoe laughed in an odd recognition: 'Like those folks out there in the Hall haven't got a clue what it's like back here.'

'Yes.' Emily said. Despite the snake, the smells, the time, the place, she relaxed.

'So why aren't you there now? Were you rescued? How did you end up in London of all places on God's earth?'

'I fell in love,' Emily said. Was it that simple? From this distance, it did feel that way. 'Now I have come here to try and see my brother the Sultan.'

'A Sultan? You're kidding me!'

Zoe brought her near-empty glass up to clink against Emily's. She had both her bare feet planted on the floor between them, like the trunks of peach trees. Her moss-hair was limp, the aftermath of the beer. It clumped, more mud than moss.

'Tell me more about them Circassian ladies,' she asked. Emily felt tears coming. It was the brandy, bringing unwanted laughter and unwanted tears.

'They spent lots of time in the bathhouse, having their fat massaged by the slaves. They gossiped all day long, their voices echoing off the blue-green tiles, the water in the fountains tinkling, so, well it was like diving underwater amongst mermaids.' The brandy was doing the talking too. 'Have you seen the mermaids they have on display here?'

Zoe threw back her body. The wooden chair rocked. 'That mermaid is as much from Feejee as I am from the Black Sea. Sewn together, a fish and monkey. That's how easy it is to make a mythical beast.'

'Is nothing real?'

'Life can really knock you around. It can be a bitch you know,' was all the wisdom this strange woman had to offer Emily, who drank some more and thought of her two little bitches at home, Winzig and Babette, more than likely neglected by the maid and falling over each other to get to the door every time a carriage slowed on the road outside. Her dogs, soft and loving and waiting and loyal. Could life be like that?

'You are so lucky,' Zoe sighed, reaching down to pick up Jake from under the sofa Emily was sitting on. Zoe stroked along his diamond tessellations. 'All those wonderful things to remember from when you were a kiddy.'

Lucky. Emily rolled that word around in her mouth.

'Lucky,' she nodded. Maybe it was true. Whether she was old enough yet to be living on memories she did not know.

255

ABOUT THE AUTHOR

Jane Downing was born in Australia but was taken to live on Manus Island a month later. She has since lived in Tanzania, Ireland, Indonesia, the (then) USSR, China, the Marshall Islands and Guam. While living and working in the Marshall Islands, where truth was often stranger than fiction, she began to write. She now lives back in Australia.

ACKNOWLEDGEMENTS

Emily Ruete published an account of her life titled *Memoirs of an Arabian Princess* in 1886. It is the first known memoir by an Arab woman written for western eyes. *The Sultan's Daughter* is a work of fiction that exists within the huge silences in her memoir.

The Sultan's Daughter originated as part of a Doctor of Creative Arts degree undertaken at the University of Technology, Sydney. Special thanks go to my supervisor Debra Adelaide for her support, insights, meticulous care and patience throughout.

Gratitude must also go to Louise D'Arcy and Dorothy Simmons who gave generously of their time and their professional eye looking over an early version of *The Sultan's Daughter*, and to Margot Jensen who has long been my ideal reader.

Finally I would like to thank my family. My parents, who uprooted me and took me round the world again and again yet made everywhere we lived home, and my children who are everything.

GLOSSARY

Bibi	Swahili	mother, lady, term of respect for women
Ghazal	Arabic	a poetic form
Jambo	Swahili	hello
Jinni	Arabic	one of a class of spirits in Muslim demonology that inhabit the earth, assume various forms, and exercise supernatural power
Kafir	Arabic	unbeliever, infidel
Kasikazi	Swahili	winds in the winter months, bringing short rain
Kofia	Swahili	brimless, cylindrical hat worn by men
Kosch	Swahili	embroidered leather slipper, women's street shoe
Kubkâb	Swahili	high wooden sandal, women's indoor shoe
Meddes	Swahili	large pillow
Mwaka	Swahili	short, sharp rains that fall November to December
Schele	Swahili	large, black shawl worn by women when going out
Sefra	Arabic	low dining table
Shamba	Swahili	plantation, estate
Siku a mwaka	Swahili	first day of the new year
Streuselkuche	German	crumb cake
Suri	Swahili	concubine who has given the Sultan a child
Tekkies	Swahili	small pillow
Yaya	Swahili	nurse

Note: many of these terms are taken from Emily Ruete's memoir and their usage and spelling originates in her unique family circumstances with its mixture of Swahili and Arabic.